JADE DRAGON

Sarah Milledge Nelson

RKLOG Press

Littleton, Colorado

This book is a work of fiction. Names, characters, places, and incidents are products of the author's imagination or are used fictitiously.

For permission and information:

RKLOG Press
5878 S. Dry Creek Court
Littleton, CO 80121

Library of Congress Control Number: 2004096601

Library of Congress Cataloguing in Publication Data

Nelson, Sarah Milledge
Jade Dragon
Fiction
1. Fiction
2. China – Fiction
3. Archaeology – Fiction

ISBN 0-9675798-2-1

RKLOG Press Trade paperback printing, first edition

Cover by Marilynn Kreft
Book design by Mary Kay Gadd
Printed in the U.S.A. by Eastwood Printing, Denver, Colorado

For my sister Eleanor Decker,
my best critic since she was two
and laughed at the stories
I made up to entertain her.

Other books by Sarah Milledge Nelson

FICTION

Spirit Bird Journey

NON-FICTION

The Archaeology of Northeast China

The Archaeology of Korea

Ancestors for the Pigs

Gender in Archaeology

Denver: An Archaeological History

Ancient Queens

In Pursuit of Gender

Equity Issues for Women in Archaeology

Powers of Observation

Han River Chulmuntogi

Studies in Bella Bella Prehistory

Reviews of Spirit Bird Journey,
the first Clara Alden book

"This is a **delightful** book, whimsical yet based on solid scholarship." *Bibliophilos, James G. Patterson*

"Nelson has given us a **creative and full-of-life set of images**, a truly "peopled past." *American Antiquity, Margaret Conkey.*

"This is . . . **a lyrical novel, which both entertains and informs** without being self-indulgent." *Asian Perspectives, Brian Fagan*

"Nelson's story is a **multi-layered, complex** study of identity, gender, archaeology, and adoptee issues . . .The story is seamless and well paced." *Korean Quarterly, Andrea Lee*

"Dr. Nelson produces a more **rounded sense of life** than other [prehistoric] experiments." *Antiquity, Nicholas James*

"This is a good read . . .Would that there were **more such books** in English." *Transactions of the Royal Asiatic Society, Korea Branch, Gertrude K. Ferrar*

". . .**a marvelous read**. . .superbly crafted."
C. Leon McGahee, M.D.

"I was absolutely unable to put it down. . .**completely absorbing**."
William Dolen, M.D.

"I just finished your book and I really like it a lot!! The book **haunted me for several days after I finished it."**
Sociologist and poet Prof. Anne Rankin Mahoney

ACKNOWLEDGEMENTS

Many thanks to Marilynn Kreft, who painted the cover based on a photograph of Pig Mountain, and kept urging me to finish the book to display her painting. Mary Kay Gadd was of exceptional help designing the book and dealing with technical details. My colleagues at the University of Denver, Prof. Robert E. Stencel and Prof. Lawrence Conyers read the parts of the story that pertain to their professional expertise – astronomy and ground-penetrating radar, respectively, but they are not to be blamed for any remaining errors. My other readers, Eleanor Decker and Christina Kreps, made useful suggestions. Most especially a big, warm hug to Mitch Allen, who slogged through the first two drafts and made enough criticisms to turn the manuscript into this story. Thanks also to Hal, who kept asking when I would be finished writing this book, thus hurrying along the process. Clearly, it cut into our time together.

Funding for several expeditions to China came from The Wenner-Gren Foundation for Anthropological Research and National Geographic Society's Fund for Exploration, for which I am grateful, although they didn't fund the novel. Co-explorers over the years are too numerous to mention, but Guo Dashun and Sun Shuodao were the first excavators, who showed me the site in the first place. Yangjin Pak and Hung-jen Niu have been good co-workers throughout our years of exploring the Hongshan culture. I'm also grateful to my companions on the trip in 1987 when I first met the Hongshan people: my graduate students Ardith Hunter and Mingming Shan, who have been friends ever since.

Prologue

I don't think of myself as an adventurous person, although I enjoy foreign travel and meeting people of other cultures. I might have turned down this adventure if I could have seen the future, but maybe not. There were pluses and minuses.

It began with a phone call from my partner's father. I was just back from a year doing archaeology in Korea, and Ed and I were experimenting with living together. So I was surprised and intrigued, but not overwhelmed, to be invited to lunch by Mr. Howland. I assumed Ed would be there too, but I was wrong.

Mr. Howland is an intellectual properties lawyer, meaning copyrights and such. He's medium height and slender, with a lot of wavy gray hair. If Ed looks like him in twenty-five or thirty years, I won't mind. We met at his office, and his secretary brought chicken salads and iced tea for both of us into his conference room. He put me at ease with a friendly smile.

"I'm hoping you can help me," he began. "I understand you're extraordinarily good at languages."

When I began to say something modest, he held up his hand to stop me. "You learned Korean in a year, both speaking and reading, correct?"

"Not with native fluency in either case," I answered honestly. "But sufficiently for my purposes, yes."

"Have you ever thought of learning Chinese?"

"It would be useful for understand Korean archaeology to be able to read Chinese. Otherwise, no."

"How about adding Chinese to your studies?"

"Why?" Mr. Howland's interest in my linguistic abilities made no sense at all.

"There's someone I want you to meet. She works for a national committee and her job is returning stolen Chinese artifacts.. She has a proposal for you. Would you like to meet her?"

I put down my cloth napkin and left my half-eaten chicken salad behind, as we pushed back our chairs and went into Mr. Howland's office. On the way in he made a hand flick at his secretary, and within seconds a buxom woman in an expensive suit and lots of gold jewelry was ushered in.

"Sandra Wold, Clara Alden," Mr. Howland introduced us. We shook hands. I regretted wearing jeans and a cotton sweater. I felt it put me at a definite disadvantage.

"Sandra, Clara is an archaeology student who picked up in a year what the U.S. Army classifies as the most difficult language in the world. With some study she can certainly handle the language side of your project. Tell her about it."

Sandra folded her arms across her black-clad bosom. She was all business.

"The U.S. has signed an agreement with China which stipulates that stolen antiquities, however they get into the country, will be returned to China."

"Just as it should be," I agreed.

"I hoped you would see it that way. The problem is, tomb raiding has become an industry in China, and the amount of illegal Chinese antiquities entering the U.S. is overwhelming. We suspect that westerners are organizing and even financing some of the tomb robbing. Some auction houses, dealers, wealthy patrons, and museums are involved in this traffic, but it's hard to catch them, and even harder to prosecute them.

"This brings me to you. We need a legitimate archaeologist who is not Chinese but who speaks Chinese well, to be our eyes and ears in China."

"There are several westerners who have cooperative projects with Chinese archaeologists," I said, "and most of them are fluent in Chinese. Why not ask one of them? You wouldn't have to wait three years for me to learn Chinese."

"Some of them have been helpful to us, but the thieves avoid them. As a student or newly fledged archaeologist, you might be in a position to learn more. Would you be willing to learn Chinese well enough to perform that role?"

"Korean and Chinese are in completely different language families. All I know of Chinese are some loan words in Korean, and they aren't even pronounced the same. Surely there are Chinese-Americans who could watch for you more easily."

"We haven't found a trained archaeologist who is willing. They all believe they are watched closely, and probably they are right. We think you would be above suspicion. And we are very impressed with your linguistic skills. We'd like to sponsor you to learn Chinese for three years, in exchange for your listening in China. We agree that it's important to stop the looting of Chinese sites."

"I need to think about it." I squirmed around in my chair, crossing my legs the other way.

"Sorry, it's now or never. When people think about it, they talk to their nearest and dearest, and leaks develop. If you agree, we'll pay the tuition for your Chinese classes. Do you need other tuition aid?"

"No, I have a full scholarship. But you're assuming I can join an archaeology project in China, which isn't that easy. And supposing I do get to China with a legitimate project, what if I don't learn anything? Will I have to pay you back?"

"The tuition support will be in the form of a grant. All we ask is that you listen and report." Sandra leaned forward and handed me a document several pages long. "Read this over and decide."

I read the whole document, fine print, boiler plate and all, while Sandra watched. The idea of learning Chinese was appealing. The idea of helping to catch looters at archaeological sites was also appealing. Why was I hesitating?

I signed, and enjoyed three years of Chinese language study. Some of it interfered with my love life, but Ed was busy too. He never questioned my sudden desire to learn Chinese.

When I was invited to join a short archaeological project, I was thrilled. I tried not to think of myself as a mole, but I would keep an eye out for theft of archaeological objects. I reported my plans to Ms. Wold through Ed's father, but heard nothing back before I left.

Ɔ1

We waited until all the baggage from our flight had come around on the carousel, but no large orange instrument was in sight. It would be impossible to miss – six feet long and two feet wide, in a carrying case with both shoulder strap and handles.

Joe and I looked at each other in dismay over its non-appearance. Joe had tales of customs officials in other countries freaking out when they heard the word 'radar.' In China we didn't know what to expect. The unit is way too conspicuous to sneak through customs, since it begs for attention by both its size and its color. When Joe checked it in at the Boston airport, we heard comments of the "ha, ha, who are you going to shoot?" kind. Did they think we were going big game hunting in China? One skinny bearded guy and three young women? C'mon. But the radar unit was essential for our project, and this kind wasn't available in China.

"Report it missing, Clara. You speak the best Chinese," Joe ordered, handing me the baggage tag.

I took the tag. The order was typical of Joe. Of course as grad students we are his slaves, and we know it. Joe is likable in his gruff way, and I suspect it's a pose because he was so recently one of us. Anyway, speaking Chinese was part of my job on this expedition. My Chinese was pretty good in class, but it hasn't been tested in the real world. For example, I don't know the word for radar. If pushed, I would try "ra-da" and probably be in the ballpark. With luck, I can get away with describing the bag, and not its contents. I want to see all of China, but I don't want to see the inside of a Chinese jail.

I looked around for the desk to report lost luggage, but instead I saw a sign pointing to oversized baggage. Sure enough the radar unit was there, looking twice as big as life-sized. Okay, the first hurdle leaped like superwoman. I slung the strap over my shoulder, feeling like a bearer for the great white hunter on safari, and staggered back to where Joe, Laura and Ashley were protecting the rest of our luggage – mostly battered duffels and backpacks that wouldn't look enticing to thieves anyway.

"Ta da! Faster than a speeding bullet." I twirled around with the radar unit and almost fell over.

"Good one, Clara," Joe said with half a smile. "So far so good. Now we have to get it through customs."

Joe had requested that our hosts from the Beijing Archaeological Institute be present in case of trouble getting the radar unit through the customs procedures. But of course, even if the posse were here to rescue us, its members were outside the baggage area, and couldn't see if we had trouble or not. I hoped they were there for backup, though. The last hurdle was looming.

We inched our worldly belongings for the coming month ahead of us in the green line. A Chinese man in uniform walked up to me, pointed at the radar device, and asked, "*Shenme shi*?"

I was startled, but I tried not to look guilty.

"*Shi ige kaoguxue de dongxi*," was the best I could do for an answer. Sounded like Chinese 101 to my ears. I hoped I could do better as time went on in China.

"She said, 'it's an archaeological thing,'" Ashley giggled nervously behind her hand, explaining what I said to the others.

Joe tensed his muscles, although what he thought he could do, I can't imagine. The fight or flight readiness, I suppose.

The customs inspector showed a lot of teeth.

"*Hao, hao, kaoguxue de dongxi*," he said, as if I had made a delicious joke, and he slapped a sticker on its side and waved us through.

"Hao means good, or okay," I explained to Joe. "Let's get out of here before he changes his mind."

On the other side of the barrier, in a crush of people meeting planes, a young Chinese man anxiously scanning the crowd held high a sign we found reassuring. It read "Welcome American archaeologists."

We pushed our way through the crowd toward the sign, but the guy holding it ignored us. Joe worked his way right next to him, and asked in his ear if he was from the Beijing Archaeological Institute. The Chinese man jumped, and then looked at Joe and smiled.

"You must be the radar guy. Welcome to China," he said. "Call me Xiao Li." This means "small Li," but he was taller than any of us, and probably about our age. I had thought 'Xiao' was only used for children, but I was obviously wrong.

"Nice to meet you, Shelly," said Joe, offering his hand, which Xiao Li grasped and shook heartily.

"I saw you but I think you could not be the right people," Xiao Li said, by way of apology. "I look for four Americans."

Ashley batted her beautiful dark eyes at him, as she does in the company of any male. "We are all Americans. Four" And pointing to each of us, Joe, Laura, me, and herself, she counted, "One, two, three, four."

Xiao Li looked baffled, so I stepped in to help. "This is Ashley Woo. Her parents came from Hong Kong, but she was born in America. Thus she is American. She's a specialist in Chinese jades. I'm Clara Alden. I was born in Korea, but adopted by Americans and became a citizen before I can remember. Thus I am American, too, with an English name. My specialty is the Neolithic period. I've worked on archaeological sites in Korea, and would like to work in China."

Then, having dealt with the Asian anomalies, I presented Laura Wolsky and Dr. Joseph Martinez, experts in ground-penetrating radar.

Joe looked like an archaeologist: well tanned, with the obligatory beard and muscular arms. Laura is as tall as Joe. She has the all-American-girl kind of good looks – healthy, tall, blue-eyed, pink-cheeked. Ashley is medium height and willowy, like a princess in a Chinese painting. Even in jeans she manages to look like a fashion model. I'm the shortest of the bunch, and skinny, too, but I can do my share of the heavy work on an excavation.

Xiao Li volunteered no information about himself, but later we learned he's an advanced archaeology student at Beida, who has excavated Hongshan culture sites.

He made small talk as he guided us to a waiting taxi, and I was impressed with both his English and the ease with which he chatted. The driver, who was standing beside the taxi, shook his head when he saw what I was carrying. The small taxi was clearly not going to hold the five of us and our luggage, let alone the radar unit.

"Two taxis?" I suggested to Xiao Li.

"No, we need van. I not know you would bring something so large. That monster thing too big for taxi all by itself." We all laughed together, in my case out of relief that this had become someone else's problem.

Xiao Li disappeared, while Joe, Laura, Ashley and I huddled together on the sidewalk. I felt conspicuous holding the radar unit, with unbelievable crowds pushing by. It was bumped into several times, so I shifted it to a vertical position in my arms. With a large pack on my back and another bag over my shoulder, this wasn't easy, and my arms began to ache.

A Chinese man spoke to us, but neither Ashley nor I could understand his accent, so after several tries he gave up and walked on. Ashley thought he was trying to pick us up, but I thought he was asking directions. So much for our combined fluency in Chinese!

The crowds had begun to thin when Xiao Li reappeared with a driver and a van. Our China adventure was about to begin.

"In Beijing you stay three nights at Overseas Chinese Hotel," explained Xiao Li to Joe, as the taxi pulled out onto a wide highway. "Very convenient. Right across street from Archaeological Institute. Not far from Gate of Heavenly Peace Square."

Ashley saw that Joe didn't react to the latter, so she leaned toward him and whispered, "That's Tiananmen. You know, where the students tried to take a stand on democracy in 1989, and were run down with tanks?"

"Ah," said Joe, "Ancient history."

It was a joke, which we acknowledged with small groans. But there's some truth to his lack of investment in world events. Joe is such a techie type that he doesn't pay much attention to anything else. As a post-doc shepherding his little band of grad students, it's his considerable experience at using and interpreting ground-penetrating-radar in archaeological sites that had brought us all to China. As far as he was concerned, he could be anywhere. Often, he was.

Joe doesn't have any Indiana Jones tendencies. He doesn't search for lost treasures or raid tombs. He's a serious researcher, and I respect his knowledge. Just the same he's had many strange adventures taking his radar unit to faraway places. I smiled with the pleasure of being a member of this project, which no doubt would spawn other mythic tales to entertain future grad students.

I was eager to see the Hongshan culture sites, in the far northeastern part of China, a region once called Manchuria. I was especially interested in the site with the 'Goddess Temple.' The truth is, I hope to write my dissertation on leadership in Hongshan sites. I know a lot about what's been found in the sites, but I need a data set to work with.

"Three days in Beijing," Joe grumbled. "I hate delays. Why can't we go straight to Daling, Shelly?"

"It is holiday," explained Xiao Li, "Labor Day, May first. In China, Labor Day holiday ten days long. Liaoning province archaeologists cannot go to Daling until May 11. Better you wait in Beijing."

"We could go ahead and get a feel for the site, make a grid, and plan which areas to sample," Joe persisted.

Xiao Li said "Tsss," drawing air in over his back teeth.

"It's an order, Joe, phrased politely. Roll with it," I said in Joe's ear, recognizing the teeth sucking sound as an indirect negative from my time in Korea.

"What are we going to do here for three days?" Joe kicked the back of the seat, more or less accidentally.

"Since we're here anyway, we have to see the Great Wall of China," said Laura, her eyes sparkling. "It's one of the world's most famous sites."

"The Forbidden City is a must, too," Ashley said. "You've heard of it?" she teased, but Joe didn't react.

"And Tian Tan, the heavenly-blue-roofed Temple of Heaven. And the Summer Palace," I added, remembering the tourist places from a lesson in my first-year Chinese book. I hadn't dared to hope we actually would have time for seeing the sights. I considered the delay a gift from the fates, although Ed will come sightseeing with me after the fieldwork.

Xiao Li blinked at our list of places to go. "Well, okay, interesting places, but archaeologists at Beida and Archaeological Institute expecting you. They want to hear your thoughts about the Hongshan culture. Also already arranged for you to see History Museum and exhibit on archaeology in Gugong."

Three days to do all that? Really two, because today was almost over.

"We'll see what we can squeeze in," said Joe. "The archaeological preparation is important. Sight-seeing will have to fit into any extra time." Laura made a face behind Joe's back.

The highway from the airport was packed with cars and buses, and as we neared downtown, traffic barely moved. After edging into the right lane, the van driver said something I couldn't catch to Xiao Li, and turned off the elevated road. The ramp plunged us into the narrow streets of old Beijing.

A year in South Korea was my first venture into Asian archaeology. As I told Xiao Li, I'm an adopted Korean, and I look it except for my American clothes and attitude. Looking at the old streets, I was reminded of Korea. Down the side streets called *hutong*, the old architecture is similar – brick houses topped by roof tiles with slightly up-turned corners. The charm is in these unexpected alleyways. Otherwise, colorful, milling crowds had to compensate for drab buildings. Most newer buildings are made of concrete, giving them the look that Ed called "instant old" when he visited me in Korea. The new skyscrapers could be anywhere in the world, except for the large neon Chinese characters flashing their names.

The sights and sounds made me think back to my year in Korea. They were a reminder, too, of the strange dreams or visions I had that year - dreams of being a yellow bird participating in the life of Flyingbird, the leader of Bird

Mountain Village, home to a small segment of the Golden Clan. I learned a lot about prehistoric life at the sites I was working on. Maybe I would have visions of the sites we would be working on in China.

2

Daydreaming as I reminisced, I found I had spread yellow wings again and was flying into a small house. It was like those of Bird Mountain Village in having only one room, but the large room was divided into sections. It was clean and sunny, with light entering through an opening near the roof. Fuzzy hangings with patterns in black, white and brown adorned the walls, and reed mats almost covered the dirt floor.

Several women bustled around, helping with a birth. A black-haired woman beat a hand drum, and another woman wearing white jade ear ornaments danced barefoot around the mother-to-be, clapping her hands. The shells hanging from her belt made a rattling accompaniment a few tones higher than the drum. I could barely see the woman giving birth, squatting in the middle of all the commotion

I was perched on a high ledge made of twigs, to observe the proceedings, but when I heard the child cry, I flew to a lower ledge to have a better view – and got a shock. The baby girl had green eyes and wavy dark brown hair. Her skin was pale, too. Even the people of the Golden Clan were not as pale as this child.

Her mother, I noticed now that I could see her clearly, had eyes as dark as mine. Her straight black hair was held back from her forehead with a band of yellow flowers. I wondered about the father of such a pale child, but no men were present.

The mother was helped to sit up, leaning on the drummer. Her change of position revealed a pendant of pale green jade, winking in the firelight. The jade was carved in the shape of a small contorted head. It startled me. I'd seen jade heads like that before, when Flyingbird was on her quest to the sacred mountain. She was given one to wear while she traveled through unfamiliar territory. The heads were sometimes used for making magic, but their real use was to identify the wearer as an inhabitant or friend of Jade Village.

After the baby was bathed, she looked around with bright eyes and seemed to smile. As before, I knew I was in this place because it would be my job to protect her. I hoped I would be up to the job.

One of the women pushed aside the bearskin hanging in the doorway and beckoned to a man outside. "You have a beautiful daughter, Carver. Come in and greet her."

A tall man with a full brown beard entered and sat beside the mother and child, enveloping them warmly in his arms. The beard must have tickled the baby, but she didn't cry.

"Owl, my love, what a pair of beauties you two are."

Carver's face was turned toward me. His green eyes were so different from the others that I gave a squawk. This caught the attention of the birth assistant with the drum.

"Look at that yellow bird," she said to the others. "It has to be a good omen for this child."

They all looked in my direction. To my surprise, the baby's father recognized me. "I think this is the yellow bird in my favorite song. Haven't you heard me singing it?" Carver asked Owl. "About the bird who guided a strange woman into my village long ago?"

When Owl looked puzzled, he added, "I often sing it while I carve."

The baby's mother nodded. "Now I know, dum-ti-diddle-um" she hummed a tune, and then sang "Golden Flyingbird. . . Do you think this could the same bird?"

"I've heard you sing about the Spirit Bird protecting a girl from a tiger at the Heavenly Lake" said the smallest of the women, a teenager, I guessed.

"Yes, that's the one, Little Shell. She was real, not a made-up story. She left a feather in my village, which my mother keeps in her treasure basket to this day. It's still bright yellow. Ma uses it to cure jaundice."

That was the first I knew of the medicinal properties of my feathers, but it made me feel proud of being useful.

"Your mother told me a story about a bird once," the new mother remembered. "Flyingbird, your great-great-grandmother of the Golden Clan, was named for that bird."

Owl put her finger on her cheek. "Oh – that means our child descends from Flyingbird on your side. Do you think Flyingbird sent her Spirit Bird to watch over her?"

"The bird must have been sent by a spirit, because none of us called her."

They contemplated both the infant and me.

"What should we name this lucky baby?" Carver asked, now that her ancestry had been verified.

"She belongs to my clan of Wu, of course. But because of the bird she should be called Golden, too. Her eyes are the color of some of the jade you carve. Golden Jade? Is that a good name?"

"Of course I'll teach her to carve if she wants to learn. But you'll tutor her in your arts, like calling the rain spirits, and healing and seeing the future, won't you? Should that be part of her name, too?"

"The name Wu means those things. My clan members are diviners, magicians, and healers. I'll instruct her in music and dance, and medicine and divining. You'll teach her how to recognize good jade-stone, and how to see the spirit in the stone and carve it out. Jade can choose for herself which path to follow. They are all kinds of magic.

"Look at those long fingers," Owl smiled as she uncurled the baby's fist with her own finger. "They're made for carving. And jade is one means of clear-seeing. Golden Jade should be her name."

Carver carried Golden Jade outside, and formally announced her name to the waiting villagers.

A flutist and two drummers had been waiting for this moment, and began to play a lively tune. A tall thin man imitated a crane, as he plucked Jade from Carver's arms and began dancing with her, holding her close in one long arm. He picked up his knees high and flapped one elbow. Then everyone joined in, dancing the crane dance in a circle, joining Golden Jade to her kinfolk of the Wu clan..

I dropped a yellow feather for good luck. Maybe this one would cure some other kinds of diseases.

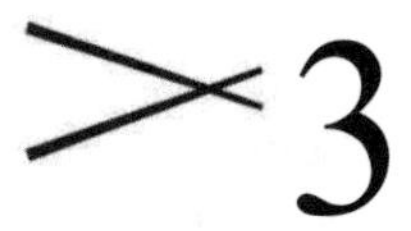

“Wake up, Clara, we’re there.”

For a moment I couldn’t think where “there” might be. A big hotel sign flashing neon Chinese characters was the clue I needed.

The sun was still high in the sky, so I suggested that we check in quickly and walk to Tiananmen Square. Xiao Li looked at his shoes, cleared his throat, and said “Tsss” over his back teeth. It got our attention, and we waited.

“Mmm. The archaeologists from the Institute want to greet you,” Xiao Li finally brought forth. “I said I would bring you over as soon as you put luggage in rooms. You already late. It is holiday, and they wish to go home. How long you need to put luggages in your rooms? I tell archaeologists you coming.”

“Ten minutes,” Joe said, just as Ashley announced, “Half an hour.” Joe narrowed his eyes at her.

“C’mon Joe, after 24 hours traveling, I need a shower. I can’t meet anybody smelling like a sewer rat. You could do with a shower yourself.” I thought Ashley was pushing her luck, but Joe smiled one of his rare full smiles.

He lifted his shoulders and sighed. “Tell them half an hour, then, Shelly. We’ll be as quick as we can.”

As we waited in line at the check-in desk, I saw Xiao Li crossing the street to the institute. Since he was out of the way, I said to Joe, “His name’s Xiao Li, not Shelly. Say Shh-ow, like be quiet, it hurts. Rhymes with ‘how.’ Li is his family name. You could call him Mr. Li.”

“Shouldn’t it be Mr. Xiao?” asked Laura.

“Good for you to know that in East Asia the family name comes first. But in this case Xiao means small, or young. He’s assuming Joe is older than he is. Or there might be another person named Li in his *danwei,* his work unit, who’s older than he is.

On the plane, Joe had held three pieces of paper, one marked with an X, so that Ashley, Laura and I could draw for the single room in Beijing. Ashley won. Laura and I suspected Joe had rigged it so he could sleep with Ashley.

"I don't care," Laura had said. "It's over between Joe and me. He can't bother me that way."

I brought only one city outfit, since I wasn't expecting to be meeting Chinese archaeologists in Beijing. It was just navy pants and a nice blue top, but for a grad student, that counts as dressed up. I examined the outfit critically. It had survived being crammed in my duffel bag pretty well. I looked at myself in the mirror, and added the gold locket that Ed gave me just before we said good-bye. It's in the shape of a heart, and says "Safe Journey" in Chinese characters on the back. How sweet of Ed to worry about me. I hadn't told him anything about my mission.

I brushed my shoulder-length hair, which is dark brown and wavy – Korean, not Chinese hair. But there's no question, I thought, examining my eyes with their epicanthic folds, that I'm Asian.

Will the archaeologists think I'm Chinese, like Xiao Li did, I wondered. They'll realize I'm not Chinese as soon as I speak. It will be easier than in Korea, though, because the Chinese won't expect me to know the culture in my bones.

Laura bounced out of the shower and slipped into hip trousers and a skimpy tee shirt. I wouldn't have worn that outfit in China, but it wasn't my business to tell her how to dress, and she wouldn't change anyway. She brushed her streaked hair into a high ponytail that swished enticingly when she walked.

At the Institute we were given a brief tour before we met the archaeologists. The front part of the compound looks like an old manor house for a noble family, but the building with the labs is a concrete addition. Serviceable, but lacking charm. I was impressed with the sophistication of the archaeological laboratories. I expected them to be crude and dusty, but that must have been old news. They had facilities for macro-floral analysis, thin-sectioning pottery, and sediment analysis, among other high-tech analyses.

Joe soon fell into conversation with their remote sensing specialist, and Laura got someone to show her Neolithic bones from the northeast. Ashley wanted to see jades, but was told that they're not stored here.

"Jades are kept in a locked room in a building with an alarm, because of the rising theft of artifacts, which are snapped up by the art market," explained Xiao Li.

"Looting and theft would never have occurred in the time of Chairman Mao," muttered a portly man in a lab coat. I glanced at his gray hair and jowls, and wondered if he was somebody whose work I had read, but I was not destined to find out.

I followed up with a question to the Director of the Institute told us that looting of archaeological sites was increasing, and we should be careful. In one recent incident a man guarding the excavation of a Han dynasty tomb had been killed while on duty at night. The thieves ransacked the dig, and got away with many treasures, even large pieces. Theft of artifacts from museums was occurring, too, including Hongshan jades. Joe thanked the Director for the warning, and promised to stay alert and report anything suspicious.

Xiao Li suggested a browse through the bookstore, which sells only archaeological publications. Ashley and I followed him like children after the Pied Piper. What scholar can resist books?

I pounced on a new publication about Hongshan, all in Chinese, which I bought to improve my Chinese reading skills. As a bonus, it's full of great color photos, which I can turn into slides. We dumped our purchases at the hotel, and went to roam the streets.

The tourist attractions were closed for the day, so we strolled through the vast spaces of Tiananmen Square. It was crowded with people out walking – small Chinese families and clots of tourists. The gate into the outer courtyard of the Forbidden City was open, and we paid a pittance to enter.

The fading light gave it magic. It looked just like the movie, The Last Emperor, except that all the colorfully dressed extras were missing. To compensate, brightly clothed kids from one-child families skipped between their parents. They were eye-catching, especially the little girls who pranced and shook their heads, causing their enormous hair bows to bobble. Ashley couldn't stop saying "how cute" and "adorable" about each child she saw. She took pictures of several of these little princesses, who graciously allowed themselves to be photographed.

Laura whispered to me that she thought most of them were rather too chubby to be cute. Joe heard the comment, and suggested it came from the whopper, the colonel, and other American fatty foods introduced into their diet. I wondered if indulgence of the only child also played a role in the new trend.

It was hard not to notice that many young Chinese women were more skimpily dressed than Laura. Spaghetti straps and bare belly-buttons were all the rage. Laura looked positively prudish in comparison

Thinking of the pseudo-American fast food available on nearly every corner, I realized I was hungry. Laura and I consulted how to avoid fast food. She suggested Peking duck. I agreed that it would be an appropriate start for our visit to China. Joe and Ashley said they were sleepy, but hungry, too. We chose food ahead of sleep.

I asked Xiao Li if he knew a good restaurant nearby for Peking duck. He mentioned a duck restaurant near our hotel, where the archaeologists sometimes ate. What an auspicious recommendation!

A hostess led us up three flights of stairs, allowing me to peek into each level as we climbed higher. Each floor was fancier than the one below. The ground floor had bare wooden tables with a litter of bones around those that were occupied. On the top floor we were seated at a round table in a room by ourselves, with old style teak furniture and painted scrolls of the four seasons hanging on the walls.

"How much is this going to cost?" Joe muttered to me, taking in the ambience.

"Relax," I whispered back. "The menu was posted outside. Our budget will cover it." Keeping track of the expenses was one if my responsibilities.

The table had a revolving tray in the middle with nothing on it yet but a glass with tiny squares of thin paper. There were five chairs, and at each place was a table setting, consisting of a bowl with a spoon on a spoon rest, a little plate, chopsticks in a paper cover, and a chopstick holder.

We could all handle chopsticks. Ashley grew up using them, and I was an old hand at it after my year in Korea. Laura and Joe had less practice, since they learned the skill in Chinese restaurants. A waiter offered them forks, which they waved away and struggled on with the chopsticks.

"What do we do with the bones, Shelly?" Joe asked. Obviously my little lesson on Chinese pronunciation was a total failure.

Ending up with bones in your mouth is inevitable when you eat meat with chopsticks, because there's no provision for cutting meat off the bone. Xiao Li made us laugh, telling us that the polite way to eat duck was to spit the bones on the floor. He explained that it's very rude to take them out of our mouths with our fingers. None of us could manage to spit on the floor, though. Instead we spat them into our tiny paper napkins, and made a pile of small bones on the table. Xiao Li looked away when one of us did that.

I recorded in my journal all the different courses made from the same duck, beginning with the skin which is served with plum sauce and scallions, all wrapped in thin pancakes (absolutely the best), and ending with a soup made of the bones. Since this duck was female, we got duck eggs, too.

The duck came up to my expectations, which is difficult when the dish is so famous. Even Ashley proclaimed it totally delicious, and Laura patted her tummy.

"How do you say, 'I'm full' in Chinese?" she sighed contentedly.

"*Chi bao le*," Xiao Li supplied. We had many opportunities to say those words.

During the meal we discovered Qing Dao beer. It tasted so good that we drank two bottles each. Xiao Li told us the beer was authentic, because beer was introduced to China through the German concession long ago, where they built the first brewery. Joe raised his last bottle high, and cheered for the beer.

We were beginning to become a crew already, making memories of China. Before we left the restaurant, Joe organized a photo of us at the table around the ruins of the feast and the row of Qing Dao bottles. We each handed a camera to Xiao Li, who therefore had to take four pictures, as we got rowdier and sillier. In the first shot we stood posed in a row behind the table, but in the second, Joe had his long arms around all three of us women. That was the one that was splashed all over the newspapers later, when I had reason to wonder whose camera it was taken with. Ashley made a presentation of duck bones, artfully arranged, for Joe for to hold in the last picture. I hoped we weren't behaving like American tourists, but I'm afraid we were. Could that be why we had a dining room to ourselves?

I was felled by jet lag after our long day, but tooth-brushing turned out to be too complicated for a lick and a promise and fall into bed. We had been sternly warned against using the tap water, so we looked around for bottled water. Laura latched onto two thermos bottles instead.

The larger one, which we opened first, was filled with very hot water. It had a bright panda painting on the outside, a thick cork, and a battered top that could be used as a cup. A smaller thermos, still colorful but a bit more restrained with a yellow and blue geometric pattern, held cold water. That was the one for tooth-brushing.

I barely extracted my sleep tee-shirt from my pack and slipped it on before I zonked out.

Naturally, I was bright eyed again at 4:00 A.M. with no hope of going back to sleep. It's one of the laws of international travel. I didn't turn on the light, because Laura was still asleep. I just lay there and thought about the chores ahead.

Our base will be at the archaeological station called Daling, a walled compound where we'll eat and sleep. We'll use the radar unit a few kilometers away. The Daling area is a large ritual precinct with sixteen "localities," at least a dozen of them having mounded tombs containing ornamental jades.

A building they call the Goddess Temple is unique for its time and place. When it was excavated, nothing was left of the structure but the floor and fragments of decorated walls, but the contents were astounding. Fragments of life-sized statues were near the surface – parts of a bird and a pig, and a woman's shoulder and breast, as well as a face with inset green jade eyes. Discovering the statues was an enormous surprise – the statues are not just rare, they're unique for the time, in this or any other part of China. They are realistic and well-executed. They demand an explanation.

The elite tombs and the temple imply a ranked society, but it's not at all clear how ranking came about. It's a hot topic in archaeology. Questions about how people became leaders, and why others would follow them, are important for understanding cultural development. I worked on Neolithic sites in Korea, which makes a good grounding for the Neolithic in China, but the Hongshan culture is much more elaborate, with its elite burials, jade specialists, and apparently centralized religion. What caused greater complexity and centralization? It wasn't warfare, or writing, or walled cities. Hongshan lacks these traits.

I brooded about what kind of data would bear on the problem. Survey data would be a good way to start. I'll try to impress the Chinese archaeologists at Daling, so they'll invite me to work with them next year.

This year my work is to help with the study Joe was commissioned to do. The area where we'll use the radar unit is a Hongshan site, which is called the Ox River site. The process is called GPR, for ground-penetrating radar. Joe wrote his dissertation on uses of radar in archaeology, and as a result was invited to China.

Joe needs assistants, so he brought along Laura, Ashley and me. Laura has worked with him several times before, in exotic places such as Turkey and Ecuador, when she was his girlfriend. By now she's learned the principles of the radar, and soon will be able to take on projects of her own. She also studies bones.

Ashley and I will do the menial chores. We'll lay out the string grid for the radar readings to follow, make notes, take photos, and generally do whatever we're told. Joe selected us because we've both studied Chinese, and presumably will be able to transmit information about our findings to the Chinese archaeologists. I'm trained in field methods, but Ashley has never been in the field before. On the other hand, she's an expert in early Chinese jades. She even has a website about the jades she has studied, in which she carefully describes each one.

Her field is Art History, and she's writing her dissertation on ancient Chinese jades, mostly Shang dynasty, a couple thousand years later than Hongshan. She knows about Hongshan jades, too, but our paths never crossed before the Chinese class. She flirted with Joe at a party Ed and I threw, and got herself invited on this expedition.

Oddly enough, Ashley's Chinese is not as fluent as mine, because her family speaks Cantonese, which is considerably different from Mandarin, or *putonghua*, the common speech, as it's known in China. She says putonghua is a whole new language for her, as different from Cantonese as Portuguese is from Romanian. My linguistic problem is different from hers. I sometimes get Chinese confused with Korean, especially when it comes to numbers. *Yi* means "one" in Chinese and "two" in Korean, for example.

I've tried to immerse myself in Chinese culture, including practicing *qigong.* It's not just an activity, it's also a philosophy. So I'm learning about *qi,* a complex Chinese concept – breath, life, and power are all qi. My teacher is not happy about having a female student – he says qigong is only appropriate for men. But he teaches me anyway.

I decided practicing qigong would be better than thinking in circles. So I sat up in bed and crossed my legs, concentrated and took deep breaths, feeling the power flow. I could feel my wings sprouting, and I was back in the past.

4

I found myself flying into a cluster of houses. On closer inspection I saw that it was really two clusters on either side of a green space with a large spreading tree shading the gap between them. The biggest house in the larger cluster had a bearskin in the doorway, helping me to recognize it as the place where Jade was born.

I flew around the village, getting to know it. I sniffed freshly cut grass and cooking fires. The houses were in five rows parallel to the creek. Between the rows were well-worn tracks that suggested constant visiting back and forth.

From the air the village looked like a little town, except that there were no stores or other public buildings, as far as I could tell. Did they live together for the sake of sociality, or to defend against wild animals? Wild animals were obviously a part of their lives. I glimpsed a tiger skin on a floor, as well as the bear pelt in Owl's doorway. Perhaps other predators, such as wolves and foxes, were nearby, too. On the sociality side, maybe it took several hundred people to do everything that needed to be done in a farming community. Or maybe that's how many it takes to have a good party.

Some agricultural fields were beside the creek, but most fields were grown in square or rectangular plots along the hillsides, where they would catch the rainfall. Some kind of grass with small grainheads was growing, along with veggies that looked like cabbage and spinach. Vines of different kinds carried squash and some kind of bean.

Nearly everyone was outside, busy at some task.

I spotted Owl coming out of her house with a basket. Owl stopped at the house next door, and called, "Sister, are you coming? We need to pick beans for dinner in time to soak them."

A tall, graceful woman carrying a black and white basket on her head stepped around the decorated deerskin hanging in her doorway. “Here I am. Don’t be impatient, big sister.”

They were joined by four other women from the same row of houses, which I learned later were occupied by Owl’s close kin. The families were headed by Owl’s sisters. They all walked tall and carried water pots on their heads gracefully, like royalty wearing crowns.

The whole valley was inhabited by the Wu clan. Their specialties were healing the sick and injured, and contacting and controlling spirits. Occasionally they would tell the future, too, but that was inviting trouble, for the future belongs to the spirits, who are jealous of their secrets.

Some of the Wu family were more talented at these activities than others, but they all had a connection with spirits. For this talent they were feared by those from other villages, as well as sought out for help. Owl had the strongest bond with Spirits, and she had become the person most often asked for help. Her services were sought even by dwellers in other villages.

When Carver married Owl, he brought his jade-carving talent to Green Valley, where no one had carved jades before. Carver rounded up five boys and girls who showed talent in wood carving, and taught them how to rough shapes out of the hard stone, and polish it until it glowed.

To work with the children on days that were rainy or cold, Carver made a lean-to workshop on the side of Owl’s house. As I flew by he was tidying up the jade chips which had fallen as he roughed out an earring. With all this activity, Green Valley was beginning to be known for its carving.

There was exchange within Green Valley, too. Some households made extra pots for daily use, and exchanged them for other necessities, like millet wine (a specialty of Owl’s brother Dancing Crane), or fine willow baskets such as those made by Little Shell. She made interesting patterns with jade beads, or feathers, or seeds – whatever came to hand that was bright or colorful. The baskets were appreciated for their evocation of spirits, who must have inspired her.

I got so involved in watching activities in the village that I didn't notice the time. After the simple evening meal, darkness was falling. I saw the villagers begin to straggle up the hill above the village. Adults watched the eastern sky with unusual concentration. Golden Jade walked between her parents, each holding one of her hands.

"Owl," said Carver, "Jade is shivering. Shall I take her inside or get her a cloak?"

"She'll be fine as soon as the moon rises. She isn't cold, she's sensitive to the moon's changes. This night is an important time, when the moon will be swallowed by the great bird's shadow. Keep Jade close to you while I lead the chanting. The noise of the chant is frightening for a small child."

Owl judged that the time for moonrise was near. She knew how to measure the sky with her fist, and using that measure she calculated how much later the moon rose each day. She kept track of which group of stars was host to the moon each night.

Owl led the people of Green Valley to the earth altar on the edge of the village, and watched for the first glow of the moon, as the villagers crowded around her. Just as the moon appeared in a notch between the hills, she began to beat her drum. Everyone joined in chanting: "Moon, watch out, moon watch out."

The word "moon" was very drawn out into four beats, and "watch out" was said in a quick staccato. The effect was eerie.

The full moon had risen two fists high in the sky before a shadow began to creep across its face. Now Owl changed the chant to, "Moon, be steadfast, moon, be steadfast." This time the words were spoken with equal stress, sounding strong. Throughout the eclipse, the villagers chanted. Owl raised her voice gradually and the people chanted louder and louder, so that when the moon was fully covered in shadow, they were shouting.

As the shadow passed across the face of the moon and began to disappear, Owl led them to sing, "Moon, you have triumphed, moon, you have triumphed." The cadence was lilting, to match the relieved faces, still turned toward the moon and bathed in moon glow.

When the moon was shining fully again, the millet beer and round acorn cakes prepared for this night were brought out of the houses, and the celebration began. Each family came to Owl and congratulated her for preserving the moon. When I saw that Jade had fallen asleep in Carver's arms, I knew no harm would come to her that night, and I flew away.

5

In my journal, I wrote, "Here I am, standing on the Great Wall of China, looking in the direction of the Goddess Temple, far in the distance." I had to ask Xiao Li which direction from here the Daling site was, so I could put this thought into action. Xiao Li and I were ahead of the others, because Ashley and Joe stopped several times to snap photos, and Laura lingered with them, although she took fewer pictures.

"The Goddess Temple is over that way," said Xiao Li, pointing north and east with his whole right arm stiffly straight from his shoulder, like a statue of Chairman Mao. "About six hours more to drive to there from here."

We had already driven just short of two hours north of Beijing, so that made it an eight-hour drive. Pretty far, but not bad compared to the eighteen hours of traveling we had just suffered through.

Xiao Li and I were speaking English, because no matter how often I tried to speak to him in Chinese, he pretended not to understand me, and doggedly used his odd English.

Now I asked him in Chinese, "*Ni bu shi leng le?*" Aren't you cold?

It was a cool day in early May, and windy on the wall, but Xiao Li wore a short-sleeved polo shirt and looked perfectly comfortable, while I huddled in my university-logo sweat shirt.

"Not cold," he answered. "Cold is when it snows and the wind blows. Now it is spring. Spring weather is pleasant."

I was amused - he sounded just like my Chinese lessons. Perhaps they used the same lessons in reverse for teaching English. I gave up on trying to have a Chinese conversation, and gazed along the wall.

The Great Wall of China is an immense construction, a highly impressive example of "material culture," as we archaeologists say. As everybody knows, it's not a continuous wall, although it stretches about three thousand miles altogether. As many as three parallel walls were built in some regions. Parts of a wall from the Jin Dynasty still exists, far north in Inner Mongolia.

The top of The Wall was crowded with tourists of many nations, jostling each other on the wide walkway. Ed will join me for a Silk Road tour after my work here is finished. It will be a graduation present for him, his last chance to play before starting to work in his father's law firm.

To get ready for the trip, Ed read aloud tidbits from the guidebook. According to his research, what we stand on is a 20th century reconstruction of the Ming dynasty 15th century wall. But parts of the wall were built at various times beginning in the third century B.C. or so. I could relate to that. Nothing about China's past is uncomplicated.

The posted signs explain that the wall was built to keep the marauding nomads out.

"Why do they insist on nomads, when in the time of the Hongshan culture, the people who lived north of the Great Wall weren't nomads?" I asked Xiao Li peevishly.

"The nomads came later," said Xiao Li. "There was no wall at all five thousand years ago. The people to the north were settled farmers growing millets and raising pigs and sheep. Yes, sheep," he said, when I raised my eyebrows. I had missed the sheep somehow. "Sheep and cow bones, as well as pig and dog, have been found in the sites. There's even one site report that mentions horse. In fact, the villages northeast of the Great Wall each had several hundred inhabitants, and they are as old as any in China."

Xiao Li went back to see where Joe was, and I wandered on, to the end of the repaired section. I like the old, crumbling wall better than the fresh newer part. I tried to think this sentence in Chinese, but I got stuck on "crumbling." I sighed. So many words to learn.

I've been studying Chinese for three years just as I promised, and I can speak it with fluency, although I admit to some imperfections. My vocabulary is limited, and I don't always get the tones right. My Chinese teacher told me that my spoken Chinese is like singing, which I took as a compliment, until I realized she meant that singing suppresses the tones, so you have to guess the meaning. Sigh again. Getting the tones right is very difficult.

Reading is a different kind of problem, with thousands of complex characters to learn, but as long as I stick to archaeological topics, I can read Chinese pretty well. Words like 'pottery' 'excavate' and 'artifacts' pop right out of the page at me. The rest of the words are filled in to my translation more slowly, and my copies of site reports have many characters underlined and translated in the margins.

Earlier I had to learn the old style characters to read Korean archaeology journals. Although China now uses simplified characters, they aren't completely different. I already recognized a lot of characters from Korean *hanja*, so learning Chinese characters wasn't as bad as starting from scratch.

I was reminded of my qigong lessons. I felt the qi at the edge of the repaired wall, and it made a barrier I was reluctant to breach. Instead of walking farther, I followed the wall with my eyes, watching it snake until the hills concealed it, before it reappeared in the distance. The hills were green and brown, with bare crags jutting far above the wall here and there.

I savored the moment. In spite of three years of preparation, I was astonished to find myself in China. My feet on this wall. Sorry to gush, but I never believed I would be here – Clara Alden, lowly graduate student in archaeology, standing on the Great Wall, thinking Great Thoughts.

But I ramble, like the supposed nomads. The Great Wall also rambles. It meanders over hills that are rugged but not high. And it never kept out a determined invader, nomad or not. The old wall runs through a desolate region, which would be uninhabited now, except for the guides, bus drivers and vendors of tourist items.

I looked again in the direction of the Goddess Temple, and I thought I saw a flash of fire, which beckoned me to Golden Jade.

6

Three children were playing near the edge of the woods, constructing miniature houses. They had made a fire in the hearth, and put tiny clay pots on the fire. Twigs in the houses represented people.

A snuffling noise caught Jade's attention. "Shh," she told her playmates, "I hear something."

She walked on tiptoe toward the sound. Small Tiger and Robin followed her. Peeking around the trunk of a tall oak, Jade saw movement in the oak leaves at the base.

"It's baby pigs!" she whispered. "Where's their mama? Look!" She picked up one that had come out of the pile, and moved toward her on uncertain feet.

"Isn't this a darling piggy? Look at its curly tail! And its cute little nose. He's trying to get milk out of my finger. It tickles," Jade laughed, as the little pig tested her thumb with its mouth. She put the piglet into her carrying sling. "See, he's my baby," she laughed.

"Be careful," warned Small Tiger, "Mama pigs are dangerous. They don't like anyone near their babies."

Robin wanted to pick up a piglet, too. She ran toward the rest of the litter, scuffing up the leaves and cracking twigs.

The sow had not gone too far away to hear that kind of commotion near her babies. The bellow that came from her throat was a warning, followed by crashing through the forest toward the three children.

"Run! Climb a tree!" yelled Small Tiger.

They each found a tree with branches low enough to reach, but the sow came to the foot of each tree, until she smelled the piglet that Jade still carried in her sling. She began to ram her head against Jade's tree, which rocked under the repeated impacts. It would only be a matter of minutes before she either shook Jade out of the tree or knocked the tree down.

Seeing the mother pig occupied, Small Tiger and Robin scooted down from their trees and ran back to the village for help. As soon as the sow was well behind them, Small Tiger began yelling.

"Help! Help! Jade is treed by a humungous pig!"

In his haste, Small Tiger knocked over the tiny fire. It began to crackle in the nearby twigs, and spread to other forest litter. The sow smelled the fire, and felt the heat as it devoured more leaves and twigs from the forest floor. She gave up on the pig in Jade's arms, and ran to move the rest of her litter away from the fire.

Carver heard Small Tiger's shouts from his jade workshop, and ran outside. Owl was coming back from a field with an armload of cabbage, and heard the noise, too. They both ran toward Small Tiger and Robin.

By now the fire had reached the tree where Jade was sitting. She had no way down except into the fire. Help was on the way, but unless they brought water to put the fire out, it would be too late for Jade. I would have wrung my claws, but I needed them to stand on. I couldn't think of a way to put out the fire myself, or rescue Jade.

I swooped down to the edge of the fire, and picked up a flaming stick in my beak, being careful to select a long one that was only burning on the far end. I flew toward the village, and intercepted Owl as she raced toward the woods. She was trying to ignore me, but I dropped the flaming stick in her path. The fire went out, but she sniffed the air and got the message.

"Fire! Bring water!" Owl yelled to Carver. "And get everyone. We have to stop the fire before it eats our homes and fields."

I flew back to Jade, who was halfway up a birch tree. It's not the best kind of tree for climbing, because the angles between the branches are acute, and the trees taper at the top. But there's a silver lining if a pig or a fire is chasing you. Birches are flexible. The fire was still crackling around the base of the tree, but it was mostly spreading the other direction. I wondered if Jade's weight could bend the tree over close enough to the ground for her to jump safely. I perched in the top of the tree and sang for her to climb up. Jade put the pig back in the sling, and climbed higher into the V-shaped branches.

Eventually she was as high as three houses – higher above the ground than she had ever been before in her life. It made her dizzy. And then the tree began to bend – the wrong way, toward the fire. My heart was pounding. I flew high in order to dive-bombed at full speed into the tree, just above the place where Jade crouched in a high notch, hanging on tightly. My momentum was enough to push the tree away from the fire. The birch tree was already weakened from being battered by the sow, and crashed down just as Jade grabbed the piglet and jumped to the ground.

Jade and piglet fell into a pile of leaves that the fire hadn't reached. Jade was scratched from the branches, and her cheek was bleeding. She saw Owl and ran toward her. "Oh, Jade! You're safe!" Owl picked her up and looked her over. She seemed okay. They'd talk about what happened later.

"Run back to the village and find Little Shell to clean the blood and put green salve on your scratches. The rest of us have to stop the fire before it turns toward Green Valley."

The villagers brought birch-bark buckets and made a water line from the creek to the fire. The fire was blazing, but it was still small enough to put out with water, and soon the village and crops were safe.

Owl and Carver were relieved that Jade was unhurt, but mad at her too. "You must not play with fire," Carver said, emphasizing each word. "You can see how dangerous it is. You might have burned up the whole village. Three of the piglets were burned in the fire."

"The sow must have rescued the other three," mused Owl.

"Did you know about the piglets, then?" Jade was feeling more contrite than ever, with this information.

"Yes, we've been keeping an eye on the mama pig. But I only saw two piglets with the sow. I wonder what happened to the other one."

Tears ran down Jade's face. She pulled the piglet out of her sling. "He's hungry," she said. "Can I give him some porridge?"

"Certainly not. Take the piglet back to his mother. He needs milk, not porridge."

Jade looked in the forest for the sow, but couldn't find her. She had moved her nest away from children who play with fire.

"Can I keep him, Mama? His name is Piggy. I gave him some porridge. He licked it off my fingers."

Owl and Carver looked at each other. Otherwise the piglet would starve. And having a pet might keep Jade out of trouble.

When we settled into the car after the Great Wall expedition, Xiao Li told us we had spent too long there, and we had time for only one more tourist sight. We would have to choose between the Summer Palace and the Temple of Heaven. A vote split two to two.

"There's an older and much better summer palace at Cheng De, on the way to Daling," Xiao Li informed us. "You'll have to stop there anyway for lunch. Nothing else is like Tian Tan."

That settled it. I changed my vote to Tian Tan. I slept all the way back to Beijing, still not adjusted to China time, halfway around the world from Boston.

According to ancient Chinese lore, the earth is square and the sky (or heaven – it's the same word in Chinese) is circular. Accordingly, the Temple of Heaven is round, with a tile roof of a deep saturated blue, so blue it seems indeed otherworldly. Inside, it's painted bright colors, with dragons climbing down the columns, and green, red and yellow geometric designs dazzling the eye.

The altar for worshiping Heaven is outside, though, not in a building but directly under the sky. It's a round marble platform encircled by a stone whispering wall. The acoustics send sound racing around the curved wall. Of course, we had to try it as soon as Xiao Li explained it.

Joe went to the opposite side and whispered to the wall. His voice came around to our ears crisply and clearly.

"Get with the program, archaeologists, we're wasting time," he whispered. We laughed.

Ashley whispered back, "Relax, Dude, and have some fun with us."

Joe gave her his half smile. "Later," he said very softly, but audible to us all. Laura walked away, poker faced .

A guy who had been watching our whispering game struck up a conversation with Joe. It looked like the serious kind that might last a while, so Ashley and I caught up with Laura to see the rest of the grounds of the Temple of Heaven, taking pictures of each other in various scenic spots. We were just like the Japanese tourists, except they were herded together by tour guides holding colored flags above their heads, while we wandered freely.

Laura and I drifted toward our meeting point with the car, while Ashley returned to the Temple of Heaven to take more pictures of the inside details. Laura has been learning Tai Chi, so we stopped to watch elderly Chinese doing their routine in a near-by park. The practitioners were gray-haired but supple and graceful.

"When you do Tai Chi everyday, you can live forever. But only to watch is not good." Xiao Li startled us. He had appeared with the car and driver.

Joe caught up with us, accompanied by the dark-haired stranger.

"This is Evan O'Connell," he said, introducing all of us. "You won't believe what a strange coincidence. He has a Hongshan project, too. He's going to stay at Daling. I invited him to go with us."

I took in Evan's dark curly hair, bright blue eyes and nice smile. He told us he was attending a university in Wales, which had given him a small grant to test some theories about archaeoastronomy at the Daling site.

Laura, always curious about other ways to learn about the past, asked, "What exactly do you hope to discover?"

"Here's a roundabout answer." Evan spoke in the kind of British accent that makes me swoon. "In the stone circles of England, like Stonehenge, people created alignments with cracking great standing stones, to watch the heavenly bodies move and learn to predict their behaviour. For example, using the central trilithon as a backsight and the Heel Stone as a foresight, each year Neolithic people could pinpoint the summer solstice, because the sun rises exactly over the Heel Stone on that day. They could predict eclipses by moving stones in the Aubry holes.

"Other peoples, like the ancient Maya, erected their buildings so that the light fell a certain way, or on a certain carving, on a day with astronomical significance. The chiefs probably used that knowledge to manipulate people, seeming to be wizards, because the heavenly bodies would appear to obey their commands. Of course, the wizard had figured out how to anticipate the behavior of the sun, moon, and planets. It must have taken generations of passed-down lore. Oral records certainly began before there was any writing, probably helped by tunes or rhymes.

"I don't know what I'll find in the Hongshan sites, since there isn't much architecture. But most of the graves were placed on hilltops, and the strange structure called the Goddess Temple offers possibilities. Orientations of graves and buildings may give me a clue to start with."

He brought out of his shirt pocket a much-folded sketch map of the site, with its sixteen localities marked with red circles.

"I plan to go to each numbered locality, and see what might be visible from there, especially to the east and west, where the heavenly bodies rise and set."

Xiao Li hovered around, anxious to get moving. He either didn't understand Evan's British accent, or wasn't interested in archaeoastronomy. Maybe both.

Our next stop would be Beida, as we had learned to call the university. Their letterhead says "Peking University." Peking is the old way to transliterate Beijing into English. The city has been called Beijing in *pinyin* since the founding of the People's Republic of China in 1950. A university is a big school, a da xue, and so the place is known within China as Beida, short for Beijing Daxue.

We couldn't leave for Beida, though, because Ashley hadn't turned up at the meeting place.

Evan announced he was going next to the Astronomy Museum, and asked if he could catch a ride that far. I realized that if we waited for Ashley, there wouldn't be room for all of us in the car. I was intrigued with the idea of ancient astronomy, so I asked if the car could drop Evan and me off, and return here for the rest. I promised to be on the street by 1:30 for the car to pick me up. Presumably Ashley would have reappeared before then.

The astronomy museum was almost deserted. Evan seemed happy to have an attentive audience, as our footsteps echoed through the exhibits. He explained a poster showing the Chinese constellations, which represent different creatures and stories from the ones we in the western world imagine in the sky.

"You could connect the star dots in millions of ways," he pointed out. "What's surprising is not that constellations are different, but that some similarities occur across cultures. The stars of Ursa Major and Ursa Minor were perceived as groupings by many cultures. In America you call them the Big and Little Dippers, but often they're seen as two bears, especially by the circum-polar peoples."

At another display, I was fascinated to learn that in China the night sky was marked by divisions translated as "lunar mansions," or "lunar lodges." Twenty-eight of them are marked along the path of the moon through the sky. The moon stops in a different lodge each night, and thus the progression of the days can be traced. Each lodge is distinguished by a specific bright star, or a cluster of stars. It must be a very ancient way of reckoning the passing of time.

I asked Evan about the sky in Hongshan times.

"How would the people of that time have understood the night sky? They could surely see the sky better than we usually do, with all the light pollution of modern cities. I've read that the Big Dipper was an important constellation in later China, but what would the Hongshan people have made of it, going round and round the North Star?"

Evan scratched his curls to ponder this question.

"In the first place," he said, "Polaris wasn't the pole star five thousand years ago. I'll have to check my computer program to see if there was such a star then, and if so, which one it was. You're right, though, that they would have seen the never-setting stars in the north."

"Do you think they sat up late looking at the stars?" I speculated.

"Sure," said Evan. "What else did they have to do? No TV. On moonlit nights they might have danced by moonlight, but they would have seen the stars better without the moon."

Then he told me an ancient Chinese story he'd read about the Cowherd and the Weaving Girl. They fell in love, but her father refused the Cowherd as a suitor, so the sky spirit took them to the heavens. To keep them apart, as the Weaving Girl's father wished, the sky spirit put them on either side of the Great River in the Sky, which we call the Milky Way. They yearned so much for each other that the sky spirit took pity, and made a bridge across for one night a year. It's good luck to cross a bridge on that day.

I could have told him that the same story was popular in Korea, because it's all part of the same large culture area, in spite of many differences. Instead, I let him tell me the familiar tale without comment.

By now we were on the roof of the museum, where large antique astronomical instruments were kept. Evan was in his element, studying each one, so I wandered to the edge and looked out over the busy street, and the tall buildings of Beijing. Beijing was interesting, but at the moment I felt some sympathy with Joe. I could hardly wait to see the Hongshan archaeological sites.

8

The night was both cloudless and moonless, but the skies were bright with a myriad stars that seemed so near that you could climb a mountain and touch them. The Milky Way was awesome. I've never seen it so clearly, so full of individually sparkling stars.

I had arrived in Green Valley. Many adults and a swarm of children were sprawled on deer hide blankets, admiring the stars. I cocked my head with one eye toward the sky. I could pick out the belt of Orion and the spread-out W that makes the constellation of Cassiopeia. In the north I found the Big and Small Dippers, but that's all I learned about the stars in Girl Scout camp.

Dancing Crane, one of Owl's brothers, was in the midst of the children as he told sky stories. Jade sat cross-legged beside him with her head resting against his arm, so she could look up at the sky.

"You know how the Great Bear rotates around the sky but never goes below the edge of the land?" Dancing Crane began. "Well, there's a reason for that.

"Once, that Bear Woman wanted to become human, so she begged the sky god to let her spend some time on earth. The sky god finally gave her permission to live on earth, if she could pass a test. The test was to stay in a cave for a whole moon cycle, without coming out to see the sun. She managed by sleeping the whole time.

"When her thirty days were over, she awoke to find that she had become a beautiful young woman. It was spring, and Bear Woman wandered through the meadows picking flowers, and through the forests enjoying the dappled sunshine that came through the trees.

"At the end of the day Bear Woman went back to her cave, but hunters had arrived. 'What happened to the bear that was in this cave,' they asked her? 'We've been watching her, waiting for the right time to capture her for our bear ceremony.'

"Bear Woman pretended she didn't know where that bear went, but she roamed with them until they found another bear with a newborn cub, still sleeping. This time the hunters captured a bear cub, and took it back to their village."

"Well," said Dancing Crane, "you'll find this hard to believe, children, but those people planned to eat the bear."

The children shuddered and squirmed and gagged.

"Bear Woman stayed in the hunters' village for a year, while they fed the bear cub human food and played with it like a child. In the meantime Bear Woman fell in love with Deer Hunter. They decided to be married in the spring at the bear festival. But when it was time to kill the bear, Bear Woman cried and cried.

"'It could have been me,' she sobbed. She asked the sky god to take her back, but to let her always be in the night sky, so she could see her beloved every night. The sky god gave her a place in the north, where bears belong.

"And because she still loved Deer Hunter, even though he was cruel to bears, she asked the sky god to give her something to do that would be helpful to him. So she has her place in the north, and she points her tail in the four directions, helping people know whether it is winter, spring, summer, or fall. That's how you can always tell which way is north, because the Bear Woman circles around the central star."

Jade found the bear in the sky, and pointed to it. "That way is always north," she repeated. "And the tail points to the east, so it is summer now."

"And it's bedtime now," said Crane, lifting her to his shoulders.

Introductions all around the archaeology department at Beida took time, but with far less ceremony than I had experienced in South Korea. The famous Professor Wu spoke excellent English, having spent a couple of years as visiting faculty at Harvard. His black hair was slicked straight back from his forehead, and a small mole on his cheek almost seemed like a beauty mark on his handsome face.

Mr. Gao was balding and stoop-shouldered, with an eager and friendly personality. When he spoke, his words sounded like Chinese, but if I listened carefully I could sort out English words.

The other archaeologists at Beida spoke no English, but they all spoke putonghua, regardless of the dialect they grew up with. Luckily I didn't have to translate. Ma Yumei was assigned as our interpreter, and we also had Xiao Li, so I was spared the embarrassment of asking the Chinese professors to repeat their words until I understood.

Miss Ma is slender and tall, with wide Manchurian cheek bones. She wore a red print dress that draped from her shoulders, no make-up, and hair gathered back at the nape of her neck. I was jealous that she looked elegant, while I would look dumpy and frumpy dressed the same. Life isn't fair.

Joe and Dr. Wu discussed ways to get to Daling. If we went by train the radar might cause a problem. It was too thick to go under the bottom berth. Where could it be stored in a small sleeping compartment, unless someone wanted it in bed with them? Even Ashley isn't skinny enough for that to be comfortable. Besides, the stop nearest to the Daling archaeological station is a small town, which meant that we couldn't take an express train. A local train stops at every station, and takes many hours. Those of us listening were divided as to whether or not it would be fun to take the overnight train. Dr. Wu suggested that we take his car from Beida, and he would come up later with Mr. Gao. But when we explained about the size of the radar unit, and the addition of Evan, he withdrew the offer. Clearly we'd need two cars, and large ones at that. But he still recommended that we drive.

"If you go by road, you'll have a chance to visit the city of Cheng De, a much older summer palace of the Manchu emperors than the recent one just outside Beijing. Although there are other contenders, it might be the place Marco Polo called Shangdu, or upper capital. The poet Coleridge poeticized the name to Xanadu.

"Even if the city doesn't date back to Marco Polo, it's ancient and interesting, and is being restored. The Lamaist temple there is called the Potala, like the famous one in Tibet. There's a lot to see. Besides, I know a good place for lunch."

That sounded promising. Joe decided to drive to Daling, whatever it might cost.

Next we were rounded up for a tour through the new Sackler museum. I let my thoughts drift as were shown a mock-up of the Paleolithic site of Zhoukoutian. It's the famous site of "Peking Man" with evidence interpreted as early fire. I learned that the site is near Beijing, across Marco Polo Bridge, of all things, but we don't have time to go there on this trip. The stratigraphy was explained in more detail than I wanted to know, so I stood watching people rather than listening. I saw Ashley give Joe a sly poke in his ribs, which he brushed off like a fly. Laura moved away from them. Something had to be going on there.

I perked up when we arrived at the exhibit with the painted pottery of the Hongshan culture, and listened attentively to Miss Ma's spiel in case I had missed something in my reading, or in case there were new unpublished discoveries.

Laura asked about the Hongshan villages, addressing our interpreter as "Miss Ma."

"Please call me Yumei. Most Americans do."

"What does your name mean?" Laura asked.

"Beautiful Jade," she said with a smile. "But I wasn't named for the Hongshan culture.

She turned back to the exhibits. "The Hongshan culture," Yumei explained, "is mostly represented by ordinary Neolithic villages. The people raised pigs and grew millets. They made brown pottery for everyday use, and fired red pots with black painted horizontal designs for ceremonial occasions. They knew how to choose the right kind of stone for different purposes. Sharp tools were chipped from the local flint-like stone, and hard granites were ground down to make plows and axes. Softer sandstone slabs were used for querns, with granite handstones for grinding the millet into flour.

"Each village had about a hundred houses in rows, but unlike the earlier cultures, most villages were not surrounded by ditches. Only a few Hongshan villages have been excavated, but hundreds have been located on surveys. The Hongshan culture would not attract so much attention except for the two ceremonial centers and the beautiful carved jades."

We came to a mock-up of a site on a hillside above the curve of a large river. Although I was familiar with the site report, and had even digitized a map of it onto my computer, it wasn't exactly as I expected. Everything looked neater, for one thing.

"The first ceremonial center excavated is called Dongshanzui, high on a hillside overlooking the Daling River. It's known for many enigmatic rock features, including stone-edged platforms and lines of rocks. Two small broken figurines were found here – one very pregnant, and the other possibly nursing an infant. Other female figures were about half life-sized. They sat cross-legged, wearing thick rope belts tied with a double loop."

I was fascinated to see a waist fragment with a rope knotted around it. In a North Korean archaeological encyclopedia there's a photograph of a rope belt of the same thickness and with the same knot, accidentally preserved by arid conditions. It piqued my curiosity, but I couldn't find a ready explanation for the same thickness of rope and identical knots being used several hundred miles apart, with probably a thousand years difference in time. Could there have been a connection through space and time? Did the knotted rope belt, so precisely tied, have a special meaning? But we were whisked on.

"The other ritual center is Daling. Sometimes," continued Yumei, "Chinese archaeologists refer to this locality as *Nushen Miao*, the Goddess Temple. On the slope of another hill about forth kilometers away, archaeologists discovered the floor of a long, low building, with life-sized statues of a woman, a pig, and a bird, along with painted pottery and fragments of a pedestal vessel with a slotted lid."

She stopped to point out a copy of the "goddess" face, with its inset green jade eyes, high cheek bones, and wide smiling lips. I didn't consider her beautiful, but definitely compelling. I found myself wishing she could talk – but then I wouldn't have a dissertation project, unless she spoke only to me.

The map of the Goddess Temple excavation showed a building with a rounded protrusion in the north, two lobes like stubby arms out to the sides, and a rectangular area at the lower end that I couldn't help thinking of as a foot. Fragments of statues were found in the center as well as in the two rounded side lobes. A photograph showed the face when it was first uncovered, without a nose. The nose turned out to be not far away, and had been replaced on the face in the second picture. The photo of the discovery showed three men in Mao caps. It definitely dated the event. No one wears them any more.

The next display case showed a map and some photos of stone piles, tumbled down so that the original arrangement of the stones was difficult to assess. Based on what I've seen elsewhere, the stones could have been parts of walls or towers. But Yumei had a different explanation.

"Above the Goddess Temple is a raised area edged with stones. We call it a platform. It is about ninety meters wide and a hundred meters long. We don't know what it was used for."

"That's about the size of two football fields side by side," Joe pontificated to us students, as if we didn't use the metric system in all our excavations. Laura rolled her eyes, but Ashley cooed, "That's really big," as if she didn't know already. On second thought, she hasn't been to a field school, so maybe she didn't know.

"The rest of the site is a necropolis, a big cemetery, with clusters of graves on hilltops, except for the biggest group of graves, which are in a valley, with a plain round mound that may be an altar." We gathered around the photos and plan drawing.

"Several graves have been excavated. They're unusual in having no tools or pottery deposited in the graves – the only objects buried with the individuals are jade ornaments, up to sixteen jades in a single grave. Pottery was found in the tombs, although it is not utilitarian and it is rarely placed in individual graves. Instead, bottomless painted pots encircle the edge of the tomb. Square tombs have a square of pottery around them. A mounded tomb may have only one or many people buried in it, but a mound of stones and dirt is piled on top of each tomb."

We stopped at the final display in this section. A photograph showed a hill with a lot of square pits sunk deeply into it. "The only other type of structure found so far is an artificial mound, as tall as a pyramid, with circles of dressed white stone embedded within it. Nobody knows what it was used for, but crucibles with traces of copper were found near the top. The copper may be later than the Hongshan era, because only one copper artifact has been excavated. It's a very simple copper wire earring, with an unworked lump of jade attached," Yumei finished her spiel.

Now it was our turn to talk. We filed into a small conference room. Joe fiddled with his computer so we could all show the power-point presentations we had prepared.

Joe showed examples of other archaeological sites where he had used radar, and the Chinese archaeologists were impressed. Then Laura discussed what could be learned from both human and animal bones. Her talk had a lot of graphs and charts in it, and in the end she showed how knowing about the nutrition of both the animals and people had allowed a better interpretation of particular sites.

With some trepidation I talked about leadership. I explained that I thought the Hongshan leaders were wu, ancient Chinese shamans, and that by means of asserting connections with spirits, they ran a peaceful society. The evidence consists of the jades themselves, some of which are masklike. Besides, there is no evidence of warfare. None of the bodies represent human sacrifices, nor are there wounds that might have been received in battle. There are no walled sites. The wu would have been leaders, I suggested, because of their knowledge, not because they were strong or had armies.

I went on to point out that the two ceremonial sites are very different from each other. One focuses on birth, and life, and the other on death and the world beyond. Both events would have required rituals to smooth the transitions.

Then I went farther out on a limb and discussed the possible effects of climate change. Perhaps decreasing precipitation made it harder to raise pigs, and that's why they are so important in the iconography. Maybe the elite owned the best places to raise pigs.

The Chinese archaeologists asked several questions of Joe, Laura and me, but the topic they really got into was Ashley's. She pointed out that, although jade-working was not new, it became much more elaborate in the Hongshan culture, and many more colors of jade were used. More jade ornaments were produced.

Ashley had also looked into the iconography of the 'goddess' face. She found jade plaques in a couple of museum collections that were similar to the face from the Goddess Temple. They had in common a headband, upturned hair ends, and an enigmatic smile. They were thought to be from the Shang Dynasty. She ended by suggesting that memory of the goddess lasted into Shang times.

Ashley clearly enjoyed the attention her paper had brought her, as she stood in the midst of an admiring crowd.

10

Looking down from a gnarled pine tree, I could see a crowd of people milling around, and hear them shouting. Jade was in the midst of the hubbub, but I couldn't yet understand what was happening. Jade had a small pig in her arms with her back turned to Small Tiger, who was yelling and waving his finger at Jade and the pig.

"You made your pig bite me," the boy screamed. "He should be butchered right now, right here. I'll get my mother's knife. It isn't right to teach pigs tricks. They are just animals to be eaten."

"Piggy didn't hurt you," Jade answered in a soft voice. "He was just trying to protect me from your teasing. Piggy loves me, you see."

"Loves you! Hah! He does what you want because you feed him by hand. He comes when you call in case you have food. He can count? Hah! He watches you to for a signal to stop. That pig has an evil spirit. Pigs shouldn't live through a fire. He should be killed before the spirit harms us."

Carver came out of his workshop, looking around to see what the commotion was about. Spotting Jade and Piggy, he waded into the knot of children and plucked Piggy from Jade's arms. "What's this about, Small Tiger? A little pig can't harbor a spirit. What a silly idea."

"He tried to bite me, Uncle Carver, it's a mean and vicious pig. You should butcher it right away." Small Tiger sounded belligerent, but he looked at the ground now that an adult was present.

"Well, let's see what wicked tricks the pig can do. Show us, Jade." Carver returned the piglet to Jade's arms.

Jade didn't want to put the piglet down, for fear that Small Tiger or one of his friends would grab him and run away. But

Carver was in charge of the situation. He sat all of the children down in a semicircle, and stood behind them.

"Show us, Jade," Carver insisted.

Jade handed the pig to her father. "Hold him while I go hide, and then I'll call Piggy with a special noise and he'll come find me."

Jade went behind a clump of bushes, and made a noise like a woodpecker. Piggy dashed to where she was. "See, he looks for me when he hears that noise."

"Hah," snorted Small Tiger. "He smells you. Any pig can do that. What else can he do?"

"He'll hide when I tell him to. Hide, Piggy." A quarter turn of her hand accompanied the command.

Piggy ran around the crowd of children, and ducked into a hole that had been dug to get clay. He stayed there without moving, until Jade called, "Come Piggy!"

"Oooh!" said some of the children.

"He'll also speak, loud or soft. Speak loud, Piggy." A terrible squeal came out of Piggy's small mouth.

"Now softly, Piggy." Piggy made a sort of grumbling noise, like a piglet nursing.

"But the best thing is, Piggy can count. How many fingers is this, Piggy?"

Jade held up three fingers. Piggy put his right front foot out and tapped three times.

"See, he's a smart pig. Too smart to be eaten."

By this time the audience had grown by several adults, who watched in surprise.

"How did you teach the pig those tricks?" asked a woman spinning dog fur as she watched.

"We were just playing. And Piggy is smart and quick."

"What use is a pig that can do those things?" asked Dancing Crane, leaning on his wooden hoe, just back from the most distant field. "He should be the main course of the harvest feast."

He tempered the meanness of his words with a smile, but Jade didn't smile back.

"No! Come Piggy" Jade had lost her good humor, and picked Piggy up again as he ran to her.

"It does seem to have an evil spirit," said an old man. "Or how would the pig know its name?"

Golden Owl came down the hill from their big house, to see what the noise was about. As the village healer and seer, Owl often had to settle disputes, so her ear was tuned to raised voices. Some adults crowded around her, asking how she could let her daughter do this kind of witchcraft with a pig.

"We'll have a ceremony tonight and throw the yarrow stalks. It's time to ask about Jade's future path. Have you noticed Jade's Spirit Bird in the pine tree? I clapped for her to come."

Owl pointed at me with her chin. All heads swiveled up in my direction, and I made sure my beautiful tail feathers were hanging straight, with all this attention.

"In the presence of the Spirit Bird we will ask all your questions, and see what the future holds. I must make preparations. We will meet when the moon rises."

The moon was just full, rising when the sun went down. As the moon changed from a large silvery ball to a smaller golden one, several hundred people gathered by moonlight in the clearing between the two groups of the houses. A sacred tree in the clearing spread its branches over all of them. The villagers sat according to households for formal occasions like this one. Nearest Owl and her family were her sisters and their families. Her brothers Dancing Crane and Eagle had married into the other section of the village, so they sat in the outer circle.

After everyone was seated and quiet, Golden Owl appeared, wearing a band made of yellow feathers around her forehead, and a belt of shells. In one hand she carried an oblong obsidian knife, and thick stems of freshly cut yarrow in the other.

"Now, please watch while I prepare the stalks."

Owl laid the stalks in a row on a flat stone. First she cut them into strips about a finger long. Then she slit each one in half the long way, creating a flat side and a round side. Laying them flat side up, she sprinkled them with red powder from a leather pouch on her belt. No one stirred. The spirits were too near for chitchat, and spirits are notoriously unpredictable.

Owl clapped her hands six times to call her spirits. "Are you here?" she called. The wind rustled through the trees, and the creek gurgled. An owl hooted from a distant tree.

"Answer first about the pig, if you please. Is it a good spirit or an evil one?"

She tossed the yarrow sticks onto the ground in front of herself, where those in the front rows could see them clearly, and later tell those not so close what they saw.

Four sticks had the round side up, and two showed the flat side. This was a good sign, although not the best.

"He's a good spirit," Owl announced, "But he has a mischievous side."

"Does the pig have something to do with Jade's future?" asked Owl as she tossed the sticks again. Once more, four round and two flat sides came up. The pig would be important for Jade, although not the most important element in her life.

"What will Golden Jade of the Wu clan become? Will she be a healer, a jade carver, a dancer for the spirits?"

Each time Owl asked the sticks fell with all curved sides up. The family heads closest to the yarrow sticks drew in their breath. Everyone knew this was the most powerful and auspicious sign.

Jade was destined to be all those things. She would be a carver, healer, and spirit dancer, but most importantly the spirits had selected her to be a leader. Perhaps a leader of many people, more than just their village.

"How many people will Golden Jade of the Wu clan lead?" asked Owl. Tens, hundreds, thousands? The tens and hundreds answered "no," the thousands, "yes."

"The spirits decree that Jade will be a leader of all the Red Mountain people," said Owl in the singsong voice of a spirit. "To prepare herself she must journey in each of the four directions, and bring back something with an inner glow from each one. Objects that glow have spirits within them."

Jade must have realized how much she would have to learn, as tears formed in her green eyes but didn't spill. The spirits had spoken. Her duties would be legion. She took a deep breath and sat up straight, hoping to live up to the expectations of the spirits.

After the augury, the villagers sat chatting, with cups of wild cherry wine to ward off the autumn chill.

"Jade is a very pleasing child," said one woman. "I think she'll be a fine leader."

"She's smart, too," added another villager.

"The best thing about her is her warm smile," said Dancing Crane. "It always makes me feel good when she greets me."

Not everyone was pleased with the idea of Jade as leader.

"True, she has a quick mind," one said, "but she isn't ambitious. How can our village become the biggest and best?"

"Perhaps," said another, "she will treat us like pigs, and expect us to count by tapping the ground."

"In any case," said a third, "she can't be our leader until she learns what her power symbol is. That won't be very soon."

Carver and Owl noted the grumbling. Talking it over, they decided that in the spring, Carver and Jade should make the first journey to discover her power symbol, and she should learn to carve it out of jade. Over the winter, they would let Piggy sleep in the house so he would come to no harm.

>11

A banquet was laid on for dinner at a local restaurant. Once again we had a room to ourselves. A big round table in the middle of the room was set with eight places, each with three sizes of drinking glasses – tiny, juice-sized, and water-sized. Several small plates of carefully arranged appetizers – peanuts, sliced meat, pickles and such were already on the table. It was Joe's place to sit on the right side of Dr. Wu, but I contrived to sit on his left. It was he who had excavated at the site, and I hoped to get some anecdotes and nitty gritty details.

The first thing that happened when we all sat down was unexpected, to say the least. Laura stared in frank curiousity. All four of our Chinese colleagues reached for the little squares of paper napkins from the center of the table and wiped off their glasses, small plates, and chopsticks. Laura caught Ashley's eye and gave her a quizzical look. Ashley lifted her shoulders slightly, and reached for the napkins to wipe her own place setting. I figured they knew something I didn't about the cleanliness of the kitchen, so I grabbed a pink napkin and performed the same ritual. Joe wasn't paying attention, deep in conversation with Dr. Wu.

Eventually, Joe looked at the table setting. He eyed the peanuts, and asked how we were supposed to eat them. "I suppose I can't just grab a handful," he said wistfully.

"No fingers. Chopsticks," I announced, and I demonstrated my skill in picking up one peanut at a time. When Joe tried it, the chopsticks kept crossing over each other, shooting the peanut across the table at Laura. We all laughed, and a waiter brought Joe a fork, which made him blush.

"Chopsticks are too low tech for me," he said, with his patented half-smile.

The toasting began over the appetizers, and continued intermittently throughout the meal. At irregular intervals someone would stand and toast our expedition, or Chinese-American friendship, or anything at all. Each toast ended with the directive, "Gambei!" which means literally 'empty cup.' If you were game enough to drain the glass, it was instantly refilled.

The innocent-looking liquid in the glass is *maotai*, a wicked white liquor that's hard for me to even sip, let alone gulp down. As the other diners became more raucous and rowdy, I began making a pretense of drinking, because I didn't need a hangover with my jetlag. Beer and water were poured into the other glasses – perfectly adequate potables, that helped to quench any unexpected mouthfuls of ginger, garlic, or red pepper. Maotai would just add to the pain.

I wasn't eating much because the cuisine of the day featured seafood, which I don't eat. I asked Yumei how to say "allergic" so Dr. Wu would stop putting crawly things with claws and antennae on my plate.

My favorite dish was an unfamiliar vegetable cut in long strips, with a taste like celery, garnished with cilantro and sesame seeds. It had tiny and very hot red peppers in it, which I learned to set aside with my chopsticks, after the first one required two glasses of beer and half a bowl of rice to quench the fire.

"You have to watch out, Clara," said Ashley unhelpfully after the fact. "The smaller the hotter." She had grown up with red peppers in her food, and she ought to know.

"Thanks for the warning," I said wryly, but Ashley's attention had shifted to Mr. Gao, across the table.

I wanted to ask Dr. Wu about the copper found at Daling, but he turned my questions away with questions of his own. Apparently serious conversation is not encouraged at banquets. He preferred to speak English, depriving me of the chance to practice Chinese, but I supposed there would be many chances in the next few weeks. I found him quite engaging.

Was I Chinese? Korean? Really? How did I come to go to school in America? So I explained about adoption, which is not common within China except for taking in orphaned relatives, and of course, Americans adopting Chinese babies, a practice which is not much publicized within China.

I noticed that Joe was talking earnestly with Prof. Gao on his other side, with the help of the attentive Yumei. I turned my attention back to Dr. Wu, who began to explain why there were so few women archaeologists in China. I hadn't asked, and in fact I hadn't had a chance to observe the gender of archaeologists yet, except for the few we met today and at the Archaeological Institute. My experience in Korea had led me to expect that not many women would be trained for the field. Dr. Wu declared earnestly that most women preferred to do museum work rather than fieldwork, especially after the birth of their only child, for China still enforces the one-child policy. The only exceptions are the countryside, where a second child is permitted if the first child is a girl, and among the National Minorities where limits were not imposed. This was a discussion I didn't want to get into now, but I did say mildly that many women archaeologists in America take their children to the field. Professor Wu's eyes opened wide. I couldn't tell if he was shocked or interested in this possibility as a solution for recruiting more women students into archaeology.

Joe claimed his attention, while I surveyed the dishes for a few last nibbles, and asked Xiao Li about them. I steered the lazy susan around so I could get the last bite of the vegetable dish I liked. Xiao Li told me its name, but it didn't stick in my mind for even the proverbial hour.

The amount of food served was incredible – platter after platter of various kinds of dishes. When the table got too crowded, the waiters just stacked the new platters on top of the old ones, balancing them on the edges so that the underneath dish was reachable, too, with determined chopsticks.

Even without touching the shellfish, the only thing that kept me from eating too much was that I am slow with the chopsticks. It made me wonder if the archaeologists who write about feasting have spent time in China.

The last dish brought to the table was delicious seaweed soup, without any sea creatures in it.

"We've had a multi-course meal, from nuts to soup instead of soup to nuts," Laura observed. "And in the old days they wrote from right to left. Is everything opposite in China?"

I asked about looting of archaeological sites. Mr. Gao said it was a pity, but now they had to be careful with artifacts that are valuable in the art market.

"Where do you keep the original artifacts from Hongshan?" Joe asked.

"Do you want to see them?" Dr. Wu might have been a trifle tipsy, but he managed to pull a huge ring of keys from his pocket.

Of course we did. After one last "gambei!" we were shown through a series of locked doors into the museum's storage area.

I was thrilled to see the real artifacts from various Hongshan sites. Nobody cared if we picked them up, even the life-sized "goddess" head. So I did, very carefully, with gloves on. It was made of coarse clay, covered by fine clay, with paint as the outermost layer. I turned it over and looked at the back. Inside the head was a piece of wood that the coarse clay was attached to.

"Could you get a radiocarbon date from this?" I asked Dr. Wu, pointing to the organic material

"We already have, but it's not published yet. More or less 3500 B.C. Surprisingly long ago, for the first life-sized statues in China, and possibly the first life-sized clay statues anywhere in the world – although I have also heard such claims for both Egypt and the Near East."

"They don't have to be the first to be remarkable," said Joe. "They're so well sculpted. So life-like."

I was impressed with the face, and wondered what she represented – a leader, a goddess, a mythical figure? I was even more anxious to learn about the leadership at the site, and to discover what this face might imply.

"Do you think this face represents a real woman?"

"Oh, no, she is a mysterious spirit. Otherwise her eyes would not be green."

"Why not?"

Wu laughed. "Like you and me, Asians have dark eyes."

I tried another topic. "Who were the leaders in the society? Who was buried in the tombs?"

"Most of those buried are men. The central burial of the biggest tomb is missing, because the tomb was looted long ago, but that person was probably a man, too. So I don't think it was a matriarchal society, if that's what you'd like to find. The site is too complex for that."

I thought I was being teased, or perhaps tested, but I tried to keep an edge out of my voice.

"I'm interested in leadership and power, regardless of the gender of the person at the top. But I don't start with any assumptions about what people thought about the abilities, duties or roles of men and women. Regardless of gender, what do you make of the burials? Are they the elite, the leaders of the society?"

"They must be chiefs. Look at all the jade they had. We found those hoof-shaped tubes under the heads of skeletons. We guess they were headdresses that the hair went through, but what happened to the hair then, or how the tube stayed on, we aren't sure. They also wore chest pendants sewn to their clothing, and bracelets, and earrings. One man held a jade turtle in each hand. They must have been resplendent in their finery."

"Where did they get the jadestone? Did it come from far away, or is it local stone?"

"Some of it is local. A white jade was used to make earrings more than three thousand years before the Hongshan culture. Pale green jade is still mined in the mountains of eastern Liaoning Province. There must have been trips to get jade stone from far away. No source has been found for some of this other jade – some yellowish, some dark green, some almost black"

"Is it jadeite or nephrite?"

"Mostly it's nephrite. But the Chinese concept of jade has to do with a glow from within, rather than the composition of the stone. Any stone that can be polished to achieve that glow is considered *yu*, which you translate as jade. Did you notice that some of the so-called 'jades' are made of a stone you call turquoise?"

"Yes – fish-shaped earrings, and an owl with outspread wings, at least. Where does the turquoise come from?"

"The nearest known sources are in Central Asia. But we don't know if a nearer source might have existed that is now mined out."

"What was the jade used for besides ornaments?"

"Only a few tools and no weapons."

"Long distance treks to obtain the raw material, coupled with fine jade-working seem like a lot of trouble for ordinary farmers. Why did the Hongshan people need leaders? What did the elite do to earn their jades? How would you persuade farmers to go on a long trek to find jade stone, and carry the heavy stuff on their backs for the return journey?"

"Maybe they managed the trade routes for jade stone."

This seemed like too circular an argument to pursue, and anyway, Joe had started to round up his gear and say good-bye. I looked forward to seeing the professors and Yumei again in Daling.

Back at the hotel, Joe beckoned me to the front desk to help him make reservations for our return stay. The price quoted was much more than we were paying. I asked why, and was told that those reservations were made on the internet, and it was a special price.

"Okay," said Joe, and we went to look for the business office, which we found on the fourth floor of the hotel. Access to the web was free. I logged on, found the hotel website, and made reservations at the cheaper rate. Is this the power of the internet, or just lack of logic?

As long as I was logged on, I sent Ed an e-mail message. I attached a digital photo of the crew at the duck restaurant, and one of me holding the goddess head. I signed it Jade Princess, which is Ed's pet nickname for me.

It wasn't hard to fall asleep, but I dreamed of Golden Jade instead of Ed.

12

As I flew in to Green Valley, I saw that Jade and Carver were packing clothing, food, and blankets. Azaleas bloomed in the forest, and the trees had a new sheen of green.

"What else do we need to take, Baba?" Jade was asking. "I have my walking stick, and some medicines that Mama taught me how to use, and food for Piggy. And my warm cloak if we're not back by snowtime."

"Food for Piggy? You don't think Piggy is coming? He would slow us down."

"I can't leave Piggy behind. Small Tiger will cook Piggy if he catches him. Mama is very busy now that Little Carver is walking. She can't be watching Piggy all the time. Piggy has to come with us. I'll carry him some of the time if he can't keep up. And as soon as we are in the forest, Piggy will find his own acorns."

"Absolutely not," growled Carver. "We're ready to go now. Say your good-byes quickly."

Jade accepted this with a silent tear, which ran down beside her nose. She was also sad about leaving Owl.

"When will I see you again, Mama?"

Both mother and daughter had watery eyes, although they had agreed that this trip was a good way for Jade to learn about the world, and that Owl should stay at home this time. There was a toddler, and Owl was pregnant.

"I went to the Ever-White Mountains on my own quest, and met Carver there. It was so exciting to see the world beyond our beautiful valley. As soon as you find your spirit emblem, and carve it from the most beautiful jade in the world, you'll be home again. You're so talented, Jade my darling daughter, it won't take you long. You'll love meeting your cousins in Jade Village. And the view from the jade hill is spectacular. You can see all the way to the big sea."

Owl knelt beside Jade and stroked her hair. "I envy you your adventures into the wide world. Maybe I can go with you on your next adventure. It's so much fun to see new places, and meet new people. You'll learn something new every day. Your journey will be useful for us here at home, too, with the knowledge you'll bring back. Knowing what the whole world is like is important, especially for a leader."

Owl offered Jade a thin bone object. "Here's a special tool for you to take along – the far-seeing needle that belonged to my mother, and generations before her. You've seen me use one to learn about distant places. Sometimes you may see us here at home when you call the spirits and use the needle. But never use it as a toy. The spirits don't like to be bothered unnecessarily. You're old enough to use it wisely."

I looked over Jade's shoulder at the needle. I would have called it an awl with a hole for thread. It had thin carvings on its flat sides. They were rubbed down with much use, but when I squinted I thought I could see a stylized bird.

Jade sniffed back her tears, and put the needle in the treasure pouch attached to her belt. Then, with the basket on her back, and her rabbit fur cloak thrown across it, she was ready to start off on her first adventure. "Good-bye, Piggy. Stay out of harm's way. Don't let a Tiger eat you."

Jade and Carver set forth on the path out of Green Valley along the river. When they came to the river crossing, they took the trail to the north, toward the mountain with pale green jade.

I was torn between going with them and staying with Piggy, who might need more watching over than Jade. Surely Carver would take care of Jade? But sometimes Carver was so involved in his own thoughts he didn't see or hear anything.

Piggy solved the problem for me. He was not about to be left behind. He waited until they were well down the path, and then followed, staying out of sight. I expected him to crash through the woods, but he stayed back and made little noise.

I followed Piggy as he crept through the bushes, tracking Jade and Carver, until they made their camp for the night, in a cave that Carver always used when he went to get jade nodules for his carvings.

Before they settled in, Carver clapped for the spirits to come, and Jade found a stick to draw a circle in the dirt around their camp. Piggy slept at the entrance, unseen, and I tucked my head under my wing in a tree nearby. After the first night Jade and Carver stayed in villages where they had relatives, and Piggy and I slept on the outskirts.

Carver was interested in the various kinds of plants that grew in the forest. He pointed them out to Jade, and told her their names and explained their uses. Jade wove wildflowers together for her hair, while she noted their scent and color, and learned their names.

Piggy was a crafty animal, now about half grown. He didn't show himself until Jade and Carver had made six camps, when it would be too late to take him back. The circumstances of Piggy's appearance were providential. The sixth day of their trek Jade and Carver entered the deep forest of conifers that separates Red Mountain territory from the Long Bow people.

Carver and Jade made a rough camp. After Carver snared a rabbit to add to their dried provisions for dinner, Jade scraped and rinsed the pelt well so that she could tan it later. They called the spirits and drew their circle, then curled around the campfire embers, wrapped in their cloaks on soft beds of leaves. As they looked through the trees at the starry sky, Carver noticed smoke rising to the east, far in the distance. "Someone from Jade Village, maybe," said Carver. "Tomorrow we'll meet them on the trail, and find out where they're going."

Piggy and I were just about to make ourselves known, when rustling leaves caught my attention, and I flew to perch on Piggy's back. Three men leapt into the clearing and pounced on Carver and Jade. Before Carver could react, two men held him and tied him up, while the third trussed Jade, cloak and all, with a long rope. Carver and Jade were completely helpless.

One man saw the jade head hanging around Carver's neck, and cut the leather thong with a sharp obsidian knife. He put the jade in his pack.

"What's this?" spluttered Carver. "Give me back my Long Bow emblem. You aren't entitled to it. Besides, you crossed our spirit circle! That's a sacrilege. This trail is free to everyone who keeps to the rules. We're not trespassing on your territory! We're

Red Mountain people, and I was born among the Long Bow people. Who are you, and what right do you have here?"

"Be quiet!" commanded the largest of the three. "Give us your jades!"

"Why?" asked Carver. "What will you give us for them? Anyway, you didn't explain why you tied us up."

"Give you?" They laughed and nudged each other. "We'll give you your lives, if you give us your jades. Or we can kill you and take all your jades and all your other possessions."

Two of the men began rooting though Carver's pack.

Piggy and I were watching from the edge of the clearing. My claws dug nervously into Piggy's back. Maybe I scared him, or maybe Piggy is as smart as Jade says. Whatever the cause, Piggy made an appalling screeching noise, the kind that Jade had taught him to do when she commanded him to "talk loud."

The robbers almost dropped the packs when they heard the noise, but when they turned around they only saw Piggy.

"Just a piglet," said one of them.

I took advantage of their distraction to swoop down behind them as they looked toward the bushes where Piggy had returned to hide. I brushed them each on the ears with my feathers, and darted away to the tree above. They looked behind them and saw nothing. Piggy howled again, and I swished behind them while he held their attention.

The lead robber crashed away into the forest, without even taking the path.

"Spirits," he yelled. "These two are protected by spirits!"

The other two men dropped the packs they had begun to rifle, and sprinted through the trees after him. When we could no longer hear their retreat, Piggy and I came into the clearing.

I looked at Jade and Carver, helpless with their arms tied behind them. Starting with Jade, I pulled at the ropes with my beak, and Piggy gently prodded with his new tusks, until we loosened the ropes enough for them Jade to wriggle free. Then she untied Carver. Neither of them was hurt, except for mild rope burns. "We should keep all this rope," observed Carter. "It might come in handy as we travel. Thick rope like this takes a long time to make."

"Piggy and Spirit Bird rescued us!" Jade picked up Piggy

and gave him a squeeze. "Those bad men thought they were spirits."

"Well, I think I believe they are spirits, too. How did you get here in time to save us?" Carver asked me, brushing the pine needles off his clothing. "Your timing was perfect. Did Jade call you?"

"I didn't," said Jade, "but I was thinking about Piggy, and wondering why the Spirit Bird didn't come on this trip. Maybe they came because the men broke the spirit circle." Neither Piggy nor I wanted to tell them that we had been following all along.

A few days later the smoke of Jade Village could be seen afar, and then finally we arrived. A farmer hoeing his field saw us coming, and ran ahead to alert the village.

"Spinner, your brother Carver is here! He has a pretty little girl with him, and a pig and a bird."

By the time we got to the center of the village, it seemed that everyone had put down their work to greet us. Jade hid behind her father when all the strangers gathered around her, but soon she and Piggy were showing off their tricks. I didn't stay for the feast in preparation.

13

No car was placed at our disposal on our second day in Beijing, but it was pleasant to walk. Xiao Li came along as guide. Laura teased him that he was afraid we'd get lost.

"Archaeologists never get lost," she explained. "We carry GPS units in our pockets." Laura demonstrated by taking hers out of a vest pocket and waving it around.

"I thought you were carrying cell phones," said Xiao Li, slapping Joe's bulging pocket.

"Ours don't work in China. And we're here too short a time to make the investment in a Chinese phone worthwhile."

Xiao Li wasn't familiar with the term GPS, but it turned out he was familiar with the gadget. "You call that Global Positioning System, GPS? I have one, too," and he pulled it out of his shirt pocket. "But you have to know more than where you are – you have to know where you are going."

"You could put that saying in a fortune cookie," Laura laughed.

"Fortune cookie?" repeated Xiao Li.

"I'll explain later," I promised.

Xiao Li took us first to the Gate of Heavenly Peace, Tiananmen itself. A giant picture of Mao still rules above the gateway, although most other Mao pictures and statues have disappeared.

"This is where Chairman Mao gave his speech to proclaim the establishment of the People's Republic of China. He stood on the wall up there," Xiao Li pointed. He turned and waved his hand at the square where people had gathered to hear the proclamation. "Everybody who could be here came. It was an exciting day for China. My grandfather still talks about being here, and what a thrill it was."

I thought of the Chinese reader I studied first year, which began with an account of that day. That's when I learned the

Chinese words for "glorious," "imposing," and "magnificent." It was certainly a historic square, as well as vast.

We went through the gate and bought tickets to see the Forbidden City properly this time. These acres were used exclusively by the Imperial family until they were supplanted in 1911 by the Republic headed by Sun Yat-Sen. It's definitely glorious, imposing, and majestic.

Courtyard follows courtyard. In each one, the walkway over which the emperor's chair was carried is intricately carved in marble with imperial five-toed dragons. On the north side of each courtyard a grand pavilion cuts off the view of the next courtyard. They all seem to be throne rooms. They can be peeked into, each with an elaborate seat and other paraphernalia, such as giant cloisonné candlesticks and bronze ritual vessels. Oddities like clocks, which had been presented to the Qing emperors by various European heads of state made the collection of objects worth observing for their quirkiness alone.

Ashley and her camera went crazy over the rooflines. At each corner of an upturned tile roof, five creatures sat in a row on the ridge. She took pictures of them silhouetted against the sky, and used her telephoto lens to make individual portraits, catching their expressions.

At the far back of the Forbidden City, Xiao Li pointed out a nine-dragon screen, made with bas-relief tiles. Each of the dragons carried a pearl in its mouth, and each had the five claws allowed only to the emperor. Elsewhere in China there are also seven-, five-, and three-dragon screens, each with five-clawed dragons. Dragons only appear in odd numbers. It's one of their quirks.

Xiao Li showed us a small museum on the east side of the complex, which of course we couldn't miss, since the current display included discoveries from the ten best archaeological sites of the previous year. Mostly the sites were tombs, which tend to have rich offerings. New discoveries at Daling had made it into the top ten. We stood and pondered the gorgeous jades newly discovered. They really do have an inner glow. Several of the new discoveries look like shaman masks. I wondered how they were used, and what they meant.

Other new finds included a pair of Han dynasty jade burial suits.

"*Two more* jade burial suits," Ashley exclaimed, in her element." Look how the jade squares are tied together with gold thread at the corners. Isn't that exquisite?"

"It's easy to get jaded with them," Laura whispered to me with a wink behind her hand. We laughed softly. She and I prefer prehistoric times, and we're more interested in the society artifacts imply than in the objects themselves.

Xiao Li had made reservations for us to line up to see Mao's mausoleum, which stands in the middle of the square. We were sternly told to take no pictures, make no noise, and be respectful. Afterwards, when we had shuffled though and out without seeing much, I was unimpressed and unmoved. I wondered if Xiao Li would be offended by my opinion.

Ashley didn't worry about what Xiao Li might think. "Mao looks like he's made of wax," she commented. "Do you think he was done by Madame Tussaud?"

"There certainly wasn't any decay visible," Joe added. "But I read that they really did mummify Mao's body, and he gets touched up from time to time."

"The glass case kind of got to me," I added, no longer troubled by reserve. "Will some princess come along and give him a kiss and wake him up?"

Xiao Li cleared his throat, and said "Tsss." We gave him our attention.

"Next we go to History Museum. It is on side of square, across street over there."

I looked where he was pointing, and saw a blocky Soviet-style building.

The exhibits were more history than prehistory, but some displays were appealing – a Zhou dynasty chariot burial attracted our attention, and I caught Ashley taking a surreptitious photo of it.

"We can skip the last floor," Xiao Li said, herding us into the foyer.

Joe never likes to skip anything, so he asked, "What's there?"

"Lots of stuff about the anti-Japanese War, the Communist struggle, and the establishment of the People's Republic of China," Xiao Li ticked off on his fingers.

I could see that Joe wanted to stay, but the rest of us were restless.

"What have you planned next?" I turned to Xiao Li.

"Do you want to go to the Friendship Store? It has five floors of beautiful things made in China."

"Will we have time to shop when we come back to Beijing?" Ashley asked. "I simply have to take things back to my family, so if this is the only chance, the answer is yes."

"We can't be sure there'll be time at the end of our trip," Joe pointed out. "It costs $200 to change a ticket, and that will be at your expense, if you want to stay and shop."

"I don't want to load up on gifts now, and have to schlep them around everywhere we go," I said, being contrary.

"I don't want to take a chance on missing the Friendship Store," Ashley insisted. "But I can go alone. I even know where it is. We passed it after we picked up Clara from the astronomy museum. You go down to the corner where the Beijing Hotel is, turn right, and then walk a long way straight ahead." Ashley switched into her persistent and persuasive mode.

"Well, I'd like to spend more time in the museum. I won't need so much time at the Friendship Store anyway. I'll meet you there," Joe suggested.

We fixed a time and place to meet.

We went our separate ways in the enormous store. I wanted to surprise Ed with a silk rug for our apartment, so I spent most of the time with rugs spread out around me. They are all so gorgeous, it was hard to choose. Finally I picked one with a navy blue border, a lighter blue in the center, and plum blossoms spilling into the center from each corner. It will look fabulous in our living room.

The clerk had me sign the corner of it, so when I received the shipment several months later, I would know that this is the carpet I picked out and paid for. The silk rug is pricey, but less than half of what it would cost as home, even with shipping added. I was amused to find myself becoming domestic. Not to mention a spendthrift.

Not much time was left before we had to meet Joe, so I decided to browse the book section. I was just examining a set of tapes called, *Joking in Chinese*, when I heard Laura's voice.

I investigated the other side of the bookshelf, and discovered Laura deep in conversation with a blond man, who wore wire-rim glasses and a small, neat goatee.

"Oh," Laura caught sight of me, "Clara, this is Lars Bock from Sweden. Clara Alden." We shook hands and murmured some pleasantries. He spoke English well, with a British accent, naturally.

"Lars is studying early Chinese documents at Beida," Laura explained. "He's interested in ancient rituals, especially those of shadowy people called *wu,* who were kind of like shamans. They danced to bring rain, and were important in state ceremonies until historic times. He thinks they go back to prehistory. So I told him about the Hongshan culture, and what we would be doing, and about your theories. He wants to come and visit our site."

"Interesting thought," I said. "Maybe the leaders I've been looking for are wu. Or began as wu."

Ashley whirled around the corner with four bags in one hand and five bags in the other.

"Can I give you a hand with those?" asked Lars, after he had made Ashley's acquaintance. "Do you know you can mail things from here? Unless you just like carrying them," he added.

"That would be so great. Where?" asked Ashley "What do I do for boxes and wrapping paper?

"I'll show you," said Lars gallantly. He gathered up Ashley's bags. Laura and I had nothing to mail, but we followed along, as soon as I bought the tape set of Chinese jokes.

The post office was amazing. First, Ashley packed her box and stood in line to have it weighed. Then she stood in another line to buy the stamps according to the weight of the package, then finished the wrapping. Instead of string, plastic ribbon in pastel colors was provided to wrap the boxes. And the stamps not only were not self-stick; they didn't have any glue at all. Lars rounded up a paste pot with a brush, and Ashley brushed the back of the stamps she had bought. Before she was finished sticking the stamps on her package it was time to meet Joe, so Laura and I went to tell him what was happening.

Joe was somewhat cool to Lars when he appeared with Ashley. When Lars expressed interest in our site, Joe explained that we were planning to rent a van with driver to go to the site, but we already had a full load.

Lars replied that he still had a few days' work to do in Beijing, and would come to the site in a couple of days. He wanted directions to the site where we would do the radar survey, and asked what had been found there. Joe explained that he hadn't been told exactly, but the Chinese archaeologists knew it was Hongshan from surface indications. And there was reason to expect structures to be found.

"By the way," Lars said, "Have you seen the Daoist temple they've just refurbished? It's quite spectacular, and not far off the highway toward Cheng De. You should see it, if you can make the time."

Joe and Lars went into a huddle while he wrote down the name and address of the temple. I took that as a hopeful sign that we would visit it on the way out of Beijing.

"I have to go," Lars looked at his watch. "Nice to meet you. See you at Daling in a couple of days." He shook everyone's hand before departing.

"How European he is," said Laura. "He practically clicked his heels when he said good-bye." She watched him walk to the stairs.

Joe turned away to look at the drums. We were next to the music department, and Joe, who plays percussion in a combo, couldn't resist a few thumps on an hour-glass-shaped drum. The rhythm sent me back to Green Valley, and Jade.

14

Jade and Carver were enjoying life in Jade Village. Carver was delighted to see his natal family again. He would have been the center of attention, since he had grown up here and was related to nearly everybody, except that his clever daughter, who had a pig and a bird for companions, was an even bigger attraction. With plenty of millet wine after dinner, the villagers were ready for some entertainment.

Carver told about the robbers, and asked if anyone had seen them, or knew who they were. Carver's brother said he had met some other people on the trail to the jade mountain, who described large men who took their food and clothes. They were not Long Bow people, nor were they Red Mountain folks. They spoke in a strange dialect, back in their throats.

"What is the world coming to?" asked Carver, "if people can't even travel through the woods safely? Wild animals are bad enough, but wild people cannot be tolerated."

The people of Jade Village were worried about the stolen symbol. "What if people they rob believe the thieves belong to this village? We'll be spoken of badly everywhere."

The Jade villagers decided to spread the word, telling travelers who visited the village to watch for the robbers, and to be prepared to defend themselves. And to warn them that a symbol of Jade Village had been stolen, so they wouldn't be fooled or confused by it.

Just the same, when they heard the story of the robbers being scared by Piggy and me, they laughed and laughed. They enjoyed it so much they made us reenact the whole episode, with three villagers playing the part of the robbers.

Before the evening ended, Jade and Piggy had to show off all their tricks, until finally everyone was satisfied, and ready to go to bed.

The next day Carver began organizing a trek to the mountain quarry where jade stone could be collected. Four jade workers of the village wanted to go, and so did Carver's sister, Spinner, and her daughter Sand Dollar and nephew, Lobster. At the last minute, Carver's brother Sandy threw together a pack and caught up with them. To protect themselves against robbers, they each carried a stout stick.

"The secret to protection may be in large numbers of people," said Spinner. "Who would dare pounce upon a group of ten people?"

The path toward the mountain begins along a rushing river. Farmers in the fields between the villages greeted them as they walked along, joking, telling stories, or singing to pass the time.

Carver told about the strange customs of Green Valley. Although he was happy there with Owl, some things took getting used to.

"They tell a different story about the bear in the sky. Of course we know that a great medicine woman, long ago, rode a tamed bear to the bedside of her dying grandmother, to receive her drum of authority and her blessings. When she died she went to the sky as a bear. But they think the stars represent a bear who wanted to become human.

"They celebrate the days when the sun stands still with dancing and drinking wild cherry wine," Carver explained. "And there's a special day in the spring when they all dance to bring the rain. I never was much of a dancer, you know, but I'm good at their steps now."

He demonstrated a one-legged hop, followed by several leaps, while humming a melody in six notes.

"I've learned to ferment wild cherries to make wine, too."

"Ah, you must show us how," said Sandy.

Only a few places were shallow enough to cross the big river, especially in spring, when snow melt makes the rivers swell. We crossed at a place where the river broke into separate streams, surrounding islands of trees and rocks. Only one branch was difficult, because of its swirling currents. To cross the swiftest part of the river, they made a human chain holding wrists tightly, so no one would get washed downstream. It was shallow, but the river was running very fast. Jade sat on Carver's shoulders, and held Piggy very tightly in her arms. I, of course, had the advantage of wings to get me across.

The mountain path wound gradually upward, through groves of trees and big sunny meadows. Wildflowers carpeted the hillsides with white, blue, and yellow patches.

"I think the jade quarry is just around the corner now," said Carver, and almost as soon as he said it, there it was.

"The jade isn't pretty when it comes out of the ground," Jade remarked, looking with disappointment at the nodules of brownish and gray stone.

"No, it's the carver who brings out the spirit of the jade," explained Carver. "You have to study each piece before you carve it, and ask the spirits for guidance. And it takes hours of rubbing before the spirits finally let it shine, to show that they are satisfied."

The travelers from Jade Village spent the night by the jade quarry. Sand Dollar and Jade taught each other songs and string finger games in the evening. Lobster watched, but didn't join in.

When they returned, Carver gave Jade a small nodule to carve.

"The first step is to call the spirits, so they will help you. Then you must rough out the object. You do that with sand stuck with pine pitch to a string if you want to cut a slab, or sand on a stone drill to make a hole. This dark red sand is the best, because it's the hardest. We collect it in special leather bags whenever we find it on our journeys."

Carver showed Jade how to make a plain earring. The basic shape was a thick doughnut-shaped ring, with a slot to slide over an ear lobe. Jade began carving her nodule in the same way, but one end was lumpy and hard to carve. As she worked with it, the end seemed to resemble a pig head, with large eyes and sticking-up ears. Still, she had to admit it didn't look like much.

"It takes a lot of practice," said Carver. "But that's a good beginning."

Lobster and Sand Dollar were also learning to carve. Lobster's father Sandy was a fisherman, so he looked to Carver for instruction. He designed a funny little head out of scrap jade. After he bored a hole through one end, he presented it to Jade.

"You should wear it on a cord around your neck. It identifies you as a member or friend of Jade Village," Lobster explained. "Your father had one before the robbers took it."

"I know. My Mama wears one, too."

Jade looked for something to give Lobster. "I don't have anything for you except this lumpy earring," Jade said.

Lobster accepted the jade object, looking at it critically.

"Don't give up on it now It looks like a pig head on this end. If you just work on it some more, the pig will break through. A pig to represent Piggy, who drove away the robbers with the help of Spirit Bird. Let me show you."

Lobster worked on the jade for an hour or so. Then he held out a fat ring of pale green jade, with a pig head on one end of the broken ring. Jade was impressed with the way it was developing.

"This is just the rough work," Lobster explained. "It needs hours more time spent polishing to make it glow. But here's your nice little pig."

"It's not a nice pig, though," objected Jade. "Where are his feet and his curly tail?"

"They aren't there because your pig is half spirit."

Carver came by to look at the object.

"It could be your symbol, you know," he said thoughtfully. "But if that's what it is, it needs a hole to hang it on a cord. You can't wear that on your ear."

Lobster showed Jade how so drill a hole by putting fine sand on the end of a stone drill, and turning it round and round. He wound a bowstring around his drill, and pushed the bow back and forth to make it drill faster through the jade.

"Making jade ornaments is a lot of work," Jade grumbled.

"The spirits will hear you and make it harder," Carver warned. "You should ask for their help to bring out the stone's inner beauty. You must make jade ornaments with love."

15

Xiao Li came early in the morning to hire a van to drive us to Daling. He asked Ashley to go with him, while the rest of us stood outside the hotel surrounded by baggage, including the conspicuous radar unit.

"Marmalade causes quite a problem," Laura said giving the radar unit a friendly pat.

"That's a good name for it. The radar now has a code name: Marmalade.We never need to use the scary word 'radar' again," Joe said.

Xiao Li and Ashley returned half-an-hour later with two taxis, pleased that they were both air-conditioned. The drivers named their price to drive us, and Joe okayed it. I checked to be sure we had enough *ren min bi* to pay them. One of the cars had a trunk large enough for the radar.

Evan turned up a little late, glad to find we hadn't left yet.

"Sorry, I overslept. Thanks for waiting for me."

The six of us with all our luggage and equipment just barely fit into the two taxis. Joe, Ashley and Laura went in the first car, and Evan, Xiao Li and I in the second. Joe instructed the lead driver to take us to the Daoist temple Lars had mentioned, and when we parked he gave us twenty minutes to see it.

Daoism, as I understand it, is a kind of nature religion, with dozens of gods or spirits. This temple was stunningly restored. Every statue was repainted, sometimes garishly, but always colorful. Every statue was resplendent in bright new paint, and the brass containers on the altars were polished to mirror brightness.

Xiao Li told us that the building had been used as a warehouse for seized objects during the long-ago Cultural Revolution. Now that most of those items have been sent to Hong Kong to be sold as antiques, the building was available to be restored for tourists. And not incidentally, a few local residents were returning to worship there.

I was entranced by the statues of the sages, with their mortar-board type hats, hung with beads dangling from the front and back.

"You'd think they'd get cross-eyed," Ashley observed.

We peeked at their eyes through their bead screen, but they were straight.

"Another perfectly good theory down the drain," I said.

One statue is a Goddess of Wisdom. I clapped my hands to her and secretly asked for a few important favors. The main one, of course, was to be invited to do more work on Hongshan sites. The other had to do with my secret mission. We'll see if she grants my requests.

After making the rounds of the temple, we still had time to wander the grounds. Ashley as usual ferreted out nooks and crannies for unusual photos. We came upon a side corridor where a ceremony was in progress. Ashley thought it was probably the one-year commemorative ritual for a deceased patriarch, because they were burning yellow silk.

"That's the widow, burning yards of silk in her husband's memory," she whispered to me, indicating a woman in white. "My Gramma burned silk for Grampa in Hong Kong, but I'm surprised to see it happening here. That would have been so forbidden in the severest years of Chairman Mao."

We watched while the silk was fed into the flame, bit by bit. After the burning, a priest (if that's the right word) brought out some numbered bamboo sticks in a box made of a bamboo cane. He had the widow choose a stick by shaking the box until one jumped out. The priest looked up the number in an ancient crumbling book, and announced that the ancestor has accepted the offerings, and that her family would continue to prosper.

I wondered where that book had been during the Cultural Revolution. If it hadn't been hidden somewhere, it wouldn't have survived.

The various corridors are pierced by windows shaped like vases, or moons, or other curvy shapes. They allowed glimpses of other corridors. Through a moon window, I saw two men talking. One was Lars, and the person with his back to me had on a shirt like Joe's.

I was surprised to see Lars here, although he had recommended the temple. Maybe it has something to do with his research. After all, we had just seen an ancient document in use. But why have a secret talk with Joe, if it was Joe?

Ashley said she hadn't seen either of the guys.

When we got back into the taxis, our driver lit a cigarette.

I am amazed at the smoking that goes on in China, including massive amounts of sharp-smelling tobacco in the taxi. Has no one told them it's bad for their lungs? The secondhand smoke is certainly bad for my nose and lungs. Joe backed me up when I requested that there be no smoking in the taxis – smoking is not among his vices. Not smoking in the car proved to be a concept that was mystifying to the drivers of both cars. Our driver smoked anyway, with his arm out the window, which was marginally better, depending on my particular seat and the wind pattern coming through the car. It did defeat the idea of air conditioning, though.

16

Jade and Carver stayed at Jade Village for a ten-day week. I popped in now and then to be sure that all was well. Since the weather was still pleasant, Carver suggested a side trip to the Heavenly Lake to collect obsidian. Carver and Jade could give nodules of the glossy black stone to the villages who fed and sheltered them on the return trip. This stone is highly prized because it's easy to flake, and makes a sharper edge than any other kind of rock. It's also quite rare, occurring only where ancient volcanoes erupted and the lava cooled quickly.

Carver and I both knew the way to the Heavenly Lake, and besides, the path was well trodden. We followed the wide river up into the mountains to its source in the Heavenly Lake. Many fishing villages with a few houses clung to the river bank. Every evening when we stopped, the village prepared a feast, followed by story-telling. Jade sighed when Carver told the robber story once again, but she loved showing off Piggy and his tricks.

They exchanged presents in each village. Carver gave jade nodules, which were gratefully received. He was often given carved wooden objects in return – bowls, spoons, and drinking cups, ornamented with geometric patterns. Once, Jade was presented with a tiger skin. It was so heavy, Carver left it to retrieve on the way back to Jade Village.

When the people of the higher villages learned that Carver was interested in plants, they pointed out special plants that grow in their high mountains. A plant with shiny green leaves and red berries was dug up, to reveal a large white root. They cut the root into small pieces to make a kind of hot drink, which gave them strength to climb the mountain better and faster. Carver liked the taste, and drank a second cup, but Jade had a hard time swallowing it.

The Heavenly Lake, in an enormous crater of the Ever White Mountains, was the biggest expanse of water Jade had yet seen. She couldn't even see across to the other side. The sides of the crater were colors of purple and lilac and maroon. I was entranced with the shades of color contrasted with the blue of the lake, as I have been each time I've been there. I flew across it just for fun, for the sheer joy of catching the updrafts.

We camped that night near the crater. Jade drew a magic circle around everyone before we settled in. I became alert on my branch as I sensed something crossing the circle. In the moonlight, I could see the shape of a big, sleek tiger padding across to Jade. When he went straight to Jade's sleeping form, I was ready to fly and peck him, but he only nudged her softly. His lick on her cheek made a small dark spot, that remained for the rest of her life. When anyone asked her about it, she would say it was the tiger's kiss.

Back at Jade Village, Piggy refused to eat with the other pigs, and stayed close to Jade. The only person he warmed up to was Sand Dollar, who scratched him behind the ears and talked to him.

Jade and Sand Dollar spent a lot of time learning to make jade objects. Jade's second try at a pig dragon was better than the first. She polished it for hours, as she talked to the other carvers of Jade Village. She was determined to learn this exacting art, but it didn't come easily.

Sandy's wife's relatives were visiting from a northern village. One of them was a boy named Frog who liked to hang around Jade and Sand Dollar while they practiced carving, attracted to Jade by her impish smile. When she finished carving a new pig dragon, Frog asked for it as a keepsake, and Jade gave it without a thought.

Lobster was furious. He chased Frog all over the beachfront, and finally caught him and began punching him.

"Wait" said Jade, "Stop it. Hitting is not a good way to solve problems. What's the trouble?"

"He wants the pig-dragon you made," Frog explained. "But you gave it to me, so it's mine."

"Then solve it peacefully, or I won't be friends with either one of you."

"I made a pig for you, and then you gave your pig to Frog. Is that fair?" whined Lobster.

"Not really fair, I can understand why you're mad. But you should be mad at me, not Frog. That pig-dragon belongs to Frog now. I'll make you another one."

Carver saw the third pig-dragon, and thought it was splendid.

"I think you've found your spirit emblem," he praised Jade.

Lobster put a string through his and wore it proudly.

When it was time to leave, Carver discussed with his sister Spinner the best way to return to Green Valley. He didn't want to risk going back through the forest, where the robbers might still be lurking, waiting for their return with jade and obsidian. This time the robbers might not be frightened by Piggy and Spirit Bird.

"Why not take a boat to the mouth of the Big West River?" suggested Carver's brother, Sandy. "After you land, you can take the paths along the riverbank back to Green Valley."

"Isn't that dangerous? I can steer a boat down a river, but I don't know how to cross the sea. Only fishing people have that skill."

"Our fishers very often go as far as the river mouth. Tall Deer and I can take you. The bay is large, but it's well protected, with many islands to land on in case of a heavy storm."

"Is there room in the boat for Piggy? And for Spirit Bird? And for all the jade and obsidian we collected?" Jade inquired, her eyebrows coming together in a frown.

"Lots of room," Sandy reassured her. We'll fill the boat with you and your baggage, and after we put you on shore, we'll have space for fish and turtles. We don't usually go so far, so on this trip we'll be able to bring home some unusual fish."

Jade didn't like the fishy smell of the boat when she first got on, but the breeze kept the odor away once they got going. The sea voyage was expected to take two days and a night. During the first day, islands were always visible on the horizon, and Sandy steered from one island to the next. Late in the first day Sandy and Tall Deer docked the boat at an island big enough to grow some crops. Friendly hands pulled the boat in. The humans enjoyed a big dinner of clams and mussels, cooked with seaweed. Gossip was exchanged, and stories told. Carver spread the word about the robbers.

The villagers helped push us off at sundown, and we watched the sun sink in the distance, in the midst of orange clouds.

"Now that the sun is gone, how will we see to find our way?" Jade asked.

"Don't worry, Little Jade, the stars will guide us. Look up and see if you can find the Bear Woman in the sky."

The clouds were all low, near the horizon. Jade scanned the sky all around the boat.

"Oh," she suddenly understood. "That way is north. And we haven't been gone from home as long as it seems, because her tail is still pointing almost in the same direction as when we left."

While we were star-gazing, dark clouds began to cover the stars, and the wind made big waves that tossed the little boat. Piggy got seasick, and Jade had to look at the distance to keep her dinner down.

"Help us roll down the sail and tie it," called Sandy, as he and Tall Deer struggled to keep the boat from turning over. Carver gave a hand by tying the sail, but the rope had become rotten in the seawater at the bottom of the boat, and soon broke.

Jade reached into her basket pack for the length of ropes the robbers had tied them up with.

"Try this. It's very strong, and I can tie it in a knot that won't come apart." Jade wound the rope around the sail, and tied it in a knot she learned from her mother. It was a magic knot that Owl used to close the robe she wore for telling the future.

With the sail down and tied, they were prepared to ride out the storm. The little boat pitched and rocked, but didn't turn over. I began to relax, but I could see Jade was still nervous, fingering the pig-dragon she now wore around her neck.

Lightning flashed, and briefly we could see a group of large rocks, in the direction the storm was pushing us. The people in the boat hunkered down, dripping with sea and rain water. I huddled near the packs, trying to keep my feathers dry in case they needed me to scout land for them when the storm passed. Piggy, unlike the rest of us, stood with his face to the rain and wind, his feet braced and his ears blowing back

When the rocks were very close, and it seemed we would be dashed on them with the next wave, Piggy brought forth one of his loudest roars. It deafened us in the boat.

I can't account for what happened next. The front of the boat turned to the right, just enough so that the wave pushed it toward the shore instead of onto the rocks. Soon the wind dropped, the rain stopped, and we were safe but sodden.

The boat landed with a grinding noise on a pebbly beach. We could see smoke, and followed it to a fishing village not far away. The kind people took us in and fed us. In return, we entertained them with stories, including the one about the robbers, and Jade and Piggy did their tricks. We also gave them both jade and obsidian, we were so grateful to be on shore.

17

The drive to Daling went through another gap in the Great Wall, where a billboard advertised a cable car to the top. When we stopped nearby to gas up, Laura asked if we could go to the top of the wall, but Joe insisted we didn't have time.

Xiao Li let me borrow his map to pore over, and I learned that we were driving through the Yan Mountains, where the Hongshan and Yangshao cultures met, transferring painted pottery to Hongshan. I wondered how that would happen. Did people walk from Hongshan to Yangshao or vice versa? Or did they meet in the middle by accident or even by prearrangement? But how could they arrange a meeting without a means of long distance communication?

My companions had an adventurous lunch in Cheng De, family style as usual. Xiao Li ordered for us – mostly seafood, which he's learned I don't eat, so he ordered me a plate of *jiaozi.* These are little packages of ground-up meat and flavorings wrapped in kiss-shaped packets of dough, and then fried. These were delicious, flavored just right. I was familiar with them, because they're eaten in Korea, too.

The most expensive dish was a huge steamed fish, served complete with head and fins and tail. Laura turned the head to point at Joe.

"That means you have to debone it" she teased.

Joe looked baffled, so Ashley deftly turned the fishover and took out the spine and ribs all still attached.

"Great trick," said Joe admiringly.

As leader of the expedition, Joe was given the pinch of meat from the fish cheeks, said to be the most delectable part of the fish. Joe's face suggested he didn't agree, but he did manage to say, "Shayshay," which is pretty close to *xiexie,* the Chinese word for thank-you.

Cheng De is a tourist city, with a summer place, a lamaist temple, the Potala Palace, and other large temples. We chose to see the Potala Palace, since it was a bright sunshiny day, and most of the sights are outside. I hoped we could see some of the rest of the buildings on our return on our way back to Beijing.

The Potala is built into a hill, like the one in Tibet, so as you visit it you are constantly climbing. The statues and shrines that line the way up the hill were so enticing Ashley used up a whole roll of film in one camera and a diskette in the digital camera. She also posed us all in various places. My favorite shows Evan with his hands out, and Laura and I on the next stage above, appearing to stand on his hands.

The views from the top are spectacular. Off in the distance I could see some yurts, which proved to be tourist cabins when we passed by them on the way out of town. The guidebook says they put on a show in Mongolian costumes, with horseback games. The concept seemed odd, because the monuments in Cheng De are covered with Manchu writing, not Mongolian.

When we returned to the taxis, we found that the drivers had declared a strike.

"How much farther?" the lead taxi driver demanded of Xiao Li.

"We've gone a bit more than halfway," Xiao Li told him.

"This is too far," said the second driver. "Give us the money you promised and we will go back to Beijing."

"How do you expect us to get to the site?" asked Xiao Li.

"We don't care. Pay us what you promised so we can go back to Beijing now."

"We promised to pay you to drive us all the way to the site. We aren't there yet. We don't owe you anything."

"Then we'll take your luggage as payment and just leave." The drivers started toward the cars.

When I told Joe what they were saying, he exploded.

"You have a contract to get us to the site," he said to the lead driver. And to us, he said, "Get in."

Xiao Li put a hand on Joe's arm. "We can't win this fight, but we can stay here arguing all night. Can I offer to pay them half? We can find other taxis in Cheng De to take us the rest of the way."

Grudgingly, Joe agreed, and we began unloading the luggage. In the end, I doled out from our money stash more than half what we had offered them, because we had gone more than half the way.

I went with Xiao Li to find two more taxis. The ones we managed to hire were not air conditioned, were a bit smaller, and cost more, but we were grateful to have any transportation at all. I had a snooze while Evan asked Xiao Li questions about Daling.

As we crossed the Daling river at Lingyuan, Ashley spotted a giant version of a pig-dragon on a pole. The taxis parked while we posed in front of it, and took the usual dozen pictures.

"We'll be at Daling in a few minutes," said Xiao Li. "After you get back in the cars."

Dr. Wu and Mr. Gao, the Chinese archaeologists from Beijing, arrived before us, and greeted us warmly. Mr. Li, a thin man with wire-rimmed glasses, was the main archaeologist at the site. He spent all his time at the Daling station. Joe was anxious to see the Ox River site, but it was too late in the afternoon to go now. Instead, we settled into our lodgings.

Anticipating public interest in the Daling site, a few rooms for guests had been built. Two pleasant gray buildings faced each other across a pleasant garden, just inside the gate. Each building had two bathrooms, four double bedrooms, and two parlors, one at each end.

"Look at this!" said Laura, throwing her pack on a bed in a corner room and thereby claiming it. "What a plush dig! Hot water! Flush toilets! Sheets! Warm covers! Luxury beyond compare!"

The rest of us swarmed all over the rooms too, taking in the comforts unaccustomed in an archaeological expedition. Usually we sleep in tents and shower with cold water. That's if there's any water at all for washing.

There were only six of us foreigners, even counting Lars who was coming later, so we designated the south building as male and the north building as female. We drew straws for the corner rooms, and Ashley and I each got one. Laura shared the bathroom with me. Joe was across from Ashley and Evan across from me, with a middle south room available for Lars whenever he came.

As soon as the rooms were sorted out, Joe called a meeting of the four of us in his parlor. We brought all the equipment and sorted it, while Laura checked it off her list. Nothing had been omitted or lost on the way. We each packed a small backpack with the things we would need on site – GPS unit, notebook, pen, twine, ribbon, knife, flags, and map. Joe and Laura each carried a fifty-meter tapes besides. Then Joe assigned each of us specific jobs, and equipment to be responsible for keeping clean and in working order. We each had log pages to record our daily activities, with specific entries required, such as the weather, any artifacts noted, artifacts picked up, and so forth.

When the organizational work was finished, Joe brought a small bottle of maotai out of his backpack, and we passed it around, toasting the project.

A commotion near the gate drew us outside. We first saw a small gray bus, and then took in the crowd disembarking from it. Seven Asian men and one woman followed each other out the door. Dr. Wu and Xiao Li went to greet them, followed shortly by Mr. Gao and Mr. Li.

"It looks like we've got company," said Evan. "We'll have to rearrange the room assignments."

I thought I heard a familiar voice, speaking Chinese with a Korean accent.

I ran to greet Professor Lee, the foremost archaeologist in Korea. The whole group, it turned out, were South Korean archaeologists, touring the Dongbei in a rented bus.

I bowed formally to Prof. Lee, but found I was tongue-tied when trying to bring forth Korean words. The Chinese in my head seemed to block the Korean language synapses.

"Anyong hasimnika," I finally blurted.

He greeted me urbanely in English. He's a nice man, although very formal. That trait may contribute to my inability to speak Korean to him. Kidok and I are buddies, and I can speak my somewhat incorrect Korean with him without inhibitions.

Kidok bounded up and gave me a big hug, in a most unKorean way. I was startled, but pleased.

"I heard you would be here. I'm studying in America now," he told me. "At Bah-ku-li. I been too busy even to e-mail to you. Very hard for me to understand lectures. I must study very hard. But I so glad to see you here."

"What state is Bahkuli in?" I asked. "Maybe I can go and visit you there."

Now Kidok frowned. "Everybody know it. In Calipornya? Across bay from Sampansisco?"

"Oh," finally I got it. My ear had to get reattuned to his Korean accent. "Berkeley. Great archaeology program there. You'll learn a lot."

Kidok took a step back to look me over. "You look wan-du-fo. You are a little older, and your hair is shorter."

How could I have forgotten this Korean-style directness? Older is good in Korea. To look older is a compliment, I reminded myself, although I am only twenty-five.

"You are skinnier," I replied with a smile. "Can't you eat American food?"

"Lots of Korean food in California," he informed me.

"How are you?" I turned to Prof. Lee, who had returned from greeting the Chinese archaeologists. "You're looking well."

"Retiring soon," he said. "But I have so many ideas to write up that I may never be really retired."

We all shared the joke. Archaeologists have a hard time retiring.

Dr. Wu joined us, and was surprised when he realized that we knew each other. Prof. Lee explained about the year I had spent with them in South Korea. "She's a good fieldworker," he ended up, which was high praise from him. It gave me a glow.

Apparently the Koreans had been expected, it was just that nobody told us. Behind them, huge piles of luggage were being unloaded from the bus. I suspected that the oversized luggage included liquid presents for our Chinese hosts. This would be expected in Korea; they were following their own customs.

The eight Koreans included six single males and one married couple. Eight people take up a whole building, so we hastily rearranged ourselves into the other building. Joe still got a corner unit, and Evan was next to him, sharing the bath. Lars could share the room with Evan if the Koreans were still here when he arrived. Laura and I kept the other corner room, with Ashley next door sharing our bath. We still weren't very crowded, and it was the plushest living arrangements I'd ever seen at a dig.

In my excitement at unexpectedly seeing Kidok and Prof. Lee again, I had failed to notice other old friends in the bunch. Two of the students from the Osanni excavation were here, both working on Ph.D.s. They were now engaged to each other. I wished them both well.

"Remember the jade bird we found at Osanni?" said Hwang-ok.

I smiled and nodded. "That was exciting. Do you remember how you refused to work in the same square as a boy? When I tell people about that dig I remember you singing American pop songs, strumming on your guitar."

"You encouraged me to get serious about archaeology. I'll never forget that. It was so wonderful to have your example."

Further chat with Prof. Lee and Kidok confirmed that the Koreans were touring archaeological sites in the Dongbei. Some archaeological discoveries suggest to them that the Korean culture was formed in this region, and now that they are allowed to visit here, they are eager to explore it.

Joe gathered our group together and we exchanged name cards with the Koreans. Name cards are a must in Asia. It's virtually impossible to remember people's names without a card, and it contains other useful information, too, such as the person's title, telephone, fax, and e-mail addresses. Most of the Korean cards have English on one side, which is a big help.

Before dinner Kidok and I took a stroll around the compound. We discovered a combined chicken coop and rabbit hutch, whose inhabitants would probably wind up on the dinner table.

"You can come by here and pick out your dinner," teased Kidok. It was a disagreeable thought to me. I decided to become a vegetarian for the duration. We also came across a vegetable garden with Chinese cabbage, cilantro, spinach-looking stuff, and much more.

"It's nice to know that the ingredients for our food are grown here," said Kidok. "And, I hope, washed in the water of that well over there. We should be safe from chicken flu." I was pleased, too, because the veggies would be fresh.

Ashley beckoned us toward the back of the compound, where the Chinese archaeologists live. "Come see the pig. He's enormous!" She led us to a pen where a pink pig stood, eating veggie peelings. We contemplated each other. I thought I saw a mean gleam in its eye. I was not tempted to pat it.

"What do you think it weighs?" asked Kidok. "Three hundred pounds?"

I had no idea how to judge its weight, but it certainly was impressive. "I suppose it will provide many dinners. But not while we're here, I hope."

Three round tables were set up for the large number of visitors and the local archaeologists. It was a convivial group. I sat with my Korean friends and caught up on the archaeological gossip. We reminisced about my year in Korea. The meal was simple but much to my liking. The dishes were mostly vegetables, with tiny pieces of meat. I did not inquire what animal they came from.

The Korean archaeologists had indeed brought liquid gifts, which were heartily enjoyed by most of the crowd. They passed around *soju,* a Korean wine, and ginseng whiskey. On the Chinese side, Qing Dao beer and *Baijiu* were served. Baijiu literally means white wine, but it's more like brandy in its alcohol content. I never got used to its strength – I always felt like my eyes were popping out of their sockets, even from a sip of it.

As the noise level rose, I tried the ginseng whiskey again, thinking I might like it this time, but it still tastes like dirt to me.

Must be something defective about my taste buds. All Koreans are supposed to appreciate it.

When we had toasted everyone present and absent friends besides, and friendship, and archaeology, we could finally leave the dining room. I was surprised to see that everyone could stand, but few were even tottery. I concluded that archaeologists everywhere can hold their liquor.

18

In Green Valley, preparations were in hand for another trip. The traveling basket packs were out, and clothing was being sorted into piles. Food for the road was stacked on the side. Owl had chosen presents to bring for various hosts along the way, and arranged them by layers in another basket.

"Ah, Spirit Bird, you've come," said Owl. "Good. Jade and Piggy and I will enjoy your company, as well as your protection. This time we're going south."

I hopped around to various groups of people, listening to the conversation buzzing around to learn the reason for the trip, and where we were going. Owl seemed to understand my curiosity.

"Well, if you would drop by more often, you would know," she teased me. "Jade needs more exposure to the four directions. She's had more than a year to digest her first adventure. It's time to set forth again. We're going in the red direction, where warmth and birds come from. My brother Hawk lives among the Dragon Bone people. I've been there twice, and the path is easy to follow, although it is not used a lot. We have to cross a rugged and steep mountain range, but otherwise it's an easy journey."

It sounded interesting to me. I'm an eager traveler, and being a bird has a bonus - I don't have to climb the mountains. I have time to enjoy the breezes, because flying is faster than walking.

I also learned that Jade's three younger siblings – there were now twin girls, as well as Little Carver – would stay at home. Carver would look after the children, with the help of Little Shell, who was still unmarried.

The weather was pleasant as we set out for the south. Flying along with Owl and Jade and Piggy, I could enjoy the hilly scenery by taking side trips up enticing valleys. Spring was blooming again, and plowing was just beginning. The first night we made camp in a grove of walnut trees opposite a mountain that looked like a pig's head. Piggy was in fine spirits, and played hide and seek with Jade.

The fine weather only held for a week. Clouds began to form as we approached the mountain range that stood in the way. We had just started up the foothills when a clap of thunder, followed by a bolt of lightning, made us look for shelter. Soon it became a drenching thunderstorm. Piggy raced to an opening which turned out to lead into a large cave.

At first it was nice to be inside the dry cave, looking out at the storm. But it rained and rained, without let-up. Jade made a fire with dry twigs, and Jade, Owl and I huddled around it to dry out. Piggy, on the other hand, liked being wet. He wandered around inside the cave, rooting here and there in the dirt. In his explorations, he found an enormous bone and brought it to Jade.

"Look at this!" Jade nudged Owl, while examining the bone, turning it over and around, considering it from every side.

"It looks like a leg bone," she said at last, "but I've never seen any animals with legs that big."

"That's a dragon bone," Owl explained to Jade. "It's well known that huge dragons lived here in ancient times. Dragon bones are rare, but very useful. They can be ground up into a powder that makes an effective medicine, that's good for healing broken bones, and for stomach trouble. We should collect some bones to take along, and give to the families that feed and shelter us on the other side of the mountains. We'll get some more for ourselves on the way home. We can remember the cave opening by the bent pine outside."

Jade and Owl followed Piggy back to his diggings in the back of the cave, and picked through the bones to find suitable ones to take along as presents. Jade set them outside to get clean in the downpour. They had to be rinsed in the next stream, because they were covered in ashy soil.

After crossing the mountains, the houses we passed were built in a different style than those of the Red Mountain and Long Bow people. The Dragon Bone people made houses that were almost square. When we stopped with a family for the night, we admired the hard white floors, as we ate river fish cooked on sticks over the fire.

The next day, our hosts gave us directions to Crooked Pine, where Owl's brother Hawk lived. Several paths criss-crossed the plain, and without a guide we could get lost. Our hosts also sent an older boy as a messenger running ahead of us with the news that two strangers were on the way, including the leader of a large Red Mountain village.

By the time we reached Crooked Pine, a formal welcome was ready. Men stood in two rows along on either side of the road. Those nearest to us as we approached were dressed in shiny crimson robes, which were draped across their backs and hung knee-length, and tied with a rope belt. The village leader stood in front to welcome us. Standing straight as a larch tree, he made a formal speech of welcome, introducing himself as Big Man. He said it was an honor to entertain a leader from a village far away. The men along the path cheered when a large man near Big Man raised his arm as a signal that the welcome talk was finished.

The men in crimson robes danced for us, holding hands in a circle. When they moved, the shine of their garments glinted up and down in the sunshine. A flutist played a tune that was not at all familiar. It sounded sad, compared to the Red Mountain flutes, and the music was high and shrill.

Next, a group of boys presented Owl with a big bouquet of scarlet flowers, and placed a crown of the same flowers on her head. Jade was given a spray of small red flowers, and a single large blossom to put behind one ear. Finally, a boy wearing a red sash offered Owl and Jade fresh spring water in red and black cups. Jade shared hers with Piggy and me, which was very welcome.

Big Man marched back down the road with his entourage, and the two rows of townspeople followed them without a word. Hawk and his two sons, Moose and Elk, stayed behind, and at last Owl and Jade could greet them. Hawk explained to Owl, as they walked into the town, that Willow was not allowed to come out and meet them, because women were forbidden to use the paths that led out of the town.

Willow was not the head of her household. Among the Dragon Bone people the fields were reallocated each year to householders. Men owned the houses, but as a foreigner, Hawk wasn't allocated space to build a house or eligible to take part in distribution of the fields. They lived in the house of Willow's brother, and farmed his fields. Hawk was not allowed to practice his healing arts, either, because Big Man had forbidden any kind of magic, including curing. Sometimes people came to Hawk anyway, especially with a sick child, but it would be disastrous for them if they got caught. Fewer and fewer people dared to come.

Willow welcomed us into their wing of her brother's house, although she clearly thought Piggy and I should stay outside. "Did you bring the pig and bird for a feast? Of course, we have pigs and chickens, too, so you needn't have bothered. That pig is scrawny from your travels, and the bird is nothing but bone and feathers to start with."

"This is my Spirit Bird," Jade introduced me. "She keeps an eye on me, and helps when trouble arises."

"It looks real to me," Willow remarked. "Does it eat and poop? Is the food and furniture safe?" I found this question insulting, and flew back outside and perched in a tree where I could watch through the door.

Jade made a noise like a woodpecker, and Piggy came running to her. "This pig is magic too. His name is Piggy. Piggy, greet Willow. She's a relative of ours."

Piggy tapped twice with his right foot, and touched his jaw to the ground.

"Oh, my," said Willow. "How did you teach the pig to do that?"

"He just has natural manners," Jade grinned. "And he's a big help on our travels."

"You'd better be careful while you're here," warned Willow. "Big Man doesn't allow any kind of magic."

"So we heard. We'll be careful."

The same evening a feast was held in our honor, arranged by Willow's relatives. We gathered in a large central square. Willow brought a dish made from some chickens with long tail feathers that ran around her courtyard. Jade wouldn't eat any, because she thought they might be my relatives. I tried to tell her that if they were my kin they were too distant to worry about.

But in my bird form, I don't eat chicken either. Neighbors brought meat and noodle dishes. They also made a dish of chopped meat wrapped in small packets of dough, and fried.

Owl tried to present obsidian nodules and a dragon bone to each household that brought food, but they refused to take them. She should give everything to Big Man, they explained. If they accepted anything, Big Man would find out and take it anyway, and punish them, besides.

Big Man came late to the feast, with three strong men, all of them wearing scarlet cloaks. Again, he greeted Owl, but this time he asked why her husband didn't come along on the trip.

"He stayed home with our other children."

"A man would stay with children? Well, I am disappointed. I have gifts for him."

Big Man signaled to a small woman wearing a crimson sash over her hempen robe. She was not introduced. She brought a large basket, and handed lengths of magenta cloth to Big Man, who presented them to Owl.

"This cloth is very beautiful. How do you make it shine?

"The spirits of worms put the shine in. But you must talk to the weavers. Perhaps they will share the secret with you."

Next Big Man presented her with a painted jar containing red powder.

"This is the source of the color. It comes from the berries of the tree the silk worms feed on, so its natural to use it to dye the cloth. I see that you wear bark-cloth while you travel. Do you have any ceremonial clothes with you?"

"I have my belt and cap that I wear when I do my spirit work. Would you like to know something about the future?"

Big Man bristled. "Your husband allows you to do those things? He lets you travel, and tell futures?

"No, my husband does not tell me what to do. I am the leader of my village. I am also a healer, a diviner, and I dance for rain."

Owl reached into her travel pack. "Here are my gifts for you. Are you familiar with this shiny black stone? It can be made into many useful tools."

"I receive it with pleasure. Do you find it in Red Mountain land?"

"No, it comes from a far away mountain toward the sunrise from our land, past the villages of the Long Bow people. It is found beside a large lake, in mountains where the snow never melts. Both my daughter and I have been there. She can tell you more about it if you like. This obsidian was collected with my daughter's own hands. It is special because she was kissed by a tiger at the lake."

"You are most kind to bring these sacred stones."

Owl reached for another packet, and opened it revealing a large tibia and scapula.

"You know about dragon bones, I'm sure. We collected these on the way here, led into a cave by the Rain Spirits. Piggy found them. These are effective against belly pains."

"Your knowledge is appreciated, as well as your gifts."

Next Owl brought out a small packet wrapped in moss and laid in a box of painted birchbark. An owl was painted on the lid.

Big Man drew in his breath when he saw the small jade bird revealed within. It was an owl with outspread wings, made of pinkish jade.

"This jade bird was carved by my husband, whose name is Carver. A secret hole in the back doesn't show in the front, so you can sew it on your cloak invisibly. My husband invented this method."

"I should ask you where this shine comes from," said Big Man. "Stone that shines from within is quite amazing. And the skill of the design is great. Your husband's carvers are very skilled."

"My husband *is* the carver. And he is very skilled. My daughter Jade can carve, too, although her designs are still simple."

"We must talk again later about your stone sources. Perhaps we can visit again."

Owl and Jade watched in amazement as they were served delicious food from jars and bowls in many more shapes than Red Mountain potters made. Painted designs were also new to them, and they exclaimed over the designs, especially a stylized fish in the bottom of one bowl used to serve fish paste seasoning.

Jade asked so many questions about the pottery that she was invited to watch the pottery being made.

An older girl named Pearl took Jade on an expedition to a river, where the clay was selected. They brought back enough to make a dozen pots. Pearl carried hers on her head, and Jade copied her, although it felt heavier than the jars she was used to carrying.

At the pottery-making grounds, they removed small stones from the clay, and added water. The final step in preparing the clay was adding ground-up seashells, and once more kneading it thoroughly.

The vessels were constructed out of coils of clay, pressed together to form the pot. This way they could make many shapes of jars and bowls. The paint was applied before the pots were fired.

The process of firing pots depended on whether it was painted or not. The plain brown pots were fired on an open fire, as the people in Red Mountain villages did. But the painted pottery needed a red base for the black paint. To make the pots red, they had to be fired hotter, in an enclosed space dug into the ground. Jade watched the ovens for the pots being made, and the way the vessels were stacked inside it. She could show the Green Valley potters how to make red pottery when she got home.

Jade was thrilled to learn how to make paints and apply them to the pot before firing. The black paint was made from burned wood ground on a sandstone slab. Pearl showed her how to make brushes by chewing the end of a willow twig until the fibers spread out. Different sized brushes could be created just by choosing twigs of different thicknesses.

For a ten-day week Jade roamed the town. Her sunny smile and cheerful ways made friends for her everywhere. She learned many things from Willow and Pearl, including how to make white plaster for the floor by pounding white chalk in a stone bowl, and mixing the powder with water, in which shiny tree leaves had been soaked. The floors were smooth and easy to keep clean.

She learned jobs boys did, too. She watched her cousin Moose make fishhooks by carving bone into the general shape he wanted, and rubbing with small pieces of pumice stone to finish them. Elk preferred to work with wood. He sometimes carved the wooden digging sticks used to weed between the rows of crops, and added designs just because he enjoyed decorating things.

In the warm summer evenings, they sat outside and made tools or clothing, and talked or sang.

Willow told us that infants who died before they were old enough to walk were buried in jars with lids under the floors of houses, so that their spirits would come back and live in another baby. In the old days the fires had been guarded by a goddess of the hearth, but Big Man had smashed the stone figures, and made it a crime to make any more.

When Jade wasn't busy with lessons at Willow's house, or potting with Pearl, she wandered around the town, talking to people and making friends. One new friend was a boy named Buffalo, a sturdy boy with broad shoulders and an easy grin.

It looked like love at first sight. After they met, they could scarcely be separated. Jade helped Buffalo weed the young plants in his family's millet field, and found eggs his chickens had laid under the bushes. She sat by him while he whittled wooden implements. They talked without stopping. Pearl was annoyed with Jade's sudden change of best friend.

Owl called me aside one day. "Spirit Bird," she said, "Is this Buffalo boy a good match for Jade? He seems like a nice, kind boy. But then, all the people in this village are very well behaved. I can't find any reason to object, but I'm not getting any signals that this is right. What do you think?"

I wasn't sure myself. Owl sensed something wrong, but she didn't know what. And neither did I. I shook my head, meaning I didn't know, but Owl took it as a negative. "Oh dear. Young love is so hard to deal with."

19

Breakfast consisted of millet gruel with some side dishes to flavor it: in this case flat white seeds, peanuts, small pickles, and tiny red peppers. I gave the peppers a miss after Ashley's lesson, but the rest of the additions were delicious. The porridge is eaten with a thick china spoon shaped like a small ladle. Buns were also served, rather tasteless, but filling. I felt as stuffed as a bean bun while we were briefed on the localities of Daling.

I thought I knew Daling by heart after reading and translating all the publications, and mapping of the sites overlaid on a satellite image. Not to mention having seen the museum exhibits at Beida. But reading and studying aren't the same as being able to walk around and experience a site.

We were shown into a one-room museum, with almost the same exhibits we had seen at Beida. The wow factor was still at work, though. I thought what a thrill it must have been to actually unearth the face with green jade eyes.

"Today," said Xiao Li, who turned out to be the son of the local archaeologist in charge of the site, "we'll go to the Goddess Temple and the localities near it before lunch. After lunch we'll go to Locality Two, which is the area of the big burials in the valley." He pointed to places on the map.

We looked like tourists, with multiple cameras slung around our necks, and knives, GPS units and compasses attached to belts or in pockets. Prof. Lee wore an amazing vest with two dozen pockets, each containing some tool or other. I watched to see how many he actually used. All that hardware must have weighed a ton, and he is a slender man.

We jounced up the road in two jeeps and a truck, over the ruts and around the pot holes. A farmer came by with a herd of goats, and Ashley demanded to stop and snap pictures. A goat-picture frenzy ensued. The farmer must have thought we were crazy. Hadn't we ever seen goats before? But I admit I took a picture, too – a cute kid nibbling on one of Ashley's cameras.

It felt quite eerie standing by the outline of the Goddess Temple, as if the spirits were still hovering nearby. The floor had been covered up as soon as the Chinese archaeologists unearthed the unbaked clay statue fragments. Some day, when the time and funding and expertise are right, they'll reopen the dig. Until then, we can study their detailed report and published map from the original excavation.

The building probably collapsed soon after the area was abandoned. All that's left is the long, irregular outline of the building. There's a brick guard shed at each locality of Daling, and a roof protecting the Goddess Temple excavation, but otherwise there is little to see above ground.

Mr. Li pointed out Pig Mountain, a large looming presence at the Goddess Temple. It doesn't show up well in photographs, but when you're there it does look like a giant pig head, with small peaks forming erect ears on either side of a rounded summit. You can even imagine two dark boulders down the slope as eyes, and a flat area in front at the snout. Whether the prehistoric people also saw it as a pig is impossible to know, but given the prevalence of pig imagery it seems likely.

We did our usual picture-taking in front of Pig Mountain, including the Korean and Chinese archaeologists in some of the shots. Our Korean colleagues were as eager and curious as we, and hard to line up, so the photos are somewhat haphazard. Evan was trying to get a picture of everyone, and correlate each picture with a name card. I wasn't so ambitious, and asked Evan to send me copies.

Adjacent to the Goddess Temple, and up the slope from it, is the area described as a platform. It took a while to walk around the area, as the places where various pits were dug were pointed out to us. One pit had contained a whole painted jar with a lid, another contained sheep bones, and a third had three layers of broken pottery.

Describing an area as a platform conjures up a flat terrace, but in fact it's uneven, with piles of stones in various places. Dr.

Wu pointed out where they thought there was an entrance from the Goddess Temple to the platform area. Archaeologists are a curious lot, and we spent at least an hour asking questions about the finds.

Meanwhile, Joe galloped around, putting samples of the soil into little bottles and estimating the depths in various places, using Laura as his assistant.

"At least there aren't any electric wires here," he told Laura, "and only our three vehicles are parked here. It's a long way down to the road and railroad, with metal stuff passing by all the time. I think this would be okay for the radar. I hope the Ox River site is far from a big road, too."

Laura ascertained that no human bones had been found in this vicinity. The sheep bones found in a pit had been thrown away. Laura gave a mini lecture to Mr. Li about how much can be learned from animal bones, but it was too late to retrieve those sheep bones.

Evan roamed around making notes on the landscape, and sketching a map of the site, including noting what other sites were visible from the temple and the platform. He had his GPS turned on constantly, and noted the readings in his notebook, in case the electronic storage should fail. I heard him asking questions like how long it would take to walk to the nearest habitation site, and whether any shrines had been found on Pig Mountain.

I sat on the edge of the Goddess Temple, and wondered about the builders. A car engine broke my reverie. I turned and saw a big white van without markings stop on the road. The back and side windows were painted white, so it was impossible to see into it. Three big men got out, gathering up shovels and buckets from the sliding door.

I went to find Dr. Wu, and pointed at the men. "Who are they? What are they doing?"

After Dr. Wu went to speak to them, they put away their equipment, got back in their vehicle, and drove away.

"What was that about?" I was curious, of course, on behalf of Sandra Wold and my duties here.

"They said they were digging dirt to put into flowerpots," explained Dr. Wu. "There's no way I could prove they were intending to loot. But I got the number of their license plate, in case they turn up around here again."

20

When I returned to Crooked Pine, Hawk and Owl and Jade were walking to Willow's family burial hill. Soon it would be time for Owl and Jade to return, before snow closed the mountain pass. This was the last chance for Owl to talk to her brother privately. Willow and her two children stayed at home, getting ready for the Harvest Moon Festival.

At first they chatted about Green Valley relatives – those who had died or were ill, those who had prospered, those who had grown up and moved away. But when we approached the hill, Hawk gestured to Owl and Jade to site on smooth rocks by a spring. Cool water bubbled up and poured down the hill.

"I will drink of this water, sacred to the spirits, and tell you the truth," said Hawk. "This place belongs to the spirits, so it is safe here. It is unknown to Big Man so far. I don't want to burden you, little sister, you already have the whole of Green Valley to take care of. But you should know how things are among the Dragon Bone people. You have sensed that something is wrong, but I think you have not discovered the secret."

Hawk described the way Big Man ruled their town. The community was peaceful because everyone was afraid of their leader.

"It is not like Red Mountain villages, where people respect each other and keep the rules of the spirits," Hawk said earnestly. "Big Man – that is what we must call him – enforces his will with a band of toughs. No one argues, because if they do, one of these strong men will come along and whip people who complain or fight. Even children cannot raise their voices without being lashed. And the whips are ugly, made of knotted leather.

"Every family must give Big Man ten bushels of grain at harvest time, and after the wine is distilled we have to give Big

Man a large jar of millet wine. We are also required to feed his toughs whenever they are in our village. It doesn't matter if a farmer has had a bad year, and won't have enough grain left to feed the family for the winter. Just like Green Valley, it gets cold here in the winter, and nothing grows. If the stored food is taken away, people starve.

"Besides that, the women must grow silkworms, care for the mulberry trees, and weave silk cloth for the use of Big Man and his wives."

"Silk? Is that the name of the shiny cloth Big Man gave me?"

"Yes. It's been recently introduced from farther south, where mulberry trees grow wild. The insects make the silk, wrapping it around themselves while they grow into moths. The worms won't eat anything but mulberry leaves, so the trees and the larvae were imported. We think this is as far north as the mulberry trees and the silkworms can live. It's too cold in the mountains you crossed."

"What does Big Man do with so much silk? Surely he can't wear it all himself?"

"Some of it he does wear, and so do his wives. You should see them, thinking they're better than the other women, who have worked so hard to make their fine robes."

"Wives? Big Man has more than one wife?"

"He has three wives, one from each of the three towns of the Dragon Bone people. You saw one of them at the feast, but she was treated as a servant. Women are taught to be subdued. "

"He must have many children."

"Altogether Big Man has ten children. And three houses.

"The only work he does is to choose the biggest young men to do his bullying for him. Otherwise he gives feasts, and drinks, and strolls through the streets wearing scarlet feathers braided into his hair.

"Big Man says that his power will continue even after he dies. He commanded that a grave be built for himself. It is much larger than our usual graves, with a space for his body in the middle. He directed the best artist in the town to create a life-sized dragon figure on the east side and a tiger on the west side of the place where his body will lie. The tiger and dragon are outlined with expensive cowrie shells, which came all the way from the southern sea. On the north is the representation of the Great Bear, which Dragon Bone people call a Great Pig. The tomb has spaces for Big Man's loyal retainers to go to the other world with him. His head will point to the south, where he says his power derives. He will become a spirit in the sky, he says, and will be able to punish people from there even better than on the earth. People are afraid that what he says is true.

"We are not happy here, Willow and I. And we worry that Moose, who has grown so large, may be chosen as one of Big Man's enforcers. Owl, can you divine for us and see whether our fate is good or bad?"

"My hat and belt for divining are back at your house. And I think it would be dangerous for you if Big Man learned of it, since he is so opposed to 'magic.' But let's think about what you could do."

Owl looked into her far-seeing needle. People were coming and going in Green Valley, bringing many things to trade. Some of the traders were people she knew, like Carver's relatives from Jade Village. Others were strangers.

"Aha!" exclaimed Owl. "In Green Valley we could use a trading partner to obtain silk. It is beautiful enough to offer to the spirits. Perhaps I could convince Big Man that you must be the one we trade with, and establish regular times to trade. Maybe Moose could carry things back and forth."

"It might be possible," said Hawk. "After the crops are harvested, but before the cold nights come would be a good time to travel to Green Valley. Moose could take things to trade with you, and stay over the winter in Green Valley, returning the following year."

"No one should go alone on that long trip. Last year Carver and Jade were tied up by men who tried to take their jade. The robbers stole only one jade emblem, but they might have taken everything. Piggy and Spirit Bird scared them, and the robbers weren't seen again. Could you send both boys? Or would you come with Moose?"

"I'll talk it over with Willow. But it might be a workable plan."

Hawk and Willow decided it would be best to request that the whole family become traders with the Red Mountain villages. Four people would provide a measure of safety, and they would argue that they could carry more goods both ways. No one would be left behind as a hostage. They could stay in Green Valley every other year, which would at least give them something to look forward to the years they were in Crooked Pine. Owl suggested that she go with them to speak to Big Man, but Willow thought it would be better to invite him and his wives and children to a picnic near their sacred hill. It could be announced as the farewell feast for the visitors from Green Valley.

The picnic began with a speech by Big Man, saying that he was delighted to have the beautiful jade that Owl brought him, and he hoped she would come again and bring more.

That was the perfect opening for Owl to bring up the subject of regular exchange of silk and jade between the two areas. She pointed out that Green Valley could supply obsidian and seashells as well, through cousins who lived even farther away.

"A very interesting proposal," Big Man beamed. "I could have jades all over my cloak. And my wood-workers and bone carvers could make finer designs using the sharp stone. I could also use some of the jade and obsidian to trade for sea turtles and other delicacies from the south. Our southern trading partners would be very impressed. Yes, I like your idea."

"You could send someone from your town with silks, and he or she could spend the winter with us and return in the summer," proposed Owl.

"How would anyone know the way?"

"Hawk already knows the way," Owl pointed out. "And his sons are strong and could carry back many jades and nodules of obsidian."

Big Man hesitated. "I had my eye on Moose and Elk for something else," he mused, with his arms folded across his chest. "But your suggestion does make sense. On the other hand, what if they take my silk cloth and never return?"

Owl cocked her head to one side, thinking about the best answer.

"I will guarantee that they will return the next summer, carrying jade, obsidian, and shells. There is no place for the family to live permanently in Green Valley. In our villages, women own all the land. Hawk has no right to good farm land."

"Then it's decided."

"One more thing," Owl said. "It would be nice for us to have silk in a different color. The crimson you use is beautiful, but it's not right for us. Our color is yellow, like the bird who travels with us. Do you have a flower that would produce that color? Could you make golden silks, just to trade with us?"

Big Man called to the same woman who had handed him presents at the first feast.

"Can you dye silk yellow? They would like silk the color of this bird. What would you use for the dye?"

The tiny woman looked at her toes. "There's the early spring flower that grows in the woods on long branches. We sometimes crush the flowers to paint our house floors," she said softly

"Then you are in charge of it. And we will need ten bolts of silk cloth, for Hawk and his family to carry to Green Valley. How long will it take to make so much extra cloth?"

She spoke again hesitantly. "It will take me a week or more to experiment with the color. We will have to raise more silkworms next spring, and then the weavers will have to make the cloth. At least a year, I think."

"Very well." Big Man turned to Owl. "You can expect the traders to come at the end of the next growing season."

"May I know your name?" Owl asked the woman.

"I am Big Man's Wife Number One," she said, surprised. "I thought you knew."

"But don't you have a name of your own? They call me Owl," she explained. "What does your family call you?"

"My children call me Ma. Others call me Big Man's Wife Number One, or sometimes just Number One, if the context is clear."

Afterwards, Owl said she couldn't believe what strange customs they had in Crooked Pine.

"Imagine, women without names of their own!" she said. "No wonder Willow doesn't like it here. I suppose no one calls her 'Willow' except Hawk. To everyone else she is Hawk's Wife."

"I certainly wouldn't like to live here," answered Jade. "But I don't want to leave Buffalo, either. Could he come with us?"

It turned out that Buffalo didn't want to go to Green Valley, where he would own neither house nor land.

"They can't be real men there," he said, scuffing his toe along the ground.

Jade defended the customs of Green Valley heatedly.

When it was time to leave, Jade said good-bye to her uncle and aunt and cousins with cheerful hopes to see them in Green Valley the following summer. Buffalo came to see us off, but the parting wasn't too difficult. Ardor had cooled on both sides.

Joe was champing at the bit, but Mr. Li told us firmly that it was too hot to go to the field between lunch and three o'clock. We would have to wait for the jeep driver to have his rest. After lunch I fell in step with Kidok as we walked through the garden. Instead of going straight to our rooms, we sat at a stone table to chat.

"How are things at home?" I asked him.

"All fine," he told me. "My younger brother married the girl my parents selected for me, and that took the pressure off me. He has two boys. They are very happy, and so am I. That's why they let me go to Berkeley. And you? Is Ed still in your life?"

"Yes, Good old Ed, the anchor of my life. He'll be finished with law school in a few weeks. Then we'll meet in Beijing and make a tour of the Silk Road, all the way out past Urumchi to Kashgar. It should be fun."

"Did you marry him?"

"You cut straight to the chase, don't you? Ed mentions marriage now and then, but I don't know. I'm afraid if I don't finish my degree first, I'll get distracted and never finish. Another thing is that Ed has decided to go into his father's law firm, and his parents think a socialite wife would be better for him than a scholar. It would be a big strain on our lifestyle, being so closely involved with them. I think we should see if our relationship could handle it before we marry."

"Ed's a nice guy. You two will be happy even with problems like in-laws. It sounds like Korea."

"Time will tell."

"Dongsu is well, too. Now and then we speak of you. He'll be glad to know I saw you, looking pretty as ever."

"Tell him hello from me, too." A little of the old magic was still there, so I didn't want to see him. But I liked hearing about him.

"What's he doing these days?"

"He has a daughter, two years old now. And he was just promoted to Associate Professor."

Since we had been instructed to take the customary Chinese rest after lunch, Kidok and I obediently trucked back to our rooms. Laura and I talked for a bit about the Goddess Temple and its discoveries, and speculated about how it would be to be part of the team that reopens it. But who knows when that will be? I wrote in my journal, catching up for the last few days' neglect, and then dropped off to sleep in the heat of the day.

By mid-afternoon we were piling into the vehicles again, although it turned out that Locality 2 was so close we could have walked. The site is squeezed between the railroad and the main highway to Beijing. Once again, we swarmed all over the site, looking for stratigraphy, soil changes, and other archaeological pursuits. Then Dr. Wu gathered us together and explained the site, adding to what we had already heard about it at the museum.

The neatly made square burial chamber was unlike anything else I knew of in China. It's a pity we'll never know what it held, because it was looted long ago. The round mound contained multiple burials. I thought of the Temple of Heaven, which is round because it represents the sky, and the Altar to Earth which is square. Did they already have such ideas in Hongshan times? Was the person buried in the square chamber associated with the Earth Spirit?

Laura was disappointed to learn that in the interest of preservation, the human bones had all been covered with some kind of preparation that looked like concrete. The bones are now accessible only in pictures. One photo shows an extended burial with an almost complete skeleton, lying on its back with crossed ankles. A hoof-shaped jade was behind the skull, and two large pig-dragons rested back to back on the chest. Laura looked regretfully at the pictures of bones that were now sealed in.

Then we walked across the railroad tracks and up a hill to Localities 3, 4, and 5. Each sits on top of a rounded hill. They all had contained burials, and were line-of-sight from the Goddess Temple. I wondered if such sightings were useful in some practical way, or if they were for the sake of getting blessings directly from the temple. Perhaps the visibility was only accidental, but it seemed to be too consistent for that.

Evan recorded the view from each site with his camcorder. He was calculating whether moon or sun or star risings might be seen from any of these places, using the Goddess Temple hill as a foresight. It seemed a long shot, because the direction was generally southeast – too far from due east for either the sun or the moon at maximum southern deviation. But Evan quite rightly thought he should check everything out.

Joe scoured the ground for any evidence of unexcavated buildings, to give him an excuse to use his radar here. He didn't find as much as a single sherd. Laura asked if they could save the next bones for her to study, explaining earnestly to Dr. Wu about all the information that could be extracted from human and animal bones these days.

22

Jade was taller the next time I flew into Green Valley. She was experimenting with ways to use yellow silk, draping it over her sister Fawn's shoulders. Flora watched with a critical eye. I greeted them with a cheery little song.

"Hello, Spirit Bird," Jade said. "You came at a good time. Did my mother call you? We're just getting ready for the trip to the north direction. I'm going with Uncle Eagle this time. He knows the way, and he wants to learn how to tell oracles with shoulder blades as the hunters in the north do."

Jade held Fawn by the shoulders and appraised her. Fawn was petite and pretty, with her mother's shiny black hair and dark eyes, while Flora was taller, with hazel eyes. Obviously they were not identical twins.

"Just look at this gorgeous yellow silk from the south. Didn't they do a great job? Carver is making extra jades for the next round of exchanges, so we can have plenty of silk. Won't we look splendid when we dance?"

I flew to Carver's workshop. He and six apprentices were gathered outside, working on the roughing out stage and letting the chips fly. Carver had made wooden eye covers with slits to see through after one of the boys had a piece of his iris torn out by a sharp chip. Owl gave him good treatment, or he would have lost his eyesight. The jades they were making for exchange were bracelets and pendants made of interlocking rings. They didn't exchange pig-dragons, or other emblematic jades, but kept those for Red Mountain use only. Carver was intent on his work, so I sang my six-note song to get his attention.

"Oh, hello, Spirit Bird. Did you come to supervise? These young jade carvers are getting pretty good. I'm teaching the apprentices to make the export jades. They make jade heads and simple earrings for the Long Bow people. For the Dragon Bone exchanges, we're trying to create a new style that won't weaken our qi or that of our relatives in the sunrise direction. What do you think?"

Carver held up a white jade made of three joined rings. I thought it was lovely, but he was right that it lacked the Hongshan power. I chirped in agreement.

I found Owl with Little Carver in the forest, seeking medicinal herbs and pulling them up to be hung and dried. She saw me before I made a sound.

"Thanks for coming, Spirit Bird," she said. "I've been waiting for you. Jade is going on a trek in her third direction, and I wanted to be sure you were with her. Piggy will go along, of course, and he is a big help for scaring robbers, and even Big Men."

I wanted to smile at the last comment. Piggy had become a formidable boar, with tusks that would terrify anyone who tried to harm Jade. I wouldn't be any threat at all. But traveling with Jade was interesting, and always eventful.

"Jade will travel with my brother, Eagle, this time," Owl explained to me. "He has a friend in the direction of the Bear Stars. Mostly the northern folk are a thinly spread people. They don't farm, like we do, but they fish in the big river to the north, and hunt deer in the thick forests. They also collect several kinds of nuts, which last well through the winter. Sometimes we meet them in the woods this far south. They give us deer and tiger skins, and we give them millet and jades in return. We'll ask Hawk and Willow to bring another color of silk next time, so we can give them silk as well as millet in exchange for the medicine root of the forest. I suppose they won't use much silk with their rough way of life, but even they have ceremonies, and like pretty things.

More trading, I thought. Will that be good for the Red Mountain people, or bring them trouble?

When I came again, Eagle and Jade were making their final preparations to travel to the north. Jade wore a band of yellow silk tied around her forehead, which marked her as an apprentice wu, as well as protecting her from unfriendly spirits.

"Here's the Spirit Bird," announced Eagle. "It's time to say good-bye."

Hawk and his family were gathered to see us off. I was glad to know that they were safe from Big Man, at least for the time being.

After three day's walk (and flying, for me), we came to a wide riverbed. It was mostly sand, though, and Eagle thought they'd be able to cross where the path came to the river. But instead, the river was deep in the middle, where it had carved out a steep canyon to run through. They could swim across, but the current was too swift to carry the packs and keep them dry. We turned back and made a camp, hoping someone would come by to show us a way to cross the river.

The only animal life we saw was a big brown bear with two cubs. She had no interest in us as long as we left her cubs alone. We watched them cavorting at a distance. After they decided the humans were not a danger to them, the family of bears went down to the water's edge. The cubs played in the water, splashing each other sometimes just like human children, and floating on their backs with four paws out of the water, while the mother bear fished. Now and then she would toss a fish their way, and the two of them scrapped over it. When they all had enough to eat, the mother called to her cubs, and walked up the river. After a bit the mother bear stopped, sniffed the air, and began wading into the water.

"The cubs will drown," said Jade in alarm. "We should go and save them." She was already slipping off her sandals to wade into the water.

"Hold on," said Eagle. "The cubs can swim. But they may know something we don't. Bears are smarter than you give them credit for. Let's watch awhile."

The bears were still walking up the stream, but nearing the far bank. When the river turned so that the bears were out of sight, I flew closer to see if they were finding a way across. Sure enough, the mother bear knew a shallow spot just above some rocks that created rapids below.

I kept an eye on them until I was sure they had found a ford, and then flew back to Jade and Eagle.

"Chirp," I said, cocking my head in the direction of the bears.

"It will get dark soon," Eagle observed. "We should stay here for the night. We don't know whether we'd find a good camping spot on the other side."

Jade looked longingly after the bears, but it made sense to stay where we were for the night.

An unseasonable rainfall in the night drenched us and all our belongings. Only Piggy was happy in our wet environment, rolling in the mud and splashing in the puddles. We delayed our start to dry out the basket packs and clothing. The river had become a rushing stream, and almost filled its bank. So much for wading across at the ford the bears showed us.

Ꞇ23

Lars arrived at the Daling archaeological station in time for breakfast. Everyone greeted him like a long lost friend, but I wondered how he got to the field station. The train arrives in the middle of the night, but there had been no talk about picking him up at the nearest railroad station at Yeibaishou. Maybe he walked from the station, but somehow he looked too fresh to have slept on the train and walked a dusty ten kilometers.

"Have you started your GPR work yet?" he asked Joe.

"No, they wanted us to see some of Daling first, to help us interpret anomalies. We start today."

"Can I come with you?"

"You'd be pretty bored. We'll just be walking over the ground, and setting up the grid. Dr. Wu will come along, and jointly we'll select the best areas to sample. We can't do the whole site, but we can do a reasonable amount of each kind of area."

"I'd really like to see it. Archaeology has always been a passion of mine. And I might find evidence of those wu that both Clara and I believe in."

"It's okay with me. But you'll have to ask Dr. Wu."

Dr. Wu pointed out that there wasn't room in the jeep, with five people and a driver, and all the equipment including Marmalade the orange monster, which was already famous in Chinese archaeological circles.

Lars kicked a stone. "Can I walk to the Ox River site? How far is it?"

"Twelve kilometers, maybe. Not an impossible distance, but you'd have to walk both ways."

"Can you show me on the map where it is?" Lars pulled out a map that he had copied from an old Japanese map. It was as good as ours, 1:10,000.

Dr. Wu pointed out a place along the river. "The site is up the hill from there."

"Just look for something bright orange," I laughed.

It was interesting to walk around the site, because it hadn't been surface-collected. Red potsherds, some with black paint, were strewn all over the ground. Looking down on the site from the top of the slope, it was possible to discern circles five to six meters across, darker than the rest of the soil.

"We think each circle is a house," Dr. Wu explained. "These sites are close to ground surface."

"Look, there's another group of ash circles over there, beyond that empty space," I blurted out, excited by discovering something.

"I think you're right," said Dr. Wu. "Shall we walk over there and see?"

The ash circles did continue after what seemed to be a blank space. "Why was there a separation between the groups of houses?"

"They could be sequential villages, although I would guess not, because they seem to be at the same depth. If they're all from the same time period, then maybe the village was divided in two. The empty space could have been their gathering area."

"Or market place," said Ashley.

"Or a dance ground," I threw in.

"Interesting thoughts," murmured Dr. Wu. "Perhaps you should sample this area. We'd like you to concentrate on the two housing areas. But there are some other spots worth examining, too."

He pointed out some mounds on the top of the slope, so overgrown with weeds that they were barely visible. One even had a tree growing out of it.

"We think those are burial mounds. Will your radar be able to see bodies inside?"

"I doubt it, but stone cists will show up. How about this one?" Joe chose one without a tree, the lowest one, presumably the most eroded, and marked it with a yellow flag.

Near the river was a raised area that seemed to be made of earth edged with stones.

"We've called this an altar," said Mr. Wu. "Perhaps an altar to the sky, because it's circular. What can you do here?"

Joe scratched his beard. "We could just take measurements along the top of it," Joe climbed on top to test how firm the earth was. "Or we could make a transect from the ground level, and up and across and down the other side. We could do one transect the long way and one the short way. Have you mapped the site in detail already? If you have, that would save us a lot of time."

"Yes, I brought a copy for you. Keep it to yourself, though. I didn't send it ahead of time because we've had so much trouble with looters around here. The jades are very valuable, and every farmer around knows they're mostly found in graves. Soon there won't be a one left."

"What do they do with the jades?" asked Laura. "Surely it's illegal to sell them in China."

"Oh, yes. Not just illegal - the penalty for looting is death."

"Death!" I shuddered.

Ashley asked, "Isn't that somewhat out of proportion?"

"By making the penalty so severe, the government hoped to stop it. But for the amount of ren min bi each jade will bring, many people are willing to risk even death."

"How do the looters dispose of the jades and get their money?" I tried to keep probing.

"They take them to Hong Kong, where several dealers are eager to buy illegal artifacts. Some dealers create phony documentation, so they can be exported 'legally.' Others have devised ways to hide them in legitimate shipments. Rich people from Europe and America buy them, sometimes from secret catalogs, and the dealer makes a huge profit. So does the auction house. The farmer who has risked death gets relatively little. But it's still a lot of money in his eyes."

"But the artifacts end up in museums when the rich people donate them for a tax deduction. So the public has them again, and in the meantime some peasants have more money. Doesn't the story have a happy ending?" asked Ashley.

I was shocked by Ashley's attitude, even though she's not trained as an archaeologist.

Joe must have felt the same. He turned to her with his hands on his hips, and spoke sharply. “Surely art historians don’t condone looting.”

Ashley shrugged. “Of course not, but why is it such a big deal?”

“Ashley, the artifacts lose their context if they haven’t been properly excavated. Artifacts in situ are much more informative than those that are ripped out of the ground. There’s a great deal to learn from the context - what else the artifact was found with, whether it was in a house or a burial or a trash dump or whatever. No matter how long you study the artifact, you can’t replace that information.”

Joe’s indignation came through loud and clear in his voice.

“For years art historians thought the Hongshan jades were from the Shang dynasty, because they didn’t have any context,” I couldn’t forbear to add. “It wasn’t until Hongshan graves were excavated that the graves were properly placed in time.”

Laura continued the lesson. “Yes, the jades are beautiful, and they could be thought of as art objects, but they’re much more important than things to admire. They’re clues to a lost culture. No one even suspected jades were here, because such fancy Neolithic jades don’t fit the paradigm of Chinese archaeology. But excavation made it clear that the jades belong to Hongshan times. You simply can’t replace excavation for extracting the most information.”

“Yes, I see why people shouldn’t loot sites,” Ashley said. “But if the jades have already been stolen, shouldn’t we study them?”

“That’s not the point, we need to stamp out looting.” Joe stamped with his boot to emphasize his statement. “Enough talking. Time to get to work.”

Joe flagged the corner locations of the three areas where we would do GPR. “Let’s start with the ash circles,” Joe directed. “It’s uncomplicated flat ground. We should get good readings there, and they should be easy to interpret. It will help us understand the more complicated parts of the site.”

Ashley and I lined up the grids with the cardinal directions. We set the strings five meters apart in the open meadow where the ash circles were located. The string was marked at five-meter intervals, where readings would be taken

While we were laying out grids, Laura and Joe checked various set-ups of the instrument until they were satisfied. Laura carried the GPR unit over the grid, stopping to push the button at each five-meter interval along the string, called out by Joe for the first test in this field.

We spent the afternoon carrying Marmalade the radar unit back and forth along the grid. Because this was an important area, we walked the grid both ways, north-south and east-west. Each way gives slightly different readings, and it was possible that something would show up in one direction that had been missed in the other.

Before dinner Joe downloaded the measurements of the day into his laptop, and we four went to discuss the colorful screens with the Chinese archaeologists.

"It's necessary to correct for various possible distortions, but for a first reading, it looks like the houses show up clearly. Here's one that may have an outbuilding, for example. See how there's a lighter extension on the south side?

"We can clearly tell that the buildings are not all the same size. The biggest house in each row is more or less in the middle. And look at this place between the two clusters of houses, in the middle of the open space. There's something round, with snaky things radiating from it. That might be the trunk and roots of a big tree."

"These are interesting results already," Dr. Wu was pleased. "Let's have a toast to your project!"

Xiao Li got out the tiny glasses, which meant baijiu was about to be poured. I gamely swallowed the whole glassful when Dr. Wu said "Gambei," and after a coughing fit, I joined the others in congratulating ourselves and each other.

"Let's not mention this yet," suggested Mr. Li.

Mr. Gao agreed. "We don't know who might be helping the looters."

After dinner, Evan and Kidok and I walked back to the foreigners' buildings looking at the stars. Fluffy horizon clouds kept us from seeing the whole sky, but the stars above were bright. When the rest of the tipsy archaeologists joined us, Evan pointed out western constellations to the Asians, and made notes when they named a few asterisms they recognized.

Evan outdid himself, having all the archaeologists for his audience. He told spell-binding tales about the stars, and explained how prehistoric people tracked the stars for a kind of calendar that would correct for the moon's lack of sync with the sun, and stay correlated with the seasons.

"It's called a luni-solar calendar," Evan explained. "Some ancient peoples used star clusters the same way others used the sun's rising and setting positions north and south of due east and west, to tell the time of year."

"The Chinese word for 'time' really means 'season,'" said Lars, reminding us that he is our authority on ancient China. "The early Chinese thought in terms of seasons of the year as the passage of time. There's some wonderful early poetry about it."

Dr. Wu and Mr. Gao looked at each other and nodded. The foreigner knows a lot about China. But luckily for us, they didn't begin to recite the poems in Chinese.

24

Eagle was a trained wu like the rest of his family, and Jade was a wu in training. They discussed the best way to cross the river, now that it was so full of water. Eagle brought out his far-seeing needle, and Jade did the same.

"I see a group of tents," said Eagle. "And there's my friend Chips, so it's the encampment of our destination. But how do we get there, if we can't cross the river here?"

"My needle shows this path continuing across the river. People are on the path. And they're coming toward us. Spirit Bird, can you go see who they are, and if they can help us find a way across the river?"

I was always glad to be useful. I flew across the river, and followed the path through the woods and into a clearing. Three men were just struggling out of big packs. The one with the black beard built a fire, while the tall man with a missing front tooth prepared the body of a freshly killed deer. The cross-eyed man cut branches to make spits to roast the deer. I thought they were hunters from Mountain Camp, and was about to fly back, when the fire reflected something shiny on the chest of the black-bearded man. It looked like a jade head. Were these Long Bow people?

I sat on a branch watching while they ate their dinner. They didn't talk much, so I waited to see what would happen. When they removed their cloaks to spread over their pine branch beds, I saw that each man had a tattoo on one shoulder that continued onto his back. The leader had a wolf tattoo, and the others a tiger and a leopard. I sneaked a better look at the jade head, too. It looked like Carver's jade, but I couldn't be sure. I tucked my head under my wing to wait for morning.

The three men set out in the direction of the river the next day. I followed discreetly behind them, to see if they planned to cross it, and if so, how they would do it. I hoped Jade and Eagle were still in the same spot, waiting for my report.

The sun was high before they reached the river. A birch bark canoe had been stashed among willow bushes on the river bank. The men threw their packs and cloaks into the boat, and steered it with a paddle into the main stream. I hoped they would be able to help Jade and Eagle, so I flew to sit in front of them on the canoe.

"Look," said the man wearing the jade, who I decided to call Wolf, after his tattoo. "It's a yellow-crested bird. We should catch it. They bring good luck from the spirits."

Leopard reached for a net and threw it over me in a continuous motion. I should have been warier. I was totally pinned down and helpless, under the weighted net.

By this time the canoe was drifting by the camp of Eagle and Jade. The smoke from their fire drew Tiger's attention.

"Steer over there," said Wolf. "I'll bet they're traders, taking valuable things to the north. We can overpower them and take whatever they have."

Leopard steered across the water. Not far upstream from the camp, Tiger grabbed an overhanging branch so they could land. I thought my song wouldn't carry as far as the camp, but I chirped as loudly as I could, hoping to warn Jade and Eagle.

I was surprised how little noise the three burly men made as they approached the camp. When they came within arm's reach, Wolf threw a net over Eagle, and Tiger trapped Jade.

"I know who you are!" Jade screamed. "You're the robbers. And that's my father's jade head, that tells strangers he's from Jade Village."

In a calmer voice she added, "Give it to me, or you'll be sorry."

Wolf laughed heartily. "What can you do to us, my pretty? I'm sure we can think of something to do with you."

Jade didn't bother with the subtle woodpecker call.

"Piggy," she called out loudly.

"It won't do any good to call us names," said Wolf with an offensive smirk.

Piggy had been out finding acorns for his breakfast, but was within calling distance of Jade's voice.

He came at a run, and butted Tiger, who was holding Jade. One of his tusks grazed Wolf's leg, and drew blood. Wolf screamed for the others to run, and began limping away as fast as he could. The other two ran also, leaving behind their nets. Piggy seemed inclined to follow them and finish the job, but Jade called him back.

"Where did they come from? And where's Spirit Bird?"

"They were up the river," said Eagle. "I'm sure, because I was looking downriver and didn't see them. Let's walk back and see what's there. Piggy should come, too, in case more robbers are hiding there."

Eventually Jade got close enough to hear my agitated chirping. Eagle found the canoe, and the robbers' supplies, and many things they had taken from other travelers. Jade laid it all out on the ground. Obsidian knives in birch bark containers, leather capes, and lots of flint arrowheads were on the top of one basket. They also had plants for curing, some of which Jade recognized. At the bottom of the pack, many of the rare white roots with several branches were wrapped in white leaves.

"These are the best medicine of all," Jade said. "The roots come from the Ever-White Mountains. We picked some there, and boiled them for tea. I didn't like the taste, but Father said it was good for me, and would strengthen my power."

"Shall we have some tea now?" asked Eagle.

I could only say "Chirp, chirp, chirp," in rising tones.

"You are right, Spirit Bird, we should leave this place before the robbers come back." Jade had armed herself with one of their bows, and a quiver of arrows. They may have other bows. They could shoot us from a distance, and even Piggy couldn't stop them," Jade mused.

"Let's take their boat across the river," suggested Eagle.

"It won't hold Piggy," Jade objected.

But Piggy plunged into the water and began swimming toward the far bank. Eagle paddled the canoe across the river as well as possible. The current took the boat downstream, but at least they were on the other side of the river from the robbers.

"I wish we could have snatched Father's jade head back," Jade said with regret "If we ever see them again, that's the first thing I'll do."

I smiled at the thought of the thin girl snatching the jade from the large robber.

25

It wasn't exactly raining, but it was drizzly off and on. Joe didn't want to drag Marmalade through the wet weeds, so we decided to go touring with the Koreans, and see more Hongshan sites. This day's excursion began with the artificial hill, and continued on to Dongshanzui. It would be a full day, and we'd return after dark. We brought flashlights and rain jackets, along with the usual archaeological paraphernalia.

The artificial hill is referred to as a pyramid, although it looks more like a stepped cone to me. As we climbed up, Dr. Wu pointed out three rings of dressed white stone. The hill was riddled with square pits, which we learned had been dug in the hopes of finding a magnificent tomb, but nothing was found. Near the top the Chinese archaeologists had found cruddy potsherds, which turned out to have traces of copper on them. The pottery objects must have been small crucibles for holding melted copper. This was a strange result.

"What would have been the reason for making a huge hill just to melt copper on the top?" Ashley asked.

Joe suggested that the wind may have been better there, allowing them to have a fire hot enough to melt copper.

"How hot is that?" I inquired.

"About a thousand degrees Fahrenheit. I'll look it up when I get home," Joe answered.

"How hot were their cooking fires? Or their pottery-fires?" asked Kidok

"They must have had pretty good control of the heat, because I read that underground kilns have been found in some settlements. That shows a lot of technological knowledge of fire," Laura commented.

"It seems a little extreme to move all this dirt, and put circles of white stone inside, just to build a better fire. There must be plenty of windy spots that wouldn't have taken so much effort," said Kidok.

"Maybe the Neolithic people considered melting stone to be some kind of magic, to be able to melt stone. I bet the people here were completely wowed with the sight of melting copper. Maybe they climbed up here to melt the ore just in order to impress the populace," I suggested.

"Maybe it was built to view the moon at its farthest northern and southern points on the eastern horizon," said Evan. "I can see two of the cairns from here that could have been used for foresights. I think you're asking the wrong question. Not, why melt copper on top, but why build the hill exactly here?"

We crowded into the Korean's bus for the drive to Dongshanzui. It's probably not more than twenty-five miles by road, and shorter as the yellow bird flies, but there's so much slow traffic on the road that it seems to take forever. It was market day, and the market stalls were spread out along both sides of the main highway, which made the going that much worse. Donkeys and carts were in the middle of the road, and sometimes piles of beans or tomatoes intruded onto the roadbed.

Once we were through the market town, every now and then the bus driver would stop the bus and get out of the bus, and then get back in and drive on a while. The third time it happened, those of us near the front got off to find out what was happening. He couldn't need that many pee stops.

The driver stood behind the bus, scooping water from a muddy puddle and pouring it into the radiator. Much of the water sloshed back out through an obvious break. Laura watched for a few seconds, and then reached into her pockets. From one she took a Swiss army knife, and from another she brought out a roll of duct tape. Without saying a word, she cut lengths of duct tape and wound them tightly around the leaking pipe, effectively fixing it. The rest of us, including the driver, stood back in amazement.

"Americans always carry red knives and a roll of tape," Kidok explained to the bus driver in Chinese. Joe and Laura thought this was very funny after I translated, and spread the story around the bus.

The bus driver had more problems. He lost the way after we went through another town, so we admired views from several hills before he found the road up the right hillside. The road was unpaved and rutted, but the bus wheels were wider apart than the ruts, so he managed to stay on the road.

It rained intermittently. At one point the bus got stuck in the mud, and we got out and pushed until the bus slid back onto the road track. Ashley complained of the mud on her boots and jeans. Worse was to come.

The upper hill slope where the ceremonial complex had been excavated has some characteristics that are similar to the placement of the Goddess temple. Dongshanzui is high on the slope of a hill, overlooking the Daling River, as the Goddess Temple must have overlooked the Mangniu River before the road and railroad were built.

Archaeologists swarmed all over the site, in our usual fashion, taking pictures and making measurements. Features are present, but it is not at all clear to me how we should understand the rows of low walls, possible earth altars, and a pile of thin rocks that lean in toward the middle. Dr. Wu and Mr. Li walked over it with us, pointing out the features.

"Is this the place where the small and medium-sized female figurines were found?" asked Lars.

"Yes," replied Dr. Wu. "Unlike most female figurines alleged to be pregnant, there's no doubt about the ones from Dongshanzui. The belly is distended beyond the possibility of any other explanation. There's also a statuette that might be depicting a nursing mother, with an arm to the chest and something missing."

Lars wanted to know exactly where the statue of a cross-legged woman with a rope belt was found.

"It was in pieces," explained Mr. Li. "We don't know where it was used.

"I think she might represent a wu. Knots like those on the belt were often considered sacred."

The rain began pelting down in earnest, and we ran for the bus. Somehow in the driving rain, the driver took a wrong turn. He stopped the bus at a ford in the river, which was running higher than usual because of the rain upstream. Joe and Kidok got out to look, but the rain, pushed by the wind into sheets of water, drove them back inside. Everyone was anxious to get back on pavement, because if we hit another spot of deep mud we would have to push the bus again, this time in the rain.

The river was wide, but shallow. The driver waded into it, and seemed satisfied that the bottom was solid. Back on the bus, he gunned the motor and plunged in. The bus kept moving until we reached the middle, when the motor drowned out. Several attempts to get it started again failed.

The driver got off the bus, and Joe and I went to the door to see what he was doing this time. While we watched, he was swept away down the river in the rapid current. There was no possibility of going after him, he disappeared so quickly.

A tree came down the river and hit the bus, causing it to tip toward the side where the door was. Clearly we were not safe staying here. We'd have to abandon the bus.

"We'll make a human chain," Joe announced. He lined people up, with strong men on each side of the smaller women and Prof. Lee. He asked Kidok to lead, and he himself would be at the end of the chain. Depth of the water wasn't a problem yet, but it was rising, and we should go as soon as possible. We put on our rain jackets, and several people pulled flashlights from their packs. The bus carried a strong flashlight, which Kidok shone ahead to lead the way.

Joe directed us to grip arms on the bus, and to get off slowly and make sure the person behind had foot traction before moving away from the bus. The rain and the river were so noisy he had to shout.

Crossing the river was one of those nightmares that seem to go on forever. I was between Evan and Joe, near the end of the line. Kidok led us at an angle to the current. I felt something hit against my shoulder, and yelped. Joe turned his flashlight toward me, and batted away a small branch. I was glad it wasn't something alive.

All of us reached the far bank totally soaked and exhausted from battling the current, but glad to be out of the roaring river. We regrouped, and found that we hadn't lost anyone. Evan had a cut on his arm, and my shoulder felt bruised, but we could all walk even with squishy boots. My teeth were chattering uncontrollably. There was nothing to do but continue up the road.

The rain darkened the sky, although it was still daylight. After a half a kilometer or so, we saw a light on the side of a hill. Joe and Laura climbed up to inspect. It was a farmer's home, where we were welcomed. With no false modesty we peeled off our wet clothes. I was too cold to enjoy the display of male buns, but quickly wrapped up in the blankets they provided, sharing with Laura because there were not enough to go around. The farmer's wife gave us hot barley water, and gradually we stopped shivering.

The farmer's house had no telephone. When the rain turned back to a drizzle, he offered his donkey cart to take us to town. We were a bedragggled lot, and the donkeys looked at us with disdain. The farmer urged them to move, and finally they did. When we came to a police outpost, Kidok and Joe put their wet boots back on, and went to see if help could be provided.

It was two in the morning when we finally returned to the field station, filthy and dripping, but glad to have survived. Ashley, Laura and I all showered together in the small space, because none of us could wait.

26

I flew into Mountain Camp just as Jade, Eagle and Piggy were approaching it. The whole camp gathered when our party was spotted from a distance, but everyone held bows in their hands, with arrows at the ready, and did not seem at all welcoming. In fact, I thought they were downright menacing, and considered trying to distract them some way. The group relaxed a bit when they saw we were just a man and a girl and a pig, but tension still filled the air.

Jade politely introduced the three of them, and then me, too, as she saw me alight on a branch. A man and a woman came forward to meet them, and Eagle recognized Chips, whom he had met hunting near Green Valley.

"Welcome," said Chips. "I'm sorry that we seemed unfriendly, but we have just had some very disagreeable visitors."

"Were they the robbers?"

"What do you know about them?"

"They're nasty characters," said Eagle, shaking his head.

"I've met them twice," said Jade. "The first time was in the hills between the Red Mountain and Longbow peoples. I guess they just roam around, taking things from other people. They ran away when Piggy gored one of them with his tusks, leaving their packs in a canoe up the river. We brought everything along by towing them in the boat up your small stream. If these things are yours, please take them back."

"Mostly they took food from us, including the grain we exchanged for deer hides last year. We wouldn't have gone hungry, even in the winter, but it's nice to have a change in diet during the long snowstorms."

"Where could these robbers come from?" asked Jade. "They speak a language we can understand, but the dialect is different from any we know. And there are just three of them. Do you suppose they are outcasts from some group here in the north?"

"Where exactly did you see them before?" Chips wanted to know. "Maybe we can figure out their movements."

"In the forest near the big river that divides Long Bow people and Red Mountain people. They knew about Long Bow insignia, and took my father's jade pendant head."

"Ah, yes, I thought they were Long Bow people at first, but I got suspicious when they didn't know any of the people I mentioned."

"How did they rob you?"

"They tied us up in the forest the first time, but Piggy and Spirit Bird scared them away. This time they had flint knives, and one had a bow and arrows. They could have harmed us. I think they are getting desperate."

"The robbers stayed here long enough to learn where things are stored, and then took them in the night, after they accepted our hospitality," said Chips' wife Poppy, with sparks in her eyes.

"We should do an augury to see where they are, and whether they will come back," suggested Poppy.

"After our guests rest a bit, and we have all eaten, will be time enough."

The humans had a fine feast of venison and berries, while Piggy and I foraged for ourselves. They drank cool fresh water from the spring, and then began telling stories.

Poppy told of a hunt when they had found a she bear that seemed almost human. The bear had stayed near their hunting camp for days, and had driven off a tiger prowling nearby. She thought the bear had been sent to protect them.

Deer Hunter had a story about a tiger they had trapped in a strong twine snare. Now they had a fine tiger skin rug to sleep on. Jade reached out to pat the fur, and it looked so appealing I wished I had a human hand to feel it with.

Eventually, Poppy took out her medicine bundle and the deer shoulder bones she had prepared for divining. Chips bored holes in the underside of a broad deer shoulder blade with a flint drill. When the shoulder bone was ready, Poppy unpinned her hair, and undid her long braid. Her black hair hung down to the back of her knees. I'm sure it had never been cut. The fire burned to embers. Poppy held the bone in her hand and stretched her arm over the fire. The others clapped to get the attention of the spirits.

Poppy began to sing in high-pitched voice.

"Tell us, tell us, tell us now, where the robbers hide and how?"

She whisked the bone through the fire six times.

"Are they near to us tonight? Are they lurking near our light?"

A piece of ember was scooped up and came to rest on one of the holes. The bone made a cracking sound.

Poppy examined the bone.

"No, they're not near," she said in her normal voice. "We don't have to worry about them for a while.

Jade took out her far-seeing needle.

"I see the robbers near a wide river. One of them lies by the fire with a wounded leg. The other two are talking, but I can't hear what they say. It looks like they won't cause more trouble at least until the one robber's leg heals."

"We found some pretty stone that Carver might like," said Poppy. "Here's a piece of it. We could go get more, if you think he could carve it."

Jade held the stone in her hand. It was mottled black and brown, and seemed quite hard, but it might be possible to carve and polish. Eagle hefted it, too, and nodded. They decided to go to the quarry the next day, in search of useful stone.

The stone quarry was a full day's walk, so we had to make an overnight camp. On the way back to our camping spot, after gathering some of the dark stone, Jade noticed something green in a rock.

"Look at this!" she called. "What is it? I thought it would be a flower, the color is so bright, or maybe a new kind of moss. But it is not any kind of plant, it's stone."

Everyone gathered around to see what Jade had found.

"Sometimes there is very soft reddish material near where you find this green," said Poppy. "Let's search around here."

"Here's a bit of it, in this rock with the green edges," said Chips.

"It's rather pretty," Jade remarked.

"You can make pendants out of it," said Chips. "It's soft and easy to mold by hitting it with a hard rock. But if you let it get too close to a very hot fire, it will turn into orange-colored water. See, we made shapes in the sand and poured the liquid in. It hardens into any shape you make in the sand."

"May I have a bit to take back?" asked Jade. "It is a very strange rock, that can go from solid to liquid in a fire. Owl will want to know about it, and to learn about its properties."

Chips presented her with a small copper in the shape of a snake.

27

Breakfast was delayed until eight o'clock after the mishap with the bus, so we were late returning to the Ox River site. The ground was wet, but not so soggy we couldn't work. We began to set up a new grid between the two house groups. The grid continued with a transect through the middle of the second group of houses. We had become a well-oiled team, and we sat down to lunch with a feeling of accomplishment. The jeep driver had left us there, but returned with a stack of steamy baskets that contained rice, two vegetable dishes and one dish with chicken.

"Which of my little friends from the rabbit hutch do you suppose this is, the spotted bunny or the brown one?" asked Laura, poking through the chicken dish.

"Cut it out, Laura," said Ashley, avoiding the dish altogether.

Joe changed the subject. "So clever, you Chinese, to eat with chopsticks on a dig. It's great for archaeology. I've worked where the rivers are too polluted to wash in, and even packaged wipes don't get your hands clean."

Dr. Wu laughed. "We invented a lot of useful things. Some of them are well-kept secrets."

"Where are the fortune cookies?" Laura asked when the meal was over, pretending to look through the basket.

"You're teasing," laughed Dr. Wu. "Everyone knows the story about how fortune cookies were invented in Boston Chinatown. Or was it San Francisco?"

"It must have been based on something Chinese," I insisted. "We saw an ancient book with numbered fortunes at a Daoist temple. Could that have been the inspiration? Just cut up a book and bake each number in a cookie?"

"Yech," Ashley responded. "That book must have been full of ancient germs. I hope fortune cookies didn't begin with old papers inside them.

"Not to mention destroying ancient documents and bits of ancient history," I pointed out.

"I read somewhere that if nothing had ever been destroyed or recycled, the entire globe would be armpit deep in Neolithic garbage." Ashley delivered this statement with a bit of heat, still smarting from Joe's cutting remarks about art historians two days before.

It was time to tackle the tombs, which would mean climbing up and down both sides of them, so Joe shouldered the GPR unit while Ashley and I gathered the materials to lay out the grid.

At the top of the hill, a scene of devastation stopped us short. The tombs were full of holes. The holes were randomly dug, and were of different sizes, with dirt strewn haphazardly around. A few bones poked up from the backdirt.

"Ohmigod," said Laura, picking up one of the bones. "Someone ransacked the burials. This is a human humerus." The usually stoic Laura began to cry.

Joe was speechless, too angry even to swear.

Dr. Wu looked like he might cry too. "We tried so hard to keep this site secret. How could this happen? It wasn't like this two days ago. The looters must have come yesterday, in the rain. But how did they find it? No one followed the jeep when we came the first day."

Joe's yellow flag had been replanted in an open stone-lined grave. "I suppose my flag led the looters right to the graves."

"But they had to know how to get here," Dr. Wu insisted. "There was a leak somewhere. I don't want to accuse you, but did you talk to anybody?"

"Nobody who wasn't at the archaeology station," Joe wrinkled his brow. "But there were three men in a white van at the Goddess Temple site day before yesterday. They could have found out the exact location of the site some way. Surely nobody would have told them?"

"Yes, I saw them too, and wrote down their license plate number."

We all stood frozen in the same posture we had been when the mess was discovered, like a game of Swing Statues.

Joe was the first to recover.

"What do you want us to do now?" he asked Dr. Wu. "Should we report the theft right away? Should we continue with the GPR? We can record the tombs even in this condition."

"Given the mess the looters made, the tombs will have to be excavated now anyway, what's left of them. You might as well skip the radar here.

"It might be a good control," suggested Joe. "Maybe we should do it anyway."

"Of course, if you like. I'll go back with the driver to report this incident. You four can continue with the GPR of the altar, and I'll be back to pick you up by the end of the day."

It was very sad walking over the ruined tombs. But the area was small, and it didn't take long to finish, so we went back to grid the possible altar.

Joe was on edge, and when Ashley read from the wrong side of the tape, he shouted at her, and then muttered, "I shouldn't have brought an untrained art historian for this work!"

"That's it!" Ashley threw down the tape and ran toward the river.

"The three of us can finish without her," said Joe in disgust.

We continued for about an hour, but Ashley didn't reappear.

When it came to break time, and still no Ashley, I couldn't stand it any more.

"I'm going to find her," and I tromped off in the direction Ashley had taken.

It was a thin trail, more like trampled grass than a track anyone used regularly. I noticed, though, that the trail hadn't been made by Ashley's boots. Archaeologists wear boots without treads, so as not to mess up the bottom of the pit they are excavating. I saw an occasional impression of at least two different sneaker treads, and possibly three. Probably the looters came this way.

I had gone about a hundred meters when I heard men's voices. Who could they be? Maybe Dr. Wu had the police investigating already. I didn't see anyone, though.

"Ashley," I hollered.

No answer.

I walked a little farther and called again.

"Run away, Clara," yelled Ashley in a voice pitched an octave higher than usual. "Get help!"

But I didn't have a chance to run. A large Chinese man grabbed me by the arm. He had noticed me at the same time Ashley did.

Ashley was looking out the front window of a white van. She was squeezed between two other men in the front seat.

"Not another one," I thought the driver said, although I couldn't be sure because he spoke in a Chinese dialect that's hard for me to understand.

"Well, throw her in the back of the van, and the other one, too," said the man on the other side of Ashley.

"These Chinese girls are a bother, but we have to follow our time table. You know what La-su said about keeping to the schedule. We can look for a place to dump them somewhere along the highway."

They took my pack, tied my hands behind my back, and made me get into the back seat of the van, behind a bunch of boxes. Ashley was soon trussed up and put in through the back door, too.

28

"You got here just in time, Spirit Bird," said Jade. "I'm almost ready for my journey to the west. This is my last chance to learn about faraway places. And to find a man to marry, I suppose. But I don't have to marry to become the Green Valley leader. Unless I can find someone who will help me as a leader, I won't marry at all."

I hopped around the baskets Jade was preparing. I could only see clothes and blankets for her. I wondered which relative would go with us this time. Maybe he or she was from another household, and was packing there.

Jade figured out my perplexity.

"It will be just the three of us on this journey. You and Piggy and me. It's a kind of trial, or a vision quest, depending on what happens. We'll go toward the sunset, because we haven't been in that direction. Nobody knows exactly what's out there, but we've heard about big lakes and grass as far as the eye can see. Long ago some herders came from that direction, and they brought us fine wool from small animals. According to the old stories, the animals were like dogs, but fluffier and not as smart.

"They told our people that they'd been walking two circuits of the seasons. They came over snowy mountains, flaming cliffs, and singing sands. But when they took a wrong track and came to a sandy place with neither grass nor water, most of their animals died, as well as many of their people. The few stragglers, including some children, spent a winter here, and learned some of our language.

"So we know there are people in the direction of the Yellow Springs, in spite of the shining mountains and the singing sands. Won't it be fun to learn what's out there? The world has so much to offer, and we know such a small part of it. But the Red Mountain people are in the middle of it!"

I hopped around in some agitation. Jade all alone except for a pig and a bird? She must be still a teenager. Is there a path? What if the robbers find us? Are there villages to take us in and feed us? It just seemed wrong for a teenaged girl to set forth with only a pig and a bird for companions. I tried to indicate my displeasure by flying rapidly in circles around her baskets.

Owl came out of the house and tried to calm me down.

"We know where the track to the west begins," she said, as if that were all that was needed. "You'll turn along the great river where you last saw the robbers. From there you'll follow the river toward the direction of the sunset. You must not go too far. There are stories of great houses and fine ornaments, but they may be a mirage, or exaggerations told by travelers. Return no later than when the moon is fully in its next lodging place, near the Bird Star."

Piggy came trotting around the corner of the house with his ears flying. He had reached his full growth, and his tusks were impressive indeed. He was no longer the lean little Piggy who went to Jade Village and Crooked Pine. With his heft alone he could certainly defend us against robbers, as he has before. And I could fly for help if needed. I felt better.

But if there would be no villages to stay in, what about food? What would Jade eat?

"You and Piggy can find your own food in the forests," said Jade as if she could read my mind. "I've packed some millet cakes for emergencies. I'll bring my bows and arrows, and cord for making traps. Red Mountain villages will feed me for at least three days walk toward the sunset, and people on the edge can tell us what is farther in that direction. It isn't dangerous. It will be fun to walk into the sunset."

We took the path to the northern river, using several days to visit with various friends Jade had made on the trip to the north. Then we followed the river into the mountains. As the river became smaller and steeper, no farming villages welcomed us along our route.

At this time of year, sleeping out under the stars was a pleasure, and we three enjoyed each other's company. I could tease Piggy by pecking at his tail, and he would chase me until I had to alight on a tree. It made Jade laugh. It was a pleasant and peaceful journey in full summer.

A path beckoned us ever higher into the mountains, but like the river, it became smaller and smaller. When Jade ate her last millet cake, she took out her packet of cord to make snares. The first one she put low in the bushes, and caught a rabbit. The meat from the small rabbit lasted two days, but there wasn't enough to save for later meals.

"I'll have to snare a deer," Jade said to Piggy and me. "If I get one, we'll have to stay in one camp for a few days to process the meat. But I guess there's no hurry, since we have no particular destination."

Her snares didn't work; the deer were too wary.

"I hate to use a bow and arrow, but I have to eat," Jade confided in us.

Jade sharpened her arrow points and lashed them to the arrow shafts. Then she strung her bow, tying it tighter until the cord was good and taut.

Early in the morning, she stalked a half-grown fawn, following until it was used to her presence. Then, with a well-placed shot, she felled it. She apologized to the spirit of the deer, before she cut the meat into strips and hung it over high limbs to dry. When the flesh was dry enough not to rot, she wrapped the dried meat in the deer skin, making another bundle to carry.

"We could go now, except that this is too much meat for me to carry. I could cache some things here, and the package would probably be still here when we return. We haven't seen any people, so I'd just need to make my things safe from animals."

Jade looked around. "Maybe I could lash a bundle to that tree."

But Piggy had a different idea. He caught up one of Jade's bundles in his tusk, and pranced around with it a bit.

"You're right, Piggy, you could carry some things for me. Thanks for offering."

Jade experimented with making a kind of harness of rope. Her first attempts slipped around. Finally, she figured out how to anchor two leather bags slung across Piggy's back. It seemed snug, so she tucked the deer meat packages into it.

"Is that too heavy?"

Piggy grunted, and took off at a trot. His legs were short for a pack animal, but he was sturdy enough. So Piggy became Jade's carrier.

We traveled on, down one mountain and up the next. There was always a path of sorts, although sometimes it was overgrown, and Jade had to hack away branches with her largest knife, especially for Piggy with his pack that made him even wider.

Waking one morning in the fresh dew, we heard human noises. It was startling after hearing only our own sounds, and those of nature, for so long.

"Could you fly out and see if you can find the source of the voices?" Jade requested of me. "We need to know how many people there are, and whether they're likely to be friendly or not. I think they've just arrived. We'd have heard them when we camped last night, if they were already here. If they seem dangerous, we can go back quietly, and they will never know that they almost met us."

I soared into the sky and tried to get my bearings. Surely there would be a fire wherever there are people. I circled high, looking for smoke. If we could hear them, they couldn't be very far away.

When at last I spotted the campfire, I saw no people, but many animals. Milling around the camp were sheep, dogs, and horses. I flew right into their camp, and perched on a birch tree conveniently near the fire.

"Look at that bird," said a child I hadn't noticed before. She was wearing leather trousers and a leather upper garment with a hood. She pointed at me. "I've never seen such a bright yellow bird in our homeland, Over the High Mountains. We must have gone very far."

A man with a light brown beard, dressed the same as the child, came out of a leather tent, set up on tall poles.

"We have gone very far, Little Pony. And still we've found no farming villages. I hope we'll find some kind people who will take us in during the snow time. We're too far away to return to our pastures beyond the rim of the world. We can't go back before next year at the soonest. So we have to keep going toward the sunrise, and trust the spirits to guide us."

"Isn't this the end of the world?"

"Our stories say there are people on this side of the singing sands and the sea of grass. The last time a party was lost out here my grandfather was with them. He was just a boy, about your age, but he told tales of the people and their strange customs all his life. I don't think he made up the tales, although his stories became more unbelievable as time went on.

"I loved his stories, though. I listened closely to all the versions of them, and memorized the paths they took and the sights they saw. I must have known I'd be out here on the edge of the sea of grass some day."

"Can you recognize any landmarks?"

"A few, but, he didn't tell that much detail. The important thing is that he said they met people at Red Mountain, and we haven't come to any red mountain yet. It must be farther along. I hope we still have time to get there before the snows fall."

As others came out of the three tents to warm up by the fire, I counted ten people, five adults and five children. Nothing about them suggested that they would be dangerous to Jade, but I wondered how I could find out for sure. Maybe I could get one of the children to follow me to Jade's camp, and I could see how the child behaved.

When the adults were busy with the horses, I flew down to the level of Little Pony, and chirped. As expected, she came closer to me. When I was sure I had her attention, I hopped toward the place we were camped, and Little Pony followed. I didn't know what she would make of Jade, who looked different from the European-like people in the tents. Still, Jade looked more like them than most of the Red Mountain people, so Little Pony probably wouldn't be frightened of her.

Then I began to worry what Jade and Piggy would think of this child. And I hoped that Piggy wouldn't startle Little Pony. He'd scare me, if I didn't know how gentle he was. How could I make the meeting friendly from the start?

I came to a clearing not far from our camp, and called for Piggy – not the anxious call when there was trouble, but a happy bird song. As soon as I saw him ambling toward us, I flew to land on his back. Little Pony was startled by his size, but not put off by a pig.

"It's a magic pig," she said with a childish chortle. "A magic bird and a magic pig. Have you come out of the woods to save us? We are looking for people to feed and shelter us through the winter."

A child who talks to animals is certainly a hopeful sign, I thought, so I left Piggy with Little Pony and went to call Jade. She had heard me calling Piggy, and followed him to the clearing. I turned around and saw her watching with amusement as the little girl ran her hand lightly over Piggy's tusks.

"Hello," Jade said to the child, "I see you've made friends with Piggy already. I am Jade, of the Red Mountain people, from the village of Green Valley. Who are you?"

Little Pony couldn't understand, but she smiled and plucked a wildflower and offered it to Jade.

In the meantime, Little Pony's absence had been noted, and the adults were looking for her. We weren't far away, so they tracked Little Pony easily.

Language was a problem, but at least it was obvious that neither party was hostile or dangerous. With gestures, the leader communicated with Jade that the people with their sheep, dogs, and horses needed to stay in a village for the winter. They would reward the village with sheep and wool.

By pointing to themselves and uttering sounds, they managed to exchange names. The adult men were Tamer, Bronco, and Palomino, and the women were called Racer and Rider. The children, besides Little Pony, were named Pinto, Mustang, Aster, and Buttercup

Taking the group to Green Valley for the winter was agreeable to Jade. She had been helped by both kin and strangers on her journeys. It had been a good year for crops, and there were lots of piglets. Green Valley should have a bumper harvest that could easily feed ten extra people for the winter. These people seemed friendly, and they had goods to trade. It would be a coup for her final journey to bring back these strangers from so far away.

Jade and Piggy and I went with them to their camp. Jade was running low on provisions herself, but she brought the dried deer meat to share.

We looked over their campground. It had a better water supply, more shelter, and fewer buzzing and biting insects. Jade decided to bring her gear over later in the day. Piggy carried most of it for her, in his harness.

The animals were out of sight of the camp, but Piggy led the way to greet them, while Jade and Tamer followed.

"Ooh look, Piggy," said Jade, pointing at the horses.

She'd never seen the tall animals with long tails, and long hair along the neck. "Are they large deer? Where are their antlers? Are they good to eat?"

While the older three children took the horses to pasture, and the younger two kept the sheep more or less together with the aid of two dogs, the adults sat and tried to make themselves understood with talk.

First they offered Jade fermented mare's milk in wooden cups. Jade asked for more, and got a little giggly with her third cup. Perhaps it smoothed the way for her language learning, for she picked up a few of their words immediately.

During the ten day week that we spent at Tamer's Camp, as Jade came to call it, the humans made progress with words. Observations helped, too. We saw that Tamer and Little Pony lived in one tent, and the other two were inhabited by what I assumed were family units – Bronco, Racer, and the boys Pinto and Mustang, in one tent, while Palomino and Rider lived in another with Aster and Buttercup, two blonde girls.

They started with nouns, Jade naming things near her in her language, and Tamer or one of the others saying the same word in their language. This wasn't very productive of information, but they were working on the sounds of each other's language, before trying to learn the way the words went together. As a bird, I can understand all human languages (I wish that carried over to my human form!), but since I can't speak, my understanding wasn't helpful to Jade.

"This is a knife," said Tamer, pulling an object from a leather sheaf. "What do you call it?"

The metal knife had a curved blade, and a handle made of carved antler.

"We don't have such a thing. What can you do with it?"

"It's good for cutting things. We can cut animal meat, or leather, or ropes – anything."

"Where do you get that kind of stone? It's so shiny."

"It's found in the earth, but it's not really rock. We heat it and it melts, and then we pour it into molds of the shape we want. Don't you have metal?"

"No, but I've seen something like it. And if that's a knife, I guess we have knives, too, but ours are made out of different materials. We have several kinds, to use for hard or soft cutting. The ones that cut meat and cloth look like this."

Jade fished in her basket pack and pulled out a package wrapped in deerskin. Inside the skin was her obsidian knife. It was oblong, with one serrated edge. She handed it to Tamer to look at, and he turned it over in his hand.

"Careful!" said Jade, "You'll cut yourself!"

But he already had – a thin trail of blood ran from his thumb.

"This kind of stone can be chipped to be very sharp. And if you keep it wrapped, it doesn't need to be resharpened very often. But you may have just dulled my knife with your thumb," she teased.

"Here's the other kind of knife we use." Jade held up a piece of bone with small flint pieces stuck with pine sap into a slot on one edge. She demonstrated its use on a nearby branch.

"It's better for coarse cutting than for fine cutting."

They told stories of looking for sources of copper and tin, which they melted together to make strong objects that could be made sharp.

Jade told them about the people from Across the River who had found some rock that melts, which they could pour into shapes they made in the sand. She showed them the snake amulet Chips gave her.

"That's pure copper," Tamer exclaimed. "Did you see the place it came from?"

"Yes, Uncle Eagle came with me, but I learned the way, and I could show you. It's in Chips' and Poppy's territory, so we would have to ask their permission."

"Do you think they would like to trade with us? If it turns out to be a good source of copper, that would be handy. We're also looking for tin, which is rarer."

"We'll have to ask them."

Tamer wore earrings made of turquoise, which Jade admired. They were in the shape of small fish.

"I've never seen jade this color," said Jade. "Where does it come from?"

"Lots of places near our home have turquoise stone. It's found near the copper mines, usually. We like the color, too, so we make ornaments out of it. If you like these, you can have them."

"That's very kind of you, but I can't accept. You see, in Red Mountain that would be a promise of marriage. Anyway, because I am a wu in training, I can only wear special jades made for me."

She showed Tamer the pig-dragon on a cord around her neck.

"I'd be pleased if later you made me something else out of turquoise. But I'm curious. What makes the fish stay in your ears? Our earrings have a slot to go over the earlobe, but yours have something shiny in them."

"It's copper wire. You have to have holes in your ears to wear them. I could make holes in your ears for you, with my copper needle. It doesn't hurt much."

"Well, maybe later."

>29

I learned later that Dr. Wu had already summoned the police because of the looting by the time the van left. They probably arrived at the Ox River site soon after the white van drove off along the river, on a barely visible track. Joe told the police that both Ashley and I had disappeared. They followed our footprints in the wet track along the river, and found the place where the place where the van had parked. But the white van had left, leaving no trail along the highway.

At the time, Ashley and I knew nothing of this, but it didn't take a crime detective to figure out that our captors were the tomb raiders. We had actually seen them, and their van, at the Goddess Temple the second day we were at the site.

Remembering that Dr. Wu told us then that he wrote down their license number gave me hope that we would be found before too long. Although we were tied up, they didn't gag us. When the driver opened the rear door and pushed us into the back seat, I saw several boxes in the middle of the van. We couldn't see out, because the windows were painted over. We also couldn't be seen from outside. The only good thing to say about our captivity was that the seat was soft enough. Maybe I was about to learn more about the looting, but I hoped I'd live long enough to tell about it. These guys were facing the death penalty if caught, and we had seen their faces.

Ashley was crying quietly. Her tears just streamed down. She tried to wipe them by putting her shoulder up, but the gesture wasn't very effective.

"Are you scared, Ashley, or mad?" I asked her in a whisper.

"A little of each," she said, her tears slowing.

"We have to make a plan, so you have to get yourself together. Can you do that?"

"What plan? If I hadn't been so pigheaded with Joe, we wouldn't be here. These guys were just hanging out, waiting until dark to get on the road. The one in the middle showed me his gun."

"They would have shot us already if they meant to kill us, I think, but they couldn't just leave us because we could identify them."

"They've been talking about what to do with me. And now you, too. Why did you come, Clara?"

"I came looking for you, of course. We thought you were pouting, but it seemed to be taking a very long time. So I came to see whether you had fallen and hurt yourself or something."

"Well, we can't make a plan until we find out where they're going, and what they intend to do with us."

"We can plan how to escape." I worried about Ashley's fatalism. "They'll have to stop for gas eventually, if they're going far. The fact that they waited until dark suggests that it's a long trip."

Ashley turned out to be right about the looters hoping to drive away unnoticed in the dark. They left the track along the river right away, but pulled into an alley about a kilometer down the road and waited until the sun was down.

"Good thing there's no moon yet," said the driver as he eased the van back out onto the highway.

Although we weren't too uncomfortable in the back of the van, it was unpleasant riding with our hands tied. I slept for a bit in spite of my discomfort.

I awoke to Ashley nudging me. "I need to pee."

"Tell the driver," I commanded.

She said "*Women xuyao xizaojian*," which means, we need the washroom, no doubt a more polite expression than *cesuo,* which means toilet. The men looked at each other. They said something rapidly in a language I couldn't understand at all, but Ashley was listening.

"What?" I whispered to Ashley.

"Ssh. They're speaking Cantonese." She strained forward to listen.

"They're going to stop soon to have something to eat. They'll bring us some food."

"But I have to get out," she told the driver in putonghua.

There was consultation among the three robbers.

Ashley whispered a translation, "They'll let us out at a roadside toilet on a side road. Later they'll bring us food, but they'll leave our hands tied. The one next to the driver threatens to shoot us if we try to run away."

"How can we eat, or for that matter take our jeans down to use the john, with our hands tied?" I complained to Ashley. "Even if we could, wouldn't it look odd for them to have tied-up women in their van? Wouldn't someone call the police? What cover story could they use, especially with foreigners?"

"You forget," said Ashley, "We don't look like foreigners to them. Remember Xiao Li's reaction to us."

Ashley spoke to the driver again. "You'll have to untie us. But we'll be good."

"Hao," he said, and when we stopped and got out he untied our hands. I rubbed my wrists, which were chafed, but I didn't see any red marks I could wave around so people would know we had been tied up.

The driver made us walk to the toilet between himself and the man with the gun. It must have been quite late, because no other cars were there. Ashley's hands were smudged with black dirt, I noticed, and she washed her hands at the tap outside both before and after. The driver made us use the toilet one at a time, covering the one outside with the gun.

My father jokes that when Americans travel, they become obsessed with the plumbing. I'm sorry to fit that stereotype, but I have to describe this facility. It consisted of two doors on opposite sides of a brick building. One side was marked with the character for man, the other said woman. The women's side opened into a space separated in the middle by a wall that didn't go to the ceiling. Still lower walls partitioned the slots for doing one's business on the women's side. In these slots were holes with concrete runways that sloped directly out to the street. There was no paper, and no provision for flushing. I had a tissue in my pocket, at least. Planks on each side of the hole showed you where to put your feet. I could hear Ashley gagging inside, and then I found out why when it was my turn.

From then on we stopped at better places, I'm glad to say, because Ashley refused to go near another one of this kind. She told the driver she'd rather wet her pants than use such a place again.

When we stopped at a real rest stop, our captors had a conversation about whether to leave us alone in the van while they went to get food. They decided that was a bad idea. No one wanted to stay and guard us, so finally they let us walk between them into the restaurant. We all ate noodles. We were so hungry they tasted fabulous. As the saying goes, hunger is the best sauce.

30

One day Tamer told us that the next day would be the beginning of their summer festival. They would celebrate with games on horseback, and a mutton feast. I was surprised to see that each person had a horse of their own, and that even the children could ride well. They looked like they had been born on horses, or perhaps they rode horses before they could walk.

Jade spread out a leather robe to sit on, and Piggy and I occupied a piece of robe on either side of her. We must have seemed a strange trio to the horse breeders.

The games they played all involved racing on horses. In one game they competed to grab a sheepskin from horseback. I was amazed how even Buttercup could hang onto her horse at a gallop, and reach down to the ground to pick up the sheep skin. Then they played a game where the girls taunted the boys, but dashed away on their ponies at the last moment. Finally the girls let the boys catch them. The adults were all laughing.

The sheep had been cooking all day over a bed of coals. Racer found tasty herbs of the forest to cook with it. They also had cooked some roots they found in the meadows, and put sprigs of wild mint on the meat. Rider chopped the whole sheep into fist-sized pieces, which they ate with their hands, gnawing the meat off the bones. The stomach and tongue were served separately, in slices. By the time it was ready to eat, the meat was tender and juicy. Jade kept exclaiming how delicious it was – even better than the deer she snared and ate.

When he realized that Jade had never seen a horse, Tamer offered to teach her to ride. First, though, she had to have leather trousers so that her legs wouldn't be rubbed raw by the horse. She traded her untanned hide for one that was ready to sew, and Tamer cut the hide and made trousers for her.

At first Jade rode behind Tamer on his horse, holding on to his waist, until she got the feel of the beast. The second day she could ride by herself, bareback. She laughed with pure joy at the speed of the running horse, and the wind blowing her hair behind her. She made a pretty picture, with her yellow feather headband and green eyes, astride the white horse.

Two days later, Jade and the people from Over the High Mountains agreed that it was time to leave. I watched as Racer and Rider rigged up the horses with the tent poles dragging on the ground behind them. Then they laid the other baggage across the poles, for the horses to pull. Jade looked at this rig dubiously.

"I don't think the path is wide enough for those poles," she said. "The way down the hill gets narrow and steep. The poles will catch on trees growing near the path."

"We'll figure it out," said Tamer cheerfully. "When we get stuck we'll unload, and carry the tents and baggage on our backs. In the meantime, it's nice to have the horses do the hard work."

It was slower going back with so many people and animals, especially the sheep, who wanted to wander and graze. The children and dogs kept them going in the right direction, continually urging the stragglers on.

It was several days before we came to the river crossing which was now familiar, and made a camp for the night.

"If we cross here, I can find the source of the copper. I haven't seen any tin, but the people who live in this northern territory may have seen it."

"How is the track on the other side of the river?" asked Tamer.

"The path isn't wide enough to drag your poles through the forest," said Jade. It's even narrower than the track we've been on. Some people would have to stay here, but those who go could ride horses to make the trip faster. What do you think? Shall we give it a try?"

Tamer's camp agreed to take a chance on an adventure across the wide river before the snow came. Although everyone wanted to go, they talked it over and agreed that it could be disagreeable to take the sheep through the forest. They might even attract tigers and wolves. Eventually it was decided that only Jade, Tamer, Piggy and I would go.

"Chips and his people don't stay in the same place, so we may not be able to find them," Jade warned as we set out.

We didn't find Chips and Poppy at first, but Jade remembered how to reach the source of the copper. They gathered enough copper ore so that Tamer could teach Jade how to make knives and needles. On the way back, Jade spotted Chips' tracks. Following a narrow trail, we came to another camp of Chips and his relatives. He was happy to see us, and curious about the horses.

"We have creatures like these in our grasslands, too. But they are smaller, and wilder. I can't imagine capturing one, or taming it if I did. Once in a while we hunt them. They're tasty, but kind of chewy."

Poppy said she thought the meat was tough.

"You practically have to burn it to make it edible. I like deer meat much better."

"We met some people from the far frozen north once, who ride deer, the way you ride horses" Poppy remembered. "They eat some of them, and squirt milk from the females into large birch bark buckets. They have big herds, and never have to hunt."

"I've heard of such people, too," Tamer mused. "But they are said to live far away, to the north of our pastures. Do you suppose they are the same?"

"Perhaps they're related," suggested Chips.

The prospect of meeting more people like Tamer, and seeing their horses and sheep, was exciting to Chips' encampment. So they decided to return with us to meet the rest of the group across the river.

We were surprised to find the robbers at the camp, happily settled in and talking with the people from Over the High Mountains.

Wolf flashed his knife when he saw Piggy, but Palomino explained that the pig was friendly. Using all our language skills, and gesturing expansively, we learned that the robbers were refugees from a village far away to the southwest. All the people in their village were killed in a flood while the three men were out hunting, and everything they owned was washed away.

Since then they kept to the forests and stole food from travelers. After a while they realized that people walking through the forests were carrying valuable things to trade. So they had turned to robbery as a way of life.

"How would you like to be legitimate traders instead of robbers?" Jade asked them. "We're beginning to need things from all directions. There are already traders to the south, and my father was born in a village in the east, so he often meets his relatives and exchanges goods. But I have no one to bring me things from the west. I need the colored stone that comes from far away. Are you strong enough to bring it? I can give you objects to take for trading."

"But *we* can bring you the colored stones," Tamer objected. I thought he had taken to Jade, and wanted to be sure he would see her again.

"It's very far to Over the High Mountains, but by riding horses we can cover the distance in less time, especially without sheep and children. Maybe you could find sources of copper and tin from the north of here, and bring them to us in exchange for the colored stones, which you can bring to Jade's people."

"Could we ride your horses?" asked Wolf. Tiger and Leopard looked at the horses dubiously.

"I'd rather walk," said Leopard.

"You can learn to ride," laughed Tamer.

"What will we get from it?" Chips wanted to know. "The sources of the metals are in our territory."

"What do you want?" asked Tamer.

"Horses," replied Chips. "I think they would make our hunting more efficient."

So it was decided that the three robbers would become traders between the north and west, with a detour to Jade's village to take them colored stones, and return with obsidian and silk. The Over the High Mountains people would bring horses for them the next time they came. For now, they didn't have horses to spare.

"First, though, you have to give me back my father's jade head from Jade Village."

Wolf was glad to give it to her. "It's brought us bad luck," he explained.

"I think it would be better to have one location where we all meet to exchange goods. We should choose a season, and if we can agree, a specific ten-day week, to meet." Wolf suggested.

"It should be a place that is favored by the spirits," said Jade, "but not a village where anyone lives."

Piggy began turning rapidly in circles.

"Yes, you are right, Piggy. We know a very sacred place, which is watched over by a mountain shaped like a pig. We passed by it on our trek to the south. It is not too far past Green Valley. You could come with us, and I'll show you where it is."

When this large party neared Green Valley, Jade sent me ahead to warn Owl and the others that we were on the way.

But Owl had already seen Jade in her far-seeing needle.

"Back so soon? Did you bring back treasures?"

I sang my six-note song.

Owl was still surprised when Jade and Piggy came into view, followed by thirteen people, some of them riding horses, and about fifty sheep and six dogs. There was much to tell.

>31

"What are we going to do with those Chinese girls?" the man in the middle asked the driver on the second day.

"Take them to Hong Kong and turn them loose there, I suppose," said the driver. "They've seen us, but it won't matter, because we'll be gone to America on an airplane. No point in killing them."

"But maybe they could bring us more money," said the one by the window.

"What are you saying?" asked the driver.

"These seem to be well-behaved girls, and I bet their parents are rich. Maybe their families would pay us to give them back."

"How much do you reckon they'd pay?"

"Let's find out how rich they are."

The one at the window was wearing a purple shirt, which had become our name for him. Purple Shirt turned around and spoke to us.

"Where are you from? What do your parents do?"

Ashley said, unwisely I thought, "We're American citizens. If you harm us, you'll be in big trouble."

The threesome in front digested this information. They muttered to each other.

Purple Shirt turned around again. "You, mouthy Miss, answer my questions. Where are you from?"

"Cambridge."

"Where's that?"

I thought the driver said "*Yingguo*."

"Not the Cambridge in England," Ashley actually giggled. "The one in Massachusetts. Near Boston."

"And your Papa. What is his work?"

"He's a botanist."

In Chinese she actually said, “he’s a flower man.” The three men conferred over whether a flower man could have enough money to ransom his daughter.

“What he do,” said Purple Shirt. “Sell flowers in the market?”

Ashley was insulted, and before I could stop her, she said, “He’s a university professor. At Harvard.” She pronounced it “Ha-fo.”

They had obviously heard of Hafo, and thought professors there might earn a great deal of money. And maybe I was another heiress princess.

So Purple Shirt asked me, “Now you.”

“I’m from Massachusetts too,” I admitted. “My father is a lawyer.”

“I don’t know if this is good or bad,” I whispered to Ashley. “The good news is our families will know what happened to us. They must be frantic. The bad news is, they won’t learn where we are.”

We made a late night stop for food and bathrooms. The men sat at a table eating noodles, and discussing the details of the ransom note. They kept shooting glances our way, as we sat whispering over our jiaozi at a corner table.

Now that we were valuable, they especially didn’t want to lose us. We had no where to escape to anyway.

They were writing, arguing, and crossing things out. Finally they had agreed on wording, rewrote it neatly, and borrowed an envelope from the cashier.

32

The winter in Green Valley saw many changes. The people from Over the High Mountains set up their tents. They were quite cozy for the winter, with hearths in the middle, and space for the smoke to escape around the tall poles. The tents were set up in the clearing between the two halves of the village. The central area wasn't used so much in the winter, when people spent more time indoors.

Still, there were factions. In the group of houses headed by Big Tiger, some people were unhappy about the visitors using the central space, which they considered to be half theirs. It wasn't that they had any particular need for the space, it was the principle of the thing.

In Big Tiger's eyes, the strangers were the guests of Owl and her family, and they shouldn't cause any inconvenience, however slight, to anyone else. Especially inconvenience to Big Tiger, who, after all, was a minor leader in Green Valley, and hadn't even been consulted. He grumbled, but didn't cause trouble yet.

In the meantime, the other visitors, Hawk, Willow, Moose and Elk, were made welcome. They lived in houses with members of Owl's family, and helped with the harvest. They had brought silk and seashells, and were given jades and obsidian in return. They would take these things back to Crooked Pine when spring came. The only objects presented by Tamer and his band were considered ordinary by Big Tiger. They included carved wooden objects and decorated leather shoes with soft soles. On the other hand, he coveted Tamer's copper knife and needle, but Tamer didn't have any extras to trade.

Jade spent her time with Tamer and Little Pony, learning about horses and sheep. One day Little Pony referred to Tamer as her uncle.

"Really? I thought he was your father."

"No. My mother was his sister. She was lost with his tent mate in a surprise snowstorm when they were coming across the High Mountains. Since then we've been each other's closest kin."

Jade also became close to Tamer. They talked and laughed constantly. Tamer was a kind person, and so generous with his horses, that he was welcome everywhere.

One day in the early spring, when Little Pony and the others had gone to help with the planting, Tamer invited Jade into his tent.

"Someday, I hope soon." She gave him a warm smile. "But the time isn't right. Soon I'll be prepared to lead all the Red Mountain villages. They also have to be ready to accept you. Be patient."

That wasn't all the courting going on. Moose spent a lot of time with Little Shell. They worked side by side, and went for walks together. When it snowed, they used rawhide for a seat, and slid down the hills, laughing when the spill at the bottom threw them together.

After several months, Moose made it known to Willow and Hawk that he would like to marry Little Shell. They weren't sure how this would impact their trading activities, or how Big Man would take such an arrangement. But it was clear that Moose and Little Shell were suited to each other, so plans were made for a ceremony to join them.

The festivities included a solemn ceremony of calling the spirits to witness, followed by a great feast. Some kin from other villages even came, although it was mostly a local event. The whole village gathered at the village holy place, which was an earth platform edged with cut stones. Little Shell and Moose sat on the platform in their best finery, including jade bracelets and earrings.

Owl and Jade performed the spirit-calling together. They wore robes of yellow silk, with yellow feather headbands. Shell belts and hand drums completed their costumes, to make noises and attract the spirits.

Two flute players made happy music. Mother and daughter danced between the halves of the village, and greeted the couple by encircling them six times. Then they called the spirits by clapping. Owl threw the yarrow stalks, which promised them a happy life.

After the feast there was dancing, to the music of flutes and drums. A generous amount of millet wine was provided by Hawk and Willow. As they danced, some of the guests became tipsy and loud.

Jade tried to calm the group down by asking Racer and Palomino to tell about their marriage ceremony. It turned out to be a big mistake.

"We didn't have any ceremony," said Racer. "We just made a tent together, and joined our flocks of sheep. Each of us had our own horses, and clothing and jewelry and tools. Each of our parents gave us some of the other things we needed to set up a household together. But your ceremony is very nice."

This brought the unhappiness to a head. When they were asked point blank if they were married, the whole group from Over the Mountain explained that it was not their custom to have a ceremony. When it pleased two adults, they just made a tent together. When children came along, they belonged to the tent. If the couple didn't get along, they went to tents with other people.

Big Tiger was outraged. He called out that they were immoral, and began to beat up Palomino. Racer screamed, and pandemonium broke out.

Jade had taught the children a song she made up about harmony, to quiet them when they began playing too roughly. She got one of the flutists to play it, and the children to join her, and pretty soon nearly every one was singing. Big Tiger calmed down. But he wasn't satisfied.

Early one morning Big Tiger walked to the clearing and called for the visitors to come outside. They left behind their breakfast, or whatever else they were busy with, and came out to see what the problem was. Big Tiger was one of Owl's cousins, a member of the Wu clan. He therefore had the right to wear the yellow headband, and to dance and call down the spirits. He had come dressed in his headband and belt made of shell rattles.

"In my side of Green Valley, everyone obeys the local rules," he announced. "You cannot occupy any of the space that belongs to my side of the valley, because you are offending the spirits here."

Big Tiger stalked to the edge of one tent that was nearest the southern group of houses, and began pulling up the tent stakes.

He had made his announcement in a loud voice, which brought most of the Green Valley populace to the clearing.

"What makes it your half the village?" Owl demanded. "Who gave you the right to make the rules? The spirits make rules here, not mere humans. We must ask the spirits what they think. Put back the tent pegs, and then help me with the ceremony to call the spirits. We'll do it now, since you're all dressed for the spirits."

While Owl went to get her paraphernalia, the villagers asked each other what all this could mean. Owl came back with Jade and Piggy, each wearing a yellow headband.

Big Tiger was so outraged when he saw the pig, he trembled.

"Are you trying to mock me in front of my kin, and in front of the spirits?" he ranted.

He pointed at Piggy.

"That is an offense to the sprits! They will surely punish you."

Piggy sat down in the open space, unconcerned about the shouting. He was a picture of power, with his long sharp tusks, sturdy body, and disdain of all around him.

"Now," said Owl. "We will each call the spirits in any way we choose, and ask any kind of question of them. Here are sticks with symbols on them. They will be used in this order."

In the dirt, Owl made one straight horizontal line, then two lines one above the other, and then three. The fourth sign was two lines across and two other lines crossing them.

"These marks show the order in which we may call the spirits. They are already painted onto these pieces of broken pottery, that otherwise look alike."

Owl held up the sherds so that everyone could see and appreciate them. Then she put them into a leather bag, which was marked with an embroidered spiral. The plain ends of the pottery were sticking out, but the signs could not be seen.

"Piggy gets to choose first," she announced, and put the bag in front of Piggy.

Piggy cocked his head to one side, and seemed to consider. Then he put a trotter on one of the sticks. Owl pulled it out and showed it around. It was the third turn.

"How does the pig know what to do?" people were asking each other. "He is an inspired pig." They backed away a little, making the circle around the wu bigger.

"Now you choose," Owl said to Big Tiger.

Big Tiger selected the first one. He showed it around, proud of going first.

"I'm number one," he smirked.

Jade pulled out the stick with the crisscross stripes. She would be last.

"Very well," said Owl, "My stick must be the second one."

Owl indicated that Big Tiger should address the spirits and ask his question. He danced in a circle, turning faster and faster. Sweat broke out on his face. His shells clashed together as he whirled. Suddenly he dropped to a squat and clapped six times.

"Should visitors leave if they cannot obey the rules of the spirits of this place?" he spoke in a high-pitched voice.

Jade threw the yarrow sticks. Everyone could see that the answer was "yes."

Big Tiger looked around with a satisfied smile.

Owl did no dancing. She sat cross-legged and clapped for the spirits, then paused in silence.

Raising her hands high with her palms toward the sky, she asked, "Should the smaller side of the village obey the larger side of the village, as the brother obeys the sister?"

Jade threw the yarrow sticks again, and again the answer was "yes." Big Tiger sat on his haunches and frowned.

Piggy took his turn. He scratched six times in the dirt with his trotter. Jade made a small hand motion and he went up to Tamer. Standing in front of him, Piggy nodded his head.

"What is the question, Piggy. Are you asking if Tamer can stay?"

Piggy turned in a circle.

Jade threw the yarrow sticks for the third time. The answer was a qualified "yes."

Now it was Jade's turn. She whirled around the clearing six times, stirring up dust as she went. When the dust was whirling so much it obscured her feet, she danced to where Tamer was standing and stood in front of him.

"Can Tamer stay if he will marry me according to our customs? And be faithful to Green Valley as well as to me? And belong to all the Red Mountain people, as I have promised to do?"

This time Owl tossed the sticks, and they fell in the most favorable pattern.

"It is settled," said Owl. "Tamer can stay and marry Jade, and Jade will be leader all of Green Valley."

"Uh oh," Ashley nudged me. "I think I've got my little friend."

This was not one of the many euphemisms I know for the monthly event, but I thought that was what she was talking about.

"So that means they have to stop to let us out more often," Ashley pointed out. "Unless they want their van to get icky. And they have to let me take my backpack into the toilet, because that's where my supplies are."

"I don't think my Chinese is up to discussing that problem. Maybe you'd better talk to them in Cantonese."

"No way, I'm saving that for a surprise. As long as they think we don't understand, they'll give us information when they talk to each other. You figure it out in putonghua. And hurry up, I need a stop soon."

"Excuse me," I yelled to the front seat. They ignored me.

"Excuse me," I increased the volume. "We have an emergency back here."

Purple Shirt turned around.

"Shut up."

"We need to stop. My friend has her moons. She needs to stop and fix herself. She has what she needs in her backpack, if you will hand it to her."

Some consternation was evident in the front seat. Probably a menstruating woman was considered unlucky. We usually are.

"We stop at next rest stop."

This would be our first stop in daylight. Whether that was good or not remained to be seen.

When the van parked, my eyes lit up. I saw a bus with a sign in Korean. The red sign across the top of the windshield would be hard to miss. It read, in Chinese,"South Korean Archaeological Expedition to the Northeast." The bus pulled into the parking lot near our van. Maybe I could talk to them without being noticed. I was afraid to call Ashley's attention to the bus for fear the looters would notice too.

"Your backpack," I reminded her as we were let out the back door. I glanced at the Korean bus, but no one got off. Ashley went to Purple Shirt and gestured her need for the back pack. The driver had put our packs behind the front seat, in front of their boxes. I hoped to get my pack, too, because it had power bars in it, but it was not offered. Such small things become important in captivity. Still, it was useful to get Ashley's backpack, and to hope not to have to give it back. Archaeologists carry many useful items.

No scope for escape presented itself. The driver walked in front of us and Middle Seat and Purple Shirt behind. Movement in the parking area flickered into my peripheral vision. Out of the corner of my eye I saw Kidok sneaking around cars, dashing from one to the other. He looked like something from a gangster movie. Kidok couldn't have looked more suspicious with a gun in his hand. All he needed was a white cowboy hat.

Our guardians didn't seem to notice him, though.

"I need to go with my friend to the toilet and help her," I told the driver.

He gave me a suspicious look, but we had been well-behaved so far. He grunted agreement.

In the john, I whispered to Ashley, "The Korean posse is here. They followed in a bus. They must have rented a new one since the flooding episode."

"How do we get saved, without getting shot first?"

"Somehow we have to tell Kidok not to try to rescue us here, but to follow us to Hong Kong."

"Write him a note."

"What if one of the looters finds it?"

"Can you write it in Korean?"

We "borrowed" some toilet paper and rooted around in Ashley's backpack for a felt-tip pen.

I wrote in stiff, ungrammatical Korean, "Looter car going to Hong Kong. Keep car in sight if possible without being seen. We cannot see out of windows. Do not make any signal."

"How can we get it to them?"

This didn't look like it was going to be a problem, because Kidok was outside the door.

But Purple Shirt was in line behind him, so I refused eye contact, but slipped the note into his hand as I passed.

Kidok stuck it into his pants pocket.

34

Owl wanted to make the wedding to Jade and Tamer a spectacle no one would ever forget. She and Carver were trying to think of something unusual for the ceremony.

"We want all the Red Mountain villages to be involved, and there isn't room in Green Valley. What if we have a ceremony in sight of Pig Mountain?" Carver was thinking out loud.

"That's a good thought. I was thinking of staging it at the time of a lunar eclipse. The ceremony could take place just after we have all saved the moon. According to my calculations, an eclipse of the moon will occur just when it gets to its farthest distance to the south."

"But how can you be sure? It would be seen as a disaster if the eclipse didn't occur."

"Have I ever missed a lunar eclipse? I have a system of sighting the moon that has proved accurate. But I could be surer if there was a hill to sight the moon from, so we could see it rising through a particular notch in the hills. I've been thinking about this for a long time. Let's get Jade and Tamer to come with us, and we can scout it out."

On a crisp late fall day, Owl and Carver and Jade and Tamer made an overnight trip to Pig Mountain. They found a spot where they could chart the moon rise, but it wasn't perfect.

"If we were higher, we could sight the moon perfectly from right here. How can we make something high so we can observe exactly at this spot? It has to be taller than a house. It will take too long for a tree to grow that high."

"I know," said Tamer, "Let's build a hill."

The Green Valley group looked at him in amazement.

"In Over the High Mountains we build hills out of stone," explained Tamer.

"We don't have that much stone," objected Carver.

"It could be built mostly out of earth," suggested Jade.

"Who will help?" asked Carver. "The four of us can't move that much dirt."

"Leave it to me," said Owl.

Owl sent an invitation to all the Red Mountain villages to send their strongest workers for a very special task that had been requested by the spirit of Pig Mountain. Every village that sent a work contingent would be invited to the wedding of Jade and Tamer in the spring.

When the work force had assembled, Owl instructed them to cut blocks of the white stone that outcropped on a nearby hill, and bring them to place in a large circle she had drawn on the ground.

"We will build a moon hill," Owl explained. So we will make three white circles, each one smaller and higher."

Then the villagers filled baskets with earth, and made a hill, sloping on all sides toward the top. When it was as high as one house, Owl had them make another ring of the lustrous white stone around the outside. Finally a ring of stone no bigger than a house was placed near the top.

When the hill was finished, she invited everyone on top, to wait for moonrise. It was past full, so the workers were already drinking millet wine when the moon finally shone down on their hard work. Owl noted with satisfaction that she had calculated right, and the moon would rise in the notch at the spring eclipse.

In early spring, the whole village, and many guests from outside, had a wonderful time at the wedding of Jade and Tamer. The two of them wore yellow silk, which shone in the moonlight, after the eclipse had passed.

As soon as the woods were full of wildflowers, it was time for the others from Over the High Mountains to leave for their long trek home. They gave Jade the white mare she had learned to ride, with the hopes that her horse and Tamer's would found a line of offspring. They also left six sheep for the start of a wool industry, as thanks for the hospitality of Green Valley over the winter. Jade's uncles helped to build a house for Jade and Tamer in the middle of the two halves of Green Valley, after the tents were gone. It was the biggest house of all in Green Valley when it was finished.

The horses were a continual source of wonder to the Red Mountain people. Jade and Tamer often rode them to the other villages, to see how things were going. One of their favorite rides took all day. The sacred hilltop of one of the southernmost groups of Red Mountain villages had a wide view overlooking a large river.

The sacred site was improved every year. People of the local village said that their spirits were particularly helpful with childbirth, and so it had gradually become a place of individual birth rituals for several villages nearby.

After a couple of years, when it became obvious that Jade was pregnant, it was natural that Jade and Tamer should visit the site. Tamer made small ceramic figurines to leave as an offering for the spirits of childbirth.

When the birth of Moonglow was successfully accomplished at the site, it became a famous place. A small birthing house was erected, and Jade's sisters Fawn and Flora became particularly skilled in helping difficult births. Since the small statuettes had given them a healthy daughter, Tamer molded a cross-legged statue of a wu out of clay, to sit on a small platform.

Of course I was present when Moonglow was born. She looked like a combination of her two parents, with pale eyes and dark wavy hair. This precocious and merry child became the pet of everyone, and helped solidify the notion among the Red Mountain villages that they were all one people, and that they were very lucky to have such a handsome and talented family as their leaders.

When we returned to the van and were back in our cozy spot, Purple Shirt remembered the backpack, and demanded to have it up front. Ashley frowned, but she handed it to him. As soon as he and Middle Seat snoozed off, she nudged me. When she had my attention she dug in her pants pocket and showed me her cell phone, holding it well below the level of the seat back. It was one of the slim, fold-over kind that barely make a bulge.

"Fabulous," I whispered. "But how can you ever use it?"

"You'll see," she whispered back.

We had a little nap ourselves. I actually slept until the van stopped again. This wasn't a rest stop, though. We were in a warehouse area, from the brief glimpses I got through the windshield.

Middle Seat told us to get out of the van, and hustled us at gunpoint into a shed full of boxes. I saw some Chinese characters on the building, but I didn't recognize them, so I wrote them on a scrap of paper, in case I ever had a chance to report to Sandra about this kidnapping.

When they brought us back to the van an hour or so later, it was no longer white, but blue with a Hong Kong license plate. I could tell it was the same vehicle, because the back seat had the same frayed spot. A few more boxes were shoved into the van, and then we could hear our captors consulting with the person who brought the extra boxes. Ashley leaned forward to hear better.

"Middle Seat said they could get rid of us and have more room for boxes," she reported. "But Driver said it wouldn't be a good idea to kill us, and disastrous to let us go. Besides, they'll make easy money by turning us over to our families in Hong Kong. So they're lashing some boxes to the roof."

We could hear the scraping noises as they accomplished this

I caught a glimpse of a blond man with a goatee. "That's odd," I said. "A foreigner is involved in this operation."

The foreigner had brought them new leather shoes to exchange for the sneakers they wore, and provided a jacket for each of them. They got back into the van, happy with their new clothing.

The next time we stopped, a Korean woman with a scarf around her head followed us into the ladies' room.

"It's me," whispered Kidok. "We are following, as you wisely suggested. We recognized the van when it came out of the warehouse area by a dent in the rear door, even though they repainted it and put on a different license plate. Are you two okay?"

"Just scared," I said.

"And cramped," Ashley added.

"Do you know where you're going?"

"They said Hong Kong."

"Do you know they are offering to give you up for a ransom?"

"How much are they asking?" Ashley inquired.

"Five thousand dollars each."

"We're worth more than that!" said Ashley indignantly. "I thought they'd ask a million."

"Maybe five thou is a fortune to them," suggested Kidok. "It's almost forty thousand ren min bi, for people who earn about 300 RMB per month.

"They asked about our fathers, and we told them their names. We thought they were writing a ransom note at the first stop, but we didn't give them our addresses. How did they find our families?"

"They threatened Dr. Wu at the research station, and made him send their demand to your fathers. At first he was mad, but then it seemed like the best thing to do would be to send the note along to your parents. At least they won't kill you, since you're worth so much as hostages. Dr. Wu is with us in the bus, but it wouldn't be safe for you to talk to him. Evan is with us too."

"Evan? Why on earth would Evan come?"

"Apparently some Sir Galahad idea. He says he's been in love with Ashley from the moment he laid eyes on her."

Ashley groaned. "Men!" she said.

There was a beating at the door.

"Come on out," said Purple Shirt, "We won't wait for you to eat if you don't hurry."

36

I flew over villages that were not as familiar as Green Valley. Down below, the people from Sea of Grass and Stony Water villages were in an uproar. There were speeches and shouting in Sea of Grass Village in the next valley, and farther up river at Running Water Village, people had become so excited they were hitting each other. I flew above all the other Red Mountain villages, and they seemed to be in turmoil, too. Whatever could be the matter?

The group that was talking instead of hitting and shoving seemed to be the best place to find out, so I perched in an oak tree at Sea of Grass. The Leader of the village was trying to get people to calm down and just talk, but she wasn't having much luck.

"Why should Green Valley have all the goods, and all the trading partners?" demanded a farmer, waving his hoe over his head to get people's attention. "We should just go and help ourselves to the goods. It's our as much as theirs."

A woman spinning wool claimed a spot on the high stone under the speaking tree. "It wouldn't be right just to take things. You all know that. You're just blowing off steam. But why couldn't we have trading partners in the four directions, too? Every village can do its own trading. There's nothing to stop us."

The leader stepped on the flat stone.

"Nothing but robbers!" she pointed out. "You've heard how they attacked Jade twice. I don't know what the world is coming to, with the paths so dangerous!"

Another family head stepped onto the stone. "You have to consider what we would we take to trade. At Green Valley they make carved jades to trade in all directions."

I flew to the other villages, and found more of the same. They were all jealous over the trading partners that Jade had found for Green Valley. Only Green Valley had silks from the south, fine furs from the north, green jade and obsidian from the east and copper and turquoise from the west. Green Valley was becoming splendid, leaving the other villages as they were before, but now feeling poor.

I worried about how to convey this problem to Jade. She was happily wearing her silks for ceremonial occasions, and showing off their other newly acquired goods, without a thought for the reaction of other people.

Back in Green Valley, I attracted Jade's attention by flying in to sit by her.

"Hello, Spirit Bird. I didn't call you. I wonder who did?"

Maybe the Spirit of the Wind, I thought, surely he was the god of gossip, so I ruffled my feathers and flapped my wings.

"The Wind Spirit? What's the trouble?"

So far so good, she knew there was trouble. I flew into her house and brought out a scrap of silk. Then I found a chip of green jade from Carver's workshop, and put it beside the silk. A scrap of sable fur from the north was lying by the sewing area, and I dropped it in front of Jade, too. The turquoise and copper were harder, because they were the rarest objects, and we didn't make anything from them here. So I flew to Tamer, who was working in the millet field, and hopped along until he followed me back to Jade. I sat on his shoulder and pecked at his turquoise earrings, and then at his copper knife tucked into his leather sheath.

"What's this about?" asked Tamer.

"Something about the objects we've acquired from trading, I think. Some problem? Not here, though. In the other villages?"

I sang my worried song.

"When I was out riding, I heard some people from the next valley talking about making their own trading expeditions, so they can have all the things we have. I didn't think much about it, because they don't have anything special to trade."

"Obviously, we can't have everyone going on trading expeditions But we need to share the wealth we get from trading," Jade said to Tamer. "We can do that by organizing our trade beyond the village level."

"To start with, we could get more colored stone from the west, to make more jades to trade. And what else? Maybe the painted pottery that we learned to make a few years ago? The villages that I taught how to make painted pottery and fire it in kilns could make pots to trade. Others make special baskets or clothing. We need to all think about it together."

Jade and Tamer rode their horses around to each of the villages, and proposed a meeting on the first day of the next ten day week. The moon would be full, so they could have light into the night, and make a promise to the Moon Spirit when they came to a decision.

The heads of families agreed to meet on a sacred hillside on the road to the south, and discuss what to do about the fact that Green Valley had so many things they didn't have. But there were now thousands of households among the Red Mountain people. The heads of families were too many. After discussing the matter within each village, they agreed to send the village leader to decide for the whole village.

When the full moon rose, about a hundred leaders of Red Mountain villages were assembled on the hillside. Jade and Piggy and I stood at the top of the hill, with all the village sitting on hides below us. Jade had brought strong millet wine in a large painted jar with a lid.

Jade opened the meeting by addressing the Mountain Spirit.

"We're here today to make an important decision," she intoned, after she had clapped for the spirit's attention. "Please let us know what you think."

A breeze rattled the oak leaves.

The discussion began with recriminations and what I would have called whining, but Jade sat up with her legs crossed and her back straight, and nodded at each speech. When no one else stood to talk, she stood.

"You have outlined the problem well. Now, who has a suggestion about what to do?"

No one volunteered any thoughts.

Tamer stood to be recognized. "In Over the High Mountains, where I grew up, we have trade fairs twice a year. All our trading partners know that they should come on the first full moon after the planting, and the first full moon after the harvest. We exchange many things, and everyone has fun. And we learn many things about the wide world from each other. Do you think that would work here?"

Many heads nodded. The leader of Sea of Grass Village stood.

"Maybe we should try it once a year, to start with, and see how it works."

Another leader suggested that the trading fair should be held as soon as possible after the snows had gone and the weather was warm. But not in the heat of the summer.

When it was decided to have an annual trading festival at the time in late summer when the sun stands still, everyone was satisfied.

But Jade had more to say. "The trading festival is a lot of work. We need to organize the villages to make different things. We need to organize the traders, so that they know when to come and what to bring. We need to organize food for the visitors, and places for them to sleep. Are you willing to let me do the organizing? Will each village do your part? Can I count on you, the village leaders, to make sure your village does its share of the work? If anyone grumbles, you will have to explain that without this work we cannot have the trading fair. Do you all agree?"

No dissent was heard.

"Get out your drinking cups," said Jade, "and I will pour some millet wine for each of you from this ceremonial jar, so that we will all remember this occasion. But don't drink until everyone's cup is filled."

The jar was strapped to a carrying contraption on Piggy's back. Jade and Piggy walked around, Jade scooping wine into each cup. Just when they were finished, the radiant moon shone full on Pig Mountain, lighting up its head with silver rays.

I sang my six-note song, and waved a wing to call Jade's attention to the scene across the valley.

"Look," she said. "Everyone look at Pig Mountain as we drink our wine. The Mountain Spirit approves of our plan. Now drink, and then we'll bury this jar on the mountainside in memory of this day, when all the Red Mountain villages have come together."

The black and red cups were smashed and ceremonially buried in a pit. The pit was marked above with a plank, that had carved into it the insignia of each village. The plank was a source of pride for all villages, as well as a cohesive force, and a remembrance of their coming together so that all could share in their prosperity.

37

“Why didn’t you tell Kidok about your phone?” I asked Ashley when we were in bondage again.

“I don’t know. I’m not sure who is trustworthy.”

“Kidok is entirely trustworthy.”

“But he might tell the others, and we don’t know about them. There was a leak somewhere, or they wouldn’t still be following the van, with its paint and license plate changes.”

“I wish you had told them, just the same. If you give them the phone number, they’ll know how to contact us. What if they lose sight of the van in the traffic around Hong Kong?”

“I think I’ll keep it secret for now. Pretty soon we’ll be close enough to Hong Kong that I can call my aunt. I need to call her in the daytime and leave a message first, so she doesn’t get too excited when I’m talking to her.”

We got more news from Kidok at the next rest stop. He told us that Ed and Ashley’s father were flying to Hong Kong, bringing the ransom money as demanded. Ed was using the ticket he already had to fly to Beijing for our trip. Ed and Prof. Woo will arrive tomorrow, and meet the looters in the airport. Then the looters will take the ransom money and their loot, and board a plane to San Francisco.

“You’ll be turned over to Ed and Prof. Woo after the looters’ plane takes off.”

“An unlikely scenario,” said Ashley. “What if they kill us after they get the money?”

“They won’t get it until they are inside the secure area of the airport, past immigration and security screening. So they can’t kill you after they get the money.”

“But they can kill us before they enter the terminal building. How would Ed and Prof. Woo know if we were alive or dead?

Kidok had no answer for that, but I could see it was food for thought.

At the final stop before Hong Kong, it was Evan who visited us in the ladies' room, with a scarf almost obscuring his face.

"Can't keep meeting the same Korean woman," he said. "Your captors will get suspicious."

"You look gorgeous," Ashley giggled. He had even put on lipstick.

"By the way, don't be surprised if you see your other colleagues at the airport in Hong Kong. Lars, Joe and Laura will fly there today from Beijing. They tried to get seats as soon as they knew that's where you were going, but they had to wait a couple of days for three seats on a plane. But they'll be there ahead of you, anyway."

"Dr. Wu gave the news media the story, and your pictures. People will rescue you at a rest stop if they recognize you."

"What pictures did Dr. Wu give them?" Ashley wanted to know.

"You're are all in it – Joe, Laura, and you two. Xiao Li must have taken it. It looks like you're being silly in a Chinese restaurant."

"Not that picture!" wailed Ashley. "I look terrible. My fifteen minutes of fame will be wasted."

"I'm more interested in staying alive," I said, shuddering. "I hope that's not a death warrant. There's all the more reason to dispose of us now that they know people are looking for us, and know what we look like."

When Evan was gone, Ashley crept around the corner and phoned her aunt's number, while I stood watch.

"No answer," said Ashley, "but I left a message. I told her to call me back."

"If they call in the van, the game is up."

"I indicated trouble, and left her my number, but told her not to call. If she calls anyway, I've put the phone on vibrate, so it won't make any noise. The only thing they could hear is my voice talking to my aunt, and they'll think I'm talking to you. I told her to try to be home in about four hours, when we'll stop again. I hope she gets the message."

I was feeling more hopeful when we got back on the van. The Korean bus was following us, with Dr. Wu and Evan, too. Ed and Prof. Woo were coming from the US with our ransom. And Joe, Laura and Lars would be at the airport too. What could go wrong?

38

I flew away to Green Valley as one way to escape the anxiety of being hostage. I found Jade at Carver's workshop, turning over polished jades in her hands. As the apprentices in Carver's workshop learned their craft, their designs became more intricate. Carver himself became more skilled, too, creating more ways to make the jades beautiful. He invented a rotary drill, to make circles better, and perfected the ox-nose perforation for hanging jades from the back without making a hole in the front. On another trip to Jade Village, he found some beach sand with exactly the right hardness to carve the jades. He made lines of different depths to indicate features of the birds and animals, which made the jades shimmer all the more.

Jade was thinking about how to use the objects created here. A few simple ones were used in trade, but these creations should be dedicated to the spirits, just as silk could only be worn in the presence of spirits. It was Spirits that gave both jade and silk their shine, as well as furs and copper.

Seeing me on the roof of Carver's workshop, Jade called me down to tell me what was on her mind. She had been thinking about several problems, she told me. One was that jade is a sacred material, and should belong only to those with special powers. The second problem was to decide what shapes should be made out of jade. Should they only be emblems, or should they be decorative, too? Finally, she was considering how to reward the leaders, who were working very hard to create the trade fair.

We looked over the products at Carver's workshop. There were clouds, masks, birds, and tortoises, as well as bracelets. Should there be any rules about who wears what design? Would that be a way to reward people who were managers, and had to make decisions? Of course, there were the village leaders. But now there were farmers who organized which crops to plant in order to have enough food for all the strangers at the fair, and the musicians and dancers, the potters, basket makers, and many other specialists.

I thought the idea of using jade objects as emblems was a good one. They should be a reward from the leader of the trade fair, perhaps. Jade herself had been working hard to organize the trade fair, but each village had a leader, and each working group did too – the potters, basketmakers, hide workers, cooks, tailors, farmers – so many things to do. Each kind of leader should have a jade emblem. It would mean that the spirits approved of the job they were doing. This was too complicated to say in bird language.

But Jade solved the problem.

"You approve, don't you Spirit Bird? Can I tell all the village leaders, and the group leaders, to tell those they work with that the spirits have advised me to do this? They already know that the inner shine of jade and silk attracts spirits, and they know that spirits are dangerous to those who are not prepared. Will they accept the jade as a mark of approval from the spirits?"

I trilled a six-note song in agreement.

The day for the Trading Festival had arrived. Volunteers from each of the villages made two long raised platforms on the side of the sacred hill. On one of them, temporary dwellings had been made for the traders, who came from north, south, east, and west. On the other platform, hides were spread out to display their wares. The area was shaded by a long structure of posts and boughs.

Laid out on the hides were both raw materials and finished products. Tools made of antler came from the north, some of them with decorative carving. Birch bark boxes came in many sizes and shapes, decorated with cutout bark pieces. Beautiful furs were also on display. Small furs, such as rabbit and squirrel, were brought as pelts for sale, but the dark shiny ones were given to Jade for the spirits to distribute. One trader even had a kind of trumpet made of fossil mammoth tusk, which he said would attract the male moose.

"It definitely makes a loud noise," said Owl, "but I don't think I want to call any moose. Not even my nephew," she added, making a lame joke.

Traders from the east had obsidian tools and projectile points, as well as large nodules of obsidian for anyone who was an expert knapper. They also had bone fishhooks, and shell bracelets, and square baskets, which were quite a novelty. Other, larger baskets had been made for the fish catch, but might have many other uses for those with a creative flair. Sandy had learned to dry small fish, which were a hit with the Red Mountain people to flavor their otherwise rather tasteless millet porridge. Sandy gave the raw jades to Jade, as tribute for being allowed to attend the fair and trade what he brought in his packs. But he also understood that the best jadestone belonged to the spirits.

Little Shell wanted one of the square baskets, just because she liked the design. She offered Sandy a brown beaker in exchange. He looked it over, and saw how neatly the intricate design was applied. They were both happy with the exchange.

The southern traders had likewise given Jade the silk they brought, for they knew it was only to be used in connection with the spirits. But they also had bracelets and necklaces made of cowrie shells strung on cords, as well as small pieces of painted pottery, and cups made from carved gourds. The oddest thing they brought was turtle shells.

"What are they good for?" asked Dancing Crane.

"They're good for rattles," answered the trader.

"Oh." He picked up a small one and saw that the upper and lower parts made a little box. "Will you take a carved wooden platter in exchange? It's make from oak, and it won't crack."

Another transaction was completed.

Wolf, Leopard, and Tiger, the three robbers from Jade's early journeys, all came on horses, bearing heavy packs. They also brought sheep, as well as wool, and cheese made of sheep milk. The cheese was not a big hit, but the sheep and wool were much sought after. They brought a few objects made of copper as tribute to the spirits, as well as raw hunks of obsidian and nephrite. The shininess of the copper was surely attractive to the spirits. Wolf had married a girl from the steppes, and she was there, too, knitting with the spun wool on long wooden needles.

"Knitting is just like netting and knotting, but the yarn fits tigher. Look how warm it is. And how soft. It's wonderful for winter."

The language spoken at the fair was mostly that of the Red Mountain people, although they used foreign words for materials and objects that they didn't already have a name for.

Besides the trading activities, the participants had fun. Music and dancing, and games to play went on all the time, and a big feast was held each night. Everyone agreed that, thanks to Jade, their lives were now more exciting, and more colorful. They were grateful to her for taking care of the beautiful but dangerous things from the four directions – silk, jade, fur, and copper.

We couldn’t see outside, but the van was going slower, and making a number of turns.

“Could we be already at the airport?”

“I hope so. It seems like we’ve been in this van for weeks.”

“It’s actually been five days. My cell phone has a calendar on it. We should be in Hong Kong soon. They built a new airport, did you know? I was there with my mother last year. It’s beautiful.

“I’ve never been to Hong Kong. My Dad says the landing strip is right on the edge of the water, and that it’s very scary to land there.”

“That was the old airport. The new one has longer runways.”

The men in the front seat were talking about meeting someone at the airport. Their voices were tense.

“They’re meeting someone named La-su,” whispered Ashley very softly.

“You just took the wrong turn,” said Purple Shirt.

“It’s the way to the cargo area,” answered Driver. “That’s how we’re going to get the boxes onto the plane. Our friend La-su will be here soon to help us.”

A sharp turn flung us to the right, and then another to the left. The brakes went on abruptly and we braced against the seat in front of us. The boxes shifted, but didn’t fall back on us.

The driver got out and leaned on his door. We could hear a voice speaking English with a British accent.

"Let's see if the boxes are marked right. Yes, Lars Bock, in care of the Los Angeles Museum. Excellent."

Ashley and I looked at each other. "Lars? Was Lars the one who hired the looters?"

"Maybe it wasn't an accident that he ran into us at the Friendship Store. He might have been looking for us. Was he trying to find the Ox River site and get these goons to loot it?" Ashley whispered.

"But Evan said Lars flew to Hong Kong with Joe and Laura. If Lars is on the looters' side, Joe and Laura don't know it."

"What's the deal with flying to Hong Kong, anyway? It will be all over, however it turns out, before they can see us."

"Wouldn't you want to be present when your kidnapped friends were rescued? Or whatever?"

"The point is, why should they fly down together? What information could Laura and Joe have given away to Lars? Lars knew everything from the robbers anyway."

"Once they knew where the site was, Lars may have needed to play innocent. You can't just disappear in China."

Unloading the boxes seemed to take forever. We stopped whispering and pretended to sleep on the back seat.

"Now," said the British voice. "Here is the money, in dollars as I promised you." They were standing in front of the van, and it looked like Lars. Through the front windshield I saw him hand them each a stack of $100 bills, with rubber bands around them. Each man counted his money twice.

"Let's see if you look presentable for the authorities." He considered their cotton shirts and wash trousers and new shoes. "Wear your new jackets, and you'll do."

I thought they looked scruffy enough to get caught when they presented their passports, but what do I know?

Lots of air travelers look scruffy these days, even in business class.

"As I promised, you'll start a new life in America. Here are your tickets, passports and green cards with your new names."

There was more delay as they each read through their documents.

"You will have to present all of these at passcontrol. Don't look nervous. When you get through, your carry-on luggage will be x-rayed, and then you can board the plane when your flight is called. Understand? Everything all right?"

"What about you?" asked Driver.

"I am going on a different airplane. You fly to San Francisco, where Chinese friends will meet you. I go to Los Angeles, where I'll pick up the boxes and ship them on to New York. If you ever chance to see me, I will not recognize you."

"What about the girls?"

"Girls?" Had Lars forgotten about us? "Oh, Ashley and Clara. Leave them in the van. We'll seal the doors, and if we're lucky they'll suffocate before anybody finds them."

"We could lead a hose in from the exhaust, and it would be quicker."

"It would be too conspicuous to leave the motor running. And we're in a hurry. We don't even have to tape the windows. If we seal the doors, it will look funny, and people will find and rescue them sooner. I think the van is pretty air tight."

There were some scraping noises on the top of the van, and then they left.

40

In Green Valley the situation was growing desperate. The rainstorms didn't come in the spring when they were expected, and the planted crops sprouted but were drying up. People carried water in pots from the rivers and creeks, to keep the seedlings alive. Where was the rain? Even the rivers were getting low.

Owl and Jade talked about what to do. Jade suggested consulting the spirits. Owl clapped for me, and I appeared on the ground beside them.

"We need to ask the spirits for rain. What's the best way to get the Water Spirits to cooperate? Do you suppose that we have offended them? What do you know, Spirit Bird?"

I hadn't a clue. Unless the spirits were behind an earlier Global Warming, which, come to think of it, might be a result of displeasure of the spirits with human behavior.

But I also searched for a natural reason, and I had another thought. Maybe the seasons were getting out of step with the constellation that told them when to plant their crops. For centuries, the people of this region had relied on the first sighting of Virgo in the evening sky to tell them when to plant. They relied on the Fire Star to warn them in advance of the rains. But there had been agriculture in this region for at least two thousand years – which is about how long it takes for the stars to get out of step with the seasons.

Evan had explained to me about precession of the equinoxes, in which, over a very long period of time, the stars and the seasons changed their alignment. In the 1960s the Hippies told us that, "This is the dawning of the Age of Aquarius," following Pisces for the previous two millennia. About every two thousand years, the movement is enough to make a difference to the stars and the seasons. The stars seem to slip backward through time, but the slippage is so slow that oral stories would not be expected to remain the same. On the other hand, something as important as the time to plant being attached to a particular star cluster might well be passed down for two thousand years.

I consulted Piggy, as an expert on wetness. He was't any help. I tried to remember the star charts, because if there was enough precession to make a difference, we needed to know what comes next. If the Virgo star cluster is the one they've been using to tell them when to plant, Jade could announce a big ceremony when the brightest star in Leo star rises, and be very likely to be successful in her dance for the rain.

Getting this concept across to Jade was likely to be difficult, though, given my verbal limitations. Somehow Piggy and I had to lead her through it.

First, we needed to plant the idea that the present star cluster was not the right one. To do that, I needed to know what it was called. Then it would be an elaborate game of charades.

The star that the Red Mountain people planted by is one they call the Fire Star, which is known in the west as Antares. It's a conspicuous red star, important in many cultures. I needed to do some serious naked-eye astronomy to figure out what star or star cluster should be substituted.

Each night Piggy and I began watching the eastern horizon at sunset, scanning for bright stars. It had to be about two weeks ahead of the rains. If I had been watching last year, then I would be able to select the best star. Under these circumstances, we'd have to approximate.

After several nights, I chose the Bird star in the Dragon constellation as the brightest visible star. Now it was rising about an hour after sunset. It would have had its heliacal rising two weeks ago, which would be just right.

How could I get this complex scenario across to Jade, without the power of words? First I had to make it clear that I was trying to tell her something about the stars. I got Jade to follow me to the village altar, and looked up, although it was daylight. Jade looked up, too.

"Is this about clouds?" she said.

I kept still.

"The sun, then?"

We weren't getting anywhere.

In the evening I came to Jade again, and looked up at the sky.

"The stars?"

I sang my happy song, and Piggy chased his tail.

"OK, what about the stars?"

I perched by the hearth.

"Fire," she asked. "The Fire star?"

"Chirp." I hated having such a limited vocabulary.

Now we needed to indicate the Bird Star, which I did by flying up and down.

"Bird? The Bird star?"

"Chirp."

Now how to show spring planting? I deferred to Piggy, who lowered his tusks as if they were a plow, and plowed along the ground.

"Plowing? Planting? Spring planting?"

"Chirp, Chirp, Chirp."

"Change the spring planting to the Bird star instead of the Fire star?"

Piggy and I were so glad of Jade's quick uptake that we did a kind of pig and bird dance, with me flying over Piggy's back as he ran in circles.

"So I need to change the time of the annual Calling the Rain Dance? We're planting too early, and the rain doesn't come before the seeds dry up? Well, it's too late to postpone the planting for this year, and there aren't any more seeds for this year. Maybe if I dance hard we can get the rains to come early. The villagers only care about one year at a time. If the crops all wilt now, there will be starvation among all the villages."

Jade bit the inside of her cheek.

"Let's start the preparations now. First, I think, Tamer and I need to communicate with all the villages about what has happened. We'll tell them the spirits have changed to favor a different star. I hope you are right."

As soon as Lars and the looters were out of our sight and hearing, we tried all the doors of the van, but they were locked. We couldn't roll down the electric windows, either, without the key. It was sealed up tight, with all the crevices efficiently taped over. I wondered if we could eventually run out of oxygen if someone didn't find us. Ashley sat passively, almost catatonic, as if she couldn't believe this was happening.

I rooted around for my pack. There was dirt on the floor of the van, but with the boxes gone it wasn't hard to move around. I found my pack stuffed under the front seat, and grabbed the power bars first thing. Ashley and I shared one, since we might be here long enough to need to stretch them out. There was also a water bottle in my pack, which might last us for a couple of days.

Then I rooted for my Swiss army knife. I couldn't find a crack to wiggle any one of the blades through, although I tried every one. We needed some air. I poked into the ceiling, but there was no way through the solid metal top. Why didn't they make sun roofs on these things? All I managed to do with my knife was to scrape away some of the paint so we could see out. It was not much of an accomplishment, but I felt better being able to see out the sides.

"Worse luck," Ashley finally spoke. "I thought we were out of here. What shall we do now?"

"Call your aunt again."

Ashley grunted. "Yes, I could do that, couldn't I?"

She reached into her backpack and found her address book. Then she looked up a number and dialed.

Ashley's aunt answered on the first ring, and they had a rapid conversation in Cantonese that sounded almost like hysterics. But Ashley held herself together. She recited the new license number on the van, which we had seen several times, and described the van, although of course we didn't know where at the airport we were.

I looked in my pack again and retrieved my GPS unit. Even inside the van and with buildings all around it received three satellite signals, which was marginal, but maybe the best we could do inside the van.

"Give your aunt these coordinates," I ordered. "And tell her to hurry."

Now there was nothing to do but wait. And hope that nothing had happened to Ed and Ashley's father when they handed over the money.

In twenty minutes the phone rang again.

"She says there's nothing but an empty warehouse at the location you gave her," Ashley reported. The airport authorities are looking for us, but they can't find the license plate number you gave them.

I took another GPS reading, this time with four satellites, and Ashley transmitted the numbers to her aunt.

"She says hang in there," reported Ashley as she hung up the phone.

"What choice do we have?"

42

It was a tense time to be flying into Green Valley. Or maybe it was just me that was tense. The villagers seemed to be quite confident that the dance would bring the rain.

Preparations for the feast after the Calling the Rain Dance were underway. Everyone seemed to be participating, one way or another, making feast food in the central square. Little Shell was chopping chestnuts to stir into the millet cakes, Moose stirred great pots of millet porridge, and Dancing Crane was crushing juniper berries to flavor the millet wine.

Another group headed by Fawn was preparing little baskets to place the feast food into. The baskets had been wrapped with flowers.

Everyone's best clothing was laid out, having been washed in the nearby stream and beaten with two sticks until it was without a crease anywhere. The array was colorful, with yellow silks and red flowers.

The musicians were practicing the new tune Jade had composed for the occasion. One flute player had taken the lead, and was berating a drummer for missing the beat.

With all this activity, no one seemed to need me at Green Valley, so I made a sky tour of all the Red Mountain villages. Preparations were as busy everywhere. This was to be an event for all the Red Mountain people. I felt very proud of Jade for organizing all the villages, and getting them all to agree to her representing all of Red Mountain as she danced for rain.

Circling back to Green Valley, I was greeted by Jade and Owl.

"You've been gone a long time," Jade said. "I need you and Piggy for the ritual."

I sang my cheerful song, meaning 'at your service.'

"All the people will assemble on the hills near Pig Mountain. Owl and I have made signs for them, to show them which place is for their village. Look at these signs.

She showed me a board one that had three wavy lines painted on it in green. “Which Village do you think that represents?”

I hated to be so dense, but I didn’t know.

“It’s Sea of Grass. They recognize it already. How about this one?”

The next was three irregular blobs painted in gray. Again I was stumped.

“You’re just teasing, aren’t you? This is Stony Water, represented by three rocks. We sent runners to each village, to show them their sign, and the heads of each family in Green Valley will have signs to help them find the right road.

“That’s not all, Spirit Bird. Ten days ago everyone from Green Valley walked to Pig Mountain for a rehearsal, and we had a merry picnic. I made sure everyone from here knows the words and tune of our new song, ‘Harmony Among Villages.’ ”

“I’ve been watching the sky from the top of Pig Mountain every ten days. In two more days, all the Red Mountain villagers will walk to the designated hilltops.

“Everything is planned. The musicians will play along the way, and continue when people arrive. While each village is settling into its spot, you and Piggy and I will go around to all the village groups. Piggy will show off his tricks, and you can just sit there looking beautiful.

“I’ll explain to each group that when the new Rain Stars appear at dusk that night, you and Piggy and I will climb to the top of Pig Mountain, where we will sleep and have visions of the rain spirits. The musicians will come up the next morning, so that they can make joyful sounds after the rains come. If we have calculated correctly, the rains will come as we dance.”

It seemed like a huge risk to me. What if the rains didn’t come? Everyone would be very disillusioned, at the least. At the worst they might harm Jade. Jade hadn’t asked my opinion, though. She had planned all this by herself, since we first talked about the fact that the stars had to be adjusted to agree with the seasons.

We were actually asleep when our rescuers appeared. No one we knew was allowed into the cargo area because of airport security, so the man and woman who let us out of the van were unknown to us, but we hugged them anyway.

"There, there," said a nice Chinese man who spoke perfect English. "You've had a hard time. But it's over now."

"We couldn't find you at first because the license plate was changed again. The van had an airport license on it, and didn't look at all suspicious. If you hadn't scraped some of the paint off the windows, we wouldn't have looked in and found you."

"How could you sleep?" asked the woman.

"I think we were running low on oxygen." I was yawning, taking in great gulps of air.

They took us into some sort of VIP room, gave us soap and shampoo, and showed us where we could shower and brush our teeth. What luxuries! They even gave us fresh underwear, and loose robes to wear instead of our dirty, slept-in clothes.

The woman asked if we'd like some food. I said I wasn't hungry, but she brought us orange juice and crackers anyway. Ashley stared into space and hugged her backpack as if was her only contact with reality.

Two policemen came to talk to us, with an interpreter, and we answered questions for hours, it seemed. Ashley answered most of the questions, in Cantonese. I couldn't follow what she was telling them.

They seemed to want to know about everybody, from the Chinese archaeologists to the Koreans to our group, including Evan and Lars. They asked about what we did in China, and why we were doing it. They wanted to know what everyone said and did. They asked over and over, but they didn't bully us.

After more than an hour, they still didn't seem to be satisfied. They had a conference in the hall, and the woman returned and took me into a different room.

She spoke to me in Cantonese, but when I couldn't reply, she switched to English. She told me to call her Susie.

"How much did you understand of what your friend was telling us?" she asked.

"Virtually nothing, except that it was about the archaeology and the people we've been with. I recognized names when she said them."

"I need to hear about it all from you, too, if you'll bear with me. Tell me about your capture, and what happened on the drive to Hong Kong."

I told her everything I could think of.

"Let me ask you to tell me about what happened before you were captured, then. How long have you known Lars Bock?"

"We met him in Beijing at the Friendship Store. Laura and he began talking. I don't know who spoke first. I don't know anything about him, except that he speaks Chinese like a native, and he's a China scholar, interested in early China."

"And how about Evan O'Connell?"

"He approached Joe at Tian Tan. They hit it off, and in no time Joe invited him to come with us to Daling."

"Is that typical of Joe, would you say?"

"Well, no. Joe is usually stand-offish. He wasn't so friendly to Lars."

Susie wrote this on her pad.

"Give me your impression of the Chinese archaeologists that were with you. Could any of them have been involved in the theft of artifacts?"

"Certainly not! No archaeologist would do such a thing."

"These artifacts are worth a lot of money in the right markets. Someone was behind the thefts, someone with brains and connections. Those three peasants, whom you dubbed Purple Shirt, Driver, and Middle Seat, couldn't have figured it out by themselves."

"According to what we heard, the boxes were to be sent to Lars Bock at the Los Angeles Museum. And we saw Lars when we stopped at a warehouse for more boxes. He gave the looters new shoes and coats, and had the van repainted. I guess the point was to keep them from being identified by their tracks. He might have had the tires changed, too, but we didn't notice if he did.

Susie went out of the room, and came back with tomato juice and more cheese and crackers, which I ate gratefully.

"We want to show you some people and see if you know them."

In yet another room our three captors sat a table in handcuffs. I looked at them through one-way glass.

"They are the people who tied us up and drove us to Hong Kong. Driver, Middle Seat, and Purple Shirt," I identified each one. "How did you catch them?"

"It was easy. Whoever is the brains behind this wanted them to be caught. The one you call Middle Seat tried to take a gun through the security check point. Of course it was found at the x-ray machine. All three of them were taken for questioning."

I couldn't help laughing. They definitely didn't have the worldly experience to pull off any kind of caper. "I hope you are lenient with them. They could have treated us much worse."

"It's up to the Chinese justice system."

"Did you catch Lars, too?"

"He didn't have to be caught, he volunteered to talk to us. He's talking to an agent now."

"So he's the mastermind behind the looting?"

"We're not sure. If he set up the three robbers, surely he'd realize they would tell us about him. They said the person they obey is called La-su."

"We heard them refer to him that way."

"Of course, they couldn't read the English writing on the boxes. How would they know where they were being sent?"

"I heard Lars reading them what the boxes had written on them. Why would he do that? Was it for our benefit, so we'd believe it was Lars? Or to mislead us about the destination of the boxes?"

"Yes, these discrepancies caught our attention, too."

And then, exasperated with the questioning, I had a question of my own.

"Where is everybody else? Ed must be waiting for me somewhere. I want to see him."

"You'll get to see him very soon," Susie said soothingly. "It's important to debrief you before you get involved with greeting friends and family.

"Let's go over Lars movements one more time. He strikes up an acquaintance with Laura, and then meets your group. You are going to run your radar where he presumably already knows that unexcavated jades will be found. He gives you a reason why he will go there too.

"Lars arrives without any visible conveyance, in the morning two days after you get to Daling. He asks to go with you to the site, and when he is turned down, he gets Dr. Wu to show him its precise location on a map. The Korean archaeologists don't remember seeing him that day, nor do the Chinese.

"The next day he goes with you on the excursion to Dongshanzui. This is the rainy day, when presumably the site was looted. After lunch the following day, your team discovers the mess, but continue working while Dr. Wu goes to report it. Ashley wanders by accident into the place where the looters are waiting, and you turn up there, too. This wasn't part of the plan. He uses his concern for you and Ashley to give him an excuse to come to Hong Kong.

"Let's suppose that the stop at the warehouse was prearranged. Lars has to improvise when he learns that you two are missing. He needs to look innocent, but he also needs to meet the looters, let's say in Beijing, at the appointed time, to pick up additional items for shipment. He claims he can't get airplane seats from Beijing right away, allowing him to delay a day. Somehow he leaves Laura and Joe long enough to go to the warehouse and load more boxes into the van, meanwhile having the van repainted and so forth."

Susie made a note to ask Laura and Joe about Lars' movements.

"You spot a blond man with a goatee and wire rim glasses through the front window of the van, and hear a British accent. He turns up again at the cargo area of the Hong Kong airport to help unload the van, and he announces that the boxes have his name on them. What do you think?"

"Lars surely was involved."

"But the story doesn't quite add up. Why didn't he just turn the artifacts over to a shady dealer in Hong Kong? That's the usual method. Then his hands would have been clean. Sending the stuff to America with his name on the boxes is pretty dumb."

"Lars never struck me as dumb."

"It may help to think about Evan for a bit. He also appears out of the blue, makes contact with Joe, and even goes with you in the taxis to Daling. In retrospect, doesn't that seem suspicious?"

"He played his part really well, if he isn't an archaeologist." I objected. "He had the lingo right, and knew what archaeologists do."

"Couldn't he be an archaeologist and still be a looter? You keep defending archaeologists, but archaeologists are most likely to know what's valuable in archaeological sites, and where in the site they are apt to be. Evan didn't do the tomb raiding, but couldn't he have hired the thugs in the van, and told them where to go and what to do? By the way, we're trying to find out about his university in Wales – but did he ever tell you its name?"

"No."

"Suppose he's the one who hired the looters. What would he do when he learned they had kidnapped you and Ashley? He'd find a way to keep tabs on both you and the van. He did that by going with the Koreans on their bus, and even finding an excuse to talk to you in the ladies' room. He made the lame excuse that he had fallen in love with Ashley at first sight. He must be involved some way."

"Everybody falls in love with Ashley at first sight. What's lame about that? On the other hand, somebody must have told the robbers not to harm us," I mused. "After all, there's a death penalty for looting, and we knew what they looked like. They had a gun, or various other means to kill us, like throwing us out of the van on the highway, or strangling us with rope."

Susie said, "Back in a minute," and went out and shut the door. I tried the knob and found the door locked. Well, I was now used to being locked in.

44

A few wispy clouds had formed on the western horizon when I arrived at Pig Mountain. Piggy and Jade had climbed to the top the day before. They slept in a small tent which they set up beside Pig Mountain's right ear, for protection from the wind. The view from the top was spectacular. I could see the rosy light from the sun, although it hadn't broken the horizon yet. The stars were fading, with only the brightest still visible. It was time for us all to perform our spectacle. I did an unbirdlike thing, and crossed two claws for good luck.

The three of us sat in a row, with Jade in the middle, and watched the eastern sky. Just before dawn the Bird Star asterism rose. It was only visible briefly, before the strong sunshine blotted out the sight of it. But it was all we needed. On all sides, the Red Mountain people had assembled, and they had seen the Bird Star too.

That was the first "miracle" of the day, one that was sure to occur as long as the sky in the east was clear. The other miracle would be a real one, if Jade succeeded in bringing the rain.

The sun was halfway up the eastern sky before we could see clouds gathering. They were darkest and thickest in the west, where the rain comes from. I started to hope it would turn out well.

When the sun was as high as it was going to go, Jade put on her yellow silk headband, shell belt, jade pig-dragon and jade earrings. She tied a yellow headband on Piggy, too, and a belt of shells around his waist. Then she looked at me.

"Your yellow crest and long tail are your dance costume. And shells would weigh you down if I need you to fly. You're all dressed up the way nature made you."

"Did nature make me in this form?" I wondered briefly.

The flutists and drummers and stone ringers began climbing the mountain. When they arrived, Jade clapped six times, poured out a little millet wine for the rain spirits, and then distributed wine to the musicians who had just made the tough climb.

The musicians made a wide circle around Piggy, Jade and me. At a signal from Jade, they began to play the new song that Jade wrote, called Harmony Among Villages. We could hear voices singing the words from the lower hilltops all around us.

When the song was finished, Jade took off her straw sandals and began to dance. She whirled clockwise around the ring of musicians, her shell belt rattling. Piggy ran in the other direction, also rattling his shells. The clouds had grown bigger, but they were still far in the distance. I flew in circles above Jade and Piggy, hoping to attract the clouds. The musicians began moving in a circle opposite to Jade. I could feel that we were stirring up a wind.

Without warning, Piggy screeched to a stop in the middle of the circle, and faced west. He made an impatient grunt, followed by a call that was louder than any I had ever heard him make, even the one in the boat when he stopped the storm. It looked like it was raining in the west.

"Bring the rain, Spirit Bird," called out Jade in a voice that echoed over all the hills. I doubted that I could bring rain, but I could do no less than try. I flew toward the clouds, which had definitely grown darker. I thought they were too far away to rain on Pig Mountain, but I flew in the direction of the nearest black cloud.

Piggy roared again, and lightning came out of the cloud. By the time I escaped the lightning and was back to the clearing, the thunderstorm had broken. Rain came down in torrents, and thunder boomed. The Red Mountain people on the hilltops danced in the rain.

Susie returned with a stack of papers.

"Could it have been Evan you saw and heard, and not Lars?"

"No. The person we saw was blond, with a goatee. Evan has dark curly hair, and is clean shaven."

Susie looked through her pile of papers, and selected a British passport.

"We detained everyone as they appeared at the airport. Is this Evan or Lars?" Susie handed me a copy of a passport picture with the name blotted out.

"Evan," I said immediately. And then, less certain, I said, "But this person is blonder than Evan."

"We found a wig of dark curly hair in his overnight bag, along with a paste-on goatee and glasses. Look at the picture again with the dark hair added."

"Yes, that's Evan," I said reluctantly.

"In normal circumstances you wouldn't have been fooled by the goatee – it's pretty crude. But with anxiety, dim light, and the idea planted that it was Lars, you bit."

"He must have planned to impersonate Lars from the start. But why? What did he know about Lars? A rival gang?"

"We checked up on Lars, and found that he had a legitimate reason to be investigating looting in Chinese sites. He really is who he says he is – a scholar of ancient Chinese writings, from Lund University in Sweden. Looters tend to spoil the bamboo strips that have writing on them. So he has formed the World Archaeological Sites Protection League and he is president.

"To be sure of his movements, I just asked Laura and Joe separately, and they both say Lars was with them all the time on the way to Beijing and at the airport. And that he was very concerned about what would happen to you and Ashley."

I digested this a moment. I had loved Evan's accent, and hated to think of him as a criminal.

"You think it was Evan who hired the looters?"

"Yes, we think he was behind the whole episode. We're hoping to get the three men who brought you to Hong Kong to identify him. So far they've kept mum, but I think they'll speak when they realize that the alternative is the death penalty. I haven't shown them the passport picture yet."

"Then the case is solved?"

"A few loose ends. I still need to ask you about Ashley."

"Ashley? She was one of us. And she loved jades."

"Yes, she did. Look what we found in her back pack."

Susie handed me a pale yellow jade pig-dragon with dirt clinging to it.

"In Ashley's backpack? No. I don't believe it. How did it get in there? Who tried to frame her?"

"Was Ashley tied up when you found her at the van?"

"I think so." I shut my eyes to try to remember. "She was in the front seat of the van when she called out to me to run. They tied me up and put me in the van through the back door. Then Ashley got in the van and they tied her hands."

"Ashley told us the pig-dragon was yours. She said you took it from a box when the looters weren't looking. The box she described was full of dirt and artifacts and bones, jumbled together. Any comment?"

"I never saw inside any of the boxes!" I said, indignantly. "And if I had, I wouldn't have taken anything."

"Did the boxes get shifted around at any time?"

"Not unless it happened when we were out of the van."

"We were able to have Lars Bock's luggage taken off the plane. There was no box with dirt and bones and artifacts. What happened to that box? Can you describe the boxes you saw?"

"Cardboard boxes with Chinese writing on them, for things like canned food. I didn't pay them a lot of attention. There was a seat back between us and the boxes, and we were watched through the rearview mirror the whole time. I think there may have been about a dozen boxes, but I'm not sure."

"The looters say that the foreign man called La-su told them to give Ashley the jade. She was thrilled to have it, and was looking at it when you called to her. That's when she slipped it into her back pack."

"You're saying Ashley went to meet the looters on purpose, to collect her jade? I can't believe it."

"Maybe she was more deeply involved than that."

"You mean the jade dragon was it a reward for telling someone where to find the tombs?"

"We're pursuing that angle. We've been checking on Evan's activities before he came to China. Working on the assumption that he's the mastermind behind the thefts, we looked on the web. He doesn't go through dealers or auction houses. He has a website about Chinese antiques, and follows their prices in the auction houses, then sets his a little lower for similar items. He finds buyers through their websites. Did you know that Ashley has a website about Chinese jades?"

"Well, she's a scholar. I suppose the website is about her work on the art of jades, not about their commercial aspect."

"Why do you keep defending her when she tried to frame you?"

"It just seems impossible that anyone I know could encourage looting, no matter what they would get out of it. Archaeologists don't even buy antiquities, no matter how appealing, because it only encourages more being ripped out of the ground."

"Was Ashley trained as an archaeologist?"

"No she's an art historian."

"Just so. But back to the web. It would be natural for Evan to have found Ashley through her website. We could check his e-mail, and hers, but she's already admitted that they were in touch by e-mail long before this expedition. Putting him in touch with your team was easy. She already knew you through your Chinese class, and you told her that Joe had been invited to do GPR in China. She got herself invited along, and the rest you know."

"Joe will be devastated about Ashley's involvement. She seduced him at a party at my apartment, and Laura walked out on him. He seemed happy enough with Ashley at first. But she wasn't very helpful at the site. She didn't know any archaeology, and I think he eventually realized he was besotted when he asked her to come on the expedition. She didn't even know whether to read the meters or inches side of the tape measure. Joe was getting disenchanted. He was furious with her the last day when we were working at Ox River site. She sounded like she thought it was okay to steal archaeological artifacts, as long as they ended up in museums."

I wondered if Joe and Laura would reconnect, now that Joe was no longer bewitched. Maybe the experience was too traumatic for them. Time would tell. Then I had another thought.

"How did Ashley and Evan keep in touch in China?"

"We guess that Evan gave her that phone. Ashley couldn't have bought a mobile phone that works in China – she didn't have time away from the rest of you here, and you can't buy them outside China. Somehow Evan slipped it to her. Maybe when she went missing at Tian Tan. Her photography was a convenient excuse to slip away from the group when she needed to."

"So the 'aunt' she was calling in Hong Kong was Evan?"

"The earlier calls were. He speaks Cantonese, which was how he communicated with both Ashley and the hired looters. They were not from the northeast, or they would have spoken Mandarin Chinese. Instead, they were from around here, and spoke Cantonese."

"How did we get rescued, then?"

"Ashley really has an aunt in Hong Kong. She called her after she realized you'd been abandoned in the van."

"Where is Ashley now? What will happen to her?"

"She's with her father, who has hired a lawyer. We've tried to arrange for her to go home with him, but the Chinese authorities would not agree, so she will be kept in jail for now. Her ultimate fate is unknown."

I shivered at the thought of the death penalty for Ashley. "How are her chances?"

"We can't say. Her father is influential, but the Chinese system is different from yours. Do you have any more questions?"

"What will happen to the artifacts that were taken from the Ox River site? Will anyone be able to study them and publish the result?"

"We unloaded ten boxes full of Han Dynasty artifacts off the plane. Evan had shipped them to a phony name at a post office box in L.A. Those were the boxes picked up at your stop in Beijing. Since those were the real point of the van to Hong Kong, Evan tried to see to it that they were sent on"

"Yes, but they looted the site we were working on. Where are those artifacts? They gave one jade to Ashley, but what happened to the rest of them?"

"The jade given to Ashley was almost surely from the Ox River tombs. There weren't any other boxes, though. We found some Chinese grocery boxes such as you described, flattened and put in a dumpster at the airport. There were traces of damp dirt in them, but no contents."

"What could they have done with the stuff from Ox River?" I was really distressed over this news.

"We've looked all over the airport, with no luck. Another possibility is that the theft of the jades and the capture of Ashley was intended to provide cover for sending the more lucrative Han tomb items to America. Evan would get much more for them there than in Hong Kong. It was also useful to Evan to frame Lars, who had been interfering with his operations."

"If the tomb contents were once in those boxes, what could they have done with them?" I fretted.

"You tell me. They could have been empty already when you saw them. Where would they have left them in or near Daling?"

"Well, let's think about it. Suppose they shoveled everything into cardboard boxes when they looted the tombs. If the dirt and bones and other artifacts were gone, except for a dirty jade for Ashley, they must have been dumped out nearby. The Daling area is patrolled, and they couldn't have dumped it on that property without it being found quickly. I wonder if they reburied the stuff elsewhere at Ox River."

"Could you look for it with the radar?"

"Archaeologists would spot a fresh hole without radar, unless the looters did a good job of covering it up with leaves or something else that looked natural. I'm sure there wasn't any digging visible at Ox River except for the tombs that appalled us so."

I closed my eyes to picture the way it had been.

"Wait a minute. We did transects of the site after the looters had been there. Maybe if Joe and Laura look at the downloaded results, they can find the hole."

"I'll ask them right now."

"Before you go, is that the whole picture?"

"We think so. If we need your testimony, we'll let you know. I hope at least we've put Evan out of business. You're free to see your friends now."

"Can I get my luggage and find something decent to put on?" I gestured at the robe, which made me feel like Old Mother Hubbard.

"Here it is. When you're ready, I'll take you to them."

I put on clean jeans and tee-shirt, and brushed out my hair. I felt better, but I was worried for Ashley.

"What am I allowed to tell my friends and family about this event?"

"Laura and Joe already know pretty much everything you do about Evan, and Ashley, and Lars. We've questioned them, too."

We walked around the corner to another room. It was full of most of the people I most wanted to see at that moment – Laura and Joe, Mr. Wu, Kidok and the other Korean archaeologists, and even Lars. They all hugged me. I hadn't needed to cry before, but now I did.

"You don't look too bad, after a five-day ordeal," Laura tried to stop my tears.

"The looters didn't hurt us, and did they feed us. Except for constant anxiety, it wasn't too bad. I didn't even realize how anxious I had been until now."

I looked around.

"If Ashley's father is with her, then the plane from Boston must have arrived. But where's Ed?"

Ed chose that moment to reappear from the john. He hugged me like he'd never appreciated me before. "Jade Princess," he said into my hair, "You gave me quite a scare."

He held me at arms length. "You don't look damaged. Maybe the locket I gave you protected you."

I was wearing the locket, but I'd forgotten that the Chinese characters engraved on it mean "Safe Journey."

"Did you have a premonition?"

"I only know you don't always do the safe thing. No, there are no Spirit Birds in my life. I just wanted you to come back to me. Didn't you look inside?"

"I didn't realize the locket opens."

My thumb nail did the trick. Inside was a picture of Ed and me in Korea, and a tiny folded piece of red paper, which is used for good luck in China. It took me a moment to get it unfolded to read it. The paper said, "Together, always. Will you marry me?"

"I've been waiting for an e-mail answer."

A nice kiss was interrupted by a shout from Laura. "I think we've found it! See, just next to the place where we think there was a tree. It's not as deep as the tree impression, and has a different consistency."

When the cheering died down I realized I had one more loose end to tie up. I whispered to Ed, "Did anyone ask you for the ransom money?"

"The looters were caught going through security. I waited for a long time, before Laura told the security staff to tell me you had been rescued. So now I have $5000, and you, too. What a bargain!"

"Then we can have a wonderful time on our trip, and buy something outrageously expensive. I already bought a silk rug – what else can we splurge on?"

"We'll see what we can find. Oh yes, here's a note for you that Dad gave me for you."

The note was on plain paper, and only said, "Clara, nice job. We'll talk later. Enjoy your holiday. Sandra."

46

Jade was much in demand after she solved the problem of the rains. So many people wanted to consult her that she set up a lean-to on the slope opposite Pig Mountain. Piggy and I sat on either side of her, occasionally performing some trick to impress visitors, but mostly just looking wise.

That hut was visited so often that people began to want to make it permanent. It was added to many times by Jade's devout followers. When Jade died, the building was converted into a shrine, where people could ask for favors from the spirits of statues of Jade, Piggy and me.

The last time I saw Jade was at her funeral, when Tamer volunteered to go with her to the other world, to keep her company.

Epilogue

I sit astride my white horse and wait for the dawn. Before the sun comes up, all five moving stars make tribute to Jade. The brightest one, named Wandering Dragon, has called a meeting in the house of the Bird Star to honor her. The moving stars cluster together tightly in the early morning sky.

Today, the day before the sun turns back to warm the world again, Jade's body will be entombed with love and deep respect. Today I will follow my beautiful, shining Jade into the Yellow Underworld where the suns go at night. Today the moon is almost dark. I reflect the small moon - my breath is weak, my power is weak. Tomorrow Moonglow, the new leader of all Red Mountain people, will dance the sun back to the world of the living.

Jade's powers were great. She was guided by the spirits of a pig and a bird, who brought instructions from Heaven, allowing her to choose the precise day each year to dance for rain. Each year Jade saved Red Mountain crops from the destruction of an angry sun.

Jade was an inspired leader. She helped the Red Mountain villages progress from discord to harmony, using the spirit connections of her mother, and knowledge of the five jades, taught by her father. Now she has changed even herself, into a spirit who will send rain when the leaders perform her dance. As a spirit, Jade even has a new name: Changing Woman.

The Spirit Bird waits with me, as the stars fade into the morning sky. She greets me with a sad song as I wait on the top of the moon-viewing pyramid. But I am not sad. Jade and I had a wonderful life, a life filled with wonders.

The red sun begins to bathe the earth with its glow, and a procession forms. I can hear the noisy hubbub in the distance. Every leader of a Red Mountain village, large or small, has come to honor Jade. Each carries a painted pot to place at her graveside, bottomless so that Jade's spirit can return to help them when they need her.

Some leaders have walked for days, for their villages are far. Even those from the nearest village have walked all night. I can see people awakening on the hillsides, with babies turning to their mothers to quench their morning thirst, and older children running to the bushes in the valley for another morning ritual. Everyone who could come from all the Red Mountain people are lining the roadside or sitting on the hills to watch the colorful procession,

Musicians lead the way. Flutists play a lilting tune, and drummers beat a six-stroke cadence that sets the feet dancing. It's the music Jade learned from the spirits, a song called Harmony Among Villages. The watchers on the hills know all the words by heart, and they sing along. Up and down the procession, barefoot dancers keep the beat with rattles, their yellow feathers atremble.

The twelve leaders of the trading villages have the honor of carrying Jade's body and her statue. They wear their best robes of yellow silk. Each leader carries her head high, proudly wearing the lustrous jade headdress that transforms her long black hair into a banner above her head.

The first six leaders carry Jade's body, lying on a wide plank covered with a tiger skin, for everyone to see. The tiger's legs and tail hang over the sides, swinging as the bearers move in step, creating the illusion that Jade is riding the tiger. A band woven with yellow feathers keeps Jade's white hair in place, but the wind ruffles the turned-up ends. Two jade pig-dragons, one yellow and the other white, are sewed to the front of her yellow silk robe. Her robe is tied with thick ropes, in a knot that designates a *wu*, a person who can commune with spirits. Green jade bracelets glow softly on her arms, and white jade earrings glisten on her ears. Her other ornaments are made of turquoise. It is proper for her to wear this finery to the Yellow Springs, so the Spirits Gone Before will recognize and honor her.

Following the body is an effigy of Jade, life-sized, and made of clay. The statue sits cross-legged on another tiger-skin-covered plank, dressed exactly like Jade. The clay statue looks young, although Jade lived long. Inset green jade eyes and painted cheeks give the figure life and sparkle, and a wig of springy brown hair, cut from our daughter's own head, turns up at the ends. Jade's spirit will inhabit the statue, as the spirits of the pig and the bird inhabit theirs.

The village leaders, and our new Red Mountain Leader, will be able to ask Jade about the future, just as if she had not departed to the Yellow Springs. Jade arranged for her continued presence, so that the villagers would stay calm and remember about Harmony when she went to the spirits. Our daughter Moonglow was chosen to be the new Red Mountain Leader, and she will do well. But she is yet young, and people will still want to speak to Jade, and receive her advice and comfort.

The jade carvers dance in a cluster behind the seated statue. The master carvers each have a jade cloud on the front of their clothing. They carry jade stones shaped to make sonorous music, and strike them with hardwood sticks. Each stone sounds a different tone, in harmony with the rest. Following the carvers are the statue-makers, whose leaders wear a comb-like emblem. Next comes a group of master potters, with their symbol of joined rings. The master farmers dance at the end in their straw shoes, wearing their bird-shaped jades.

The procession halts by the earth pyramid where I wait on the summit. The villagers made this hill as high as ten houses to view the moon, and to honor Pig Mountain which looms over our sacred space. I dismount to light a fire, which will draw the dancers to the top, climbing the pyramid in a spiral. When they arrive, each of the dancers claps six times to attract the attention of the Pig Mountain spirits, and bows toward the fire. Then, leaping, whirling, jumping to the cadence of the rattles, they make their homage to the older spirits, and the one newly joining them.

As I sprinkle wine into the fire it flames blue. Sweat breaks out on the dancers' foreheads. "I see Jade dancing with us," calls one dancer, and the rest become more frenzied, hoping to see her, too. Their leaf skirts flare out; their long black hair spirals toward the sky. When the fire dies down, one by one they drop in exhaustion. They reach out with two hands for the millet wine

I offer them, but give a few drops to the fire and other spirits before gulping it down in thirsty swigs.

When the dancers recover their breath, I ride my white horse to the head of the procession. Moving slowly, I lead them up the side of another hill, where a long low building glows in the dawn. It was built on the very spot where Jade used to tell oracles with Piggy. The building is round at one end and square at the other, so it is sacred to both Heaven and Earth. Since it will be the home of Jade's spirit, is gaily painted with designs on clay, in red, white, and yellow. These are the colors of earth, fire, and water. These three elements were used to construct the building.

Moonglow stands in embroidered robes and shining jades at the door of the shrine. She directs the first group of bearers to place the bier with her mother's body on a prepared platform. Although she is my beloved daughter, we greet each other formally, rubbing our palms together. We have already said our family good-byes.

Moonglow chants in front of the statue. The words are so ancient that I can only understand a little, but I know she is imbuing the statue with Jade's spirit. Intoning a refrain of the ancient words, the six leaders carry the statue inside. The rest of us wait outside, encircling the building so that no evil can enter. The yellow-robed leaders place the statue against the wall, between statues of a pig and a bird. In life they were Jade's spirit familiars, called Piggy and Spirit Bird. When the statue is seated comfortably, and her clothing is neatly arranged, each of the six village leaders claps before it.

I cannot see them, but I know the leaders will pad in single file down the long dim hallway, to the storage area on the end. They will return with six bundles arranged on their plank. The bundles are handled with care, for they contain the bones of village leaders who died before her, and will serve Jade in the Yellow Springs. Sweet-smelling wood chips from far-away spirit trees flare up in a censer, and wine is poured out for the spirits.

As the procession leaves the building, the incense burner wafts smoke in front of the cross-legged statue, whose green eyes glimmer with the light of the rising sun. Moonglow joins me, and we walk on either side of the horse, zigzagging downhill again. On reaching the valley floor, we stand aside while the bier carriers approach an elaborate construction in the middle of a large clearing. Two squares, one inside the other, outline a sacred space with shining white rock, carefully edged. The white stones stand for the tiger of the west. They also mean water, and the square represents the earth. They show Jade's close relationship with the rain spirits, and remind us that the water enriches the earth.

In the center of the concentric squares is another square, this one like a small building, about waist high, made of trimmed stones of bluish-gray, with a long narrow space in the center. Their color represents the sky dragon of the east, who controls the rain.

The leaders stop, and rest their burden on the edge of the central structure. With formal movements, they wrap the tiger skin tightly around Jade's body, and tie the legs across it. As they lift the body, we all begin to chant the ancient words that will give Jade peace in the Yellow Springs.

An empty space surrounding Jade's grave is filled with branches of sweet-smelling pine. In a round tomb next to it, other smaller graves edged with stone slabs are ready for their new occupants. Each bone bundle brought from the building above is lowered into a prepared stone cist. When each body is in its appointed place, every village leader, from the major villages to the minor ones, sets a bottomless pot upright around the edge of both tombs. They are bottomless so that communications with Jade will remain open. Decorations painted on the vessels represent plants, to show that our lives depend on crops. The clay is fired red, for the south, and the paint is black, the color of the north. Thus all the directions are represented, and none are slighted.

The pots are legion. They stand touching all the way around the perimeter of the tomb. The Red Mountain villages have grown to be many, and prospered under Jade's leadership. One final song is chorused when the pots have been set up, a song of thanks to Jade for their prosperity and happiness.

When the music stops, in total silence I lead my horse to the central grave. My farewell to Jade is formal, rubbing my hands six times. The yellow bird flies over and drops a feather in Jade's grave.

I caress the horse's muzzle, and hand the reins to our daughter Moonglow, who will take care of this precious animal, a sacred white horse from Over the High Mountains. Moonglow offers me millet wine from a large painted beaker, with zigzag designs recalling the far-away mountains of my people. I drain the beaker, holding it over my head afterwards to show that not a drop is left. It would be offensive to the spirits to leave even a drop of wine in the cup. The village leaders bow, and clap six times for me.

I walk to the remaining empty grave and lie down within it, arranging my jade headdress carefully, and making sure the pig-dragons on my chest are aligned back to back. I settle in, crossing my ankles. Distantly I can hear the spirits being entertained with song and dance one more time. As the dancers move away, the women leaders set stone lids on each of the stone cists.

I smile inside my stone coffin. I will be with her soon. I can hear clods of earth falling on the entire tomb. The villagers will take turns adding earth and stones all day, until the mound seems to touch the sky.

AUTHOR'S NOTE

This story is a work of fiction, but it is based on archaeological data. You can read about some of the facts in *The Archaeology of Northeast China: Beyond the Great Wall,* 1995, S. M. Nelson, ed., Routledge Press. For newer references, see my bibliography under Faculty at the University of Denver, or e-mail me at snelson@du.edu and I will send you a list of references.

ABOUT THE AUTHOR

Sarah Milledge Nelson is an archaeologist who first saw the "Goddess Temple site" in 1987, and has been back many times since. She has several published papers on Chinese archaeology, as well as one edited book. She also co-teaches, with Prof. Robert Stencel, a course in Archaeoastronomy. (If you think that word has the most vowels in a row of any English word, join the queue.) She is also John Evans Professor at the University of Denver.